ASCENDANCE

ASCENDANCE

SADHNA SHANKER

RUPA

Published by
Rupa Publications India Pvt. Ltd 2018
7/16, Ansari Road, Daryaganj
New Delhi 110002

Sales centres:
Allahabad Bengaluru Chennai
Hyderabad Jaipur Kathmandu
Kolkata Mumbai

Copyright © Sadhna Shanker 2018

This is a work of fiction. Names, characters, places and incidents are either the product of the author's imagination or are used fictitiously and any resemblance to any actual person, living or dead, events or locales is entirely coincidental.

All rights reserved.
No part of this publication may be reproduced, transmitted, or stored in a retrieval system, in any form or by any means, electronic, mechanical, photocopying, recording or otherwise, without the prior permission of the publisher.

ISBN: 978-81-291-5121-6

First impression 2018

10 9 8 7 6 5 4 3 2 1

The moral right of the author has been asserted.

Printed by Parksons Graphics Pvt. Ltd., Mumbai

This book is sold subject to the condition that it shall not, by way of trade or otherwise, be lent, resold, hired out, or otherwise circulated, without the publisher's prior consent, in any form of binding or cover other than that in which it is published.

Pujya, this is for you...

Contents

Taken / 1

Depletion / 47

Search / 95

Maya's Story / 131

Alternatives / 159

Aryan / 189

Decisions / 212

Earth / 225

Entirety / 254

Farewell / 275

Elone / 313

Acknowledgements / 318

Glossary / 319

Taken

Chronicle-ii, Page nz^{23}

...had come into existence after Clash-ii, which had delineated our two worlds with precision. The Fence ensured our recovery and rebuilding. Clash-ii had changed the landscape of Elone. Many had been taken. We needed to shore up our numbers, and reconstruct our cities.

As Iwe processed the lines, she could sense a flash coming from her tag. She ignored it and continued processing.

For us, it was like starting all over again from the time of the Great Escape...

The flash came again. This time it was an emergency flash. Something unprecedented had occurred. Iwe uncoupled from processing the Chronicle and opened her eyes. On the screen before her, a message was flashing:

Someone has been taken. Discovered near the Fence.

Iwe was stunned. In all the zacs that she had been managing the Vault, such an event had never happened. Taken? Who had been taken? How? Near the Fence! It must be a mistake.

She tried to scan for images of the Fence, but the channel on her workstation had been blocked. Iwe quickly switched to the Vault. It was quiet, calm and empty. Iwe trawled through the system on her workstation. The Council channels were quiet, so were all the other important channels. Apart from the flash message, there was no other information available.

Outside the Vault, night had fallen on Elone and its three full moons were riding the sky like an arc, calmly, belying the unprecedented event flashing in Iwe's tag.

In another part of the city, Tioni was pacing the floor of the Creation Facility. A neatly laid-out building with four floors, the Creation Facility was meticulously clean with pale blue walls and long glass-paned windows. After a while, Tioni came and stood near the glass panels, looking outside. The streets were dimly lit, brightening only when a shuttle passed by. However, the three full moons were casting a silvery sheen over everything. Tioni could see the leaves of a tree in the distance swaying gently in the slight breeze. In this phase of the calante, the moons illuminated the landscape transluscently.

Tioni could see herself, her oval face, limpid brown eyes, and the crown of smooth auburn hair reflected in the glass panes. Her knee-length brown tunic was slightly crumpled. She spotted a speck on her loose black pants, and bent down to brush it off. She wondered if Tara would have the curly hair and blue eyes that she had asked for. Tioni had drawn up her wish list for Tara with a lot of thought and a little help from Seeni. Both of them had had long discussions about her height, her optimal body weight once she was an adult, her sight and hearing range, among other things. The name 'Tara' and Tioni's small apartment had been ready to receive the creation ever since her request had been granted.

It had been a rather long wait for Tioni. Her request for a creation had languished in the Creation Facility because creations had not taken place on Elone for the last many zacs. Tioni's desire for a creation was an opportunity for the facility to be reopened and refreshed. The experts and toboks were retrained in the processes of creation, which had nearly been forgotten. Afterwards, a cell had been extracted from Tioni, configured to her requirements and incubated. And tonight, her creation Tara would be handed over to her.

Tioni was alone in the silent waiting room staring at the light shining brightly outside the creation chamber. She had shut down her tag when she had entered the facility as she didn't want the incessant chatter of the tag to disrupt her first meeting with Tara. A miniscule square device, the tag was their lifeline. It not only connected them to the system that enmeshed Elone's networks but also with each other. Many had embedded the tag in their arms, while others, like Tioni, kept it separate.

Night had given way to the first rays of dawn when the light outside the chamber finally went off and the door opened. The expert, in her smart uniform of pale blue tunic and short blue skirt, emerged, followed by a rolling oblong tobok. In its aperture lay a small bundle. The expert transferred the bundle into Tioni's hands. Tara was tiny. Her hair was curly and she looked around with her blue eyes, just as Tioni had wanted.

Tioni sat down on the sofa placed on one side of the waiting area and stared in wonder at the creation in her arms. The tobok rolled back into the chamber discreetly. The expert said, 'All the directions for her well-being have been put on your tag. Follow them. The details of the cell structure from which she was cultured have also been uploaded. You can take her with you now. Are you doing well? From what I understand, managing a creation requires a lot of work and effort. So, I hope you are not due for any replacement soon. Not that you need any advice from me on replacements!'

Tioni continued gazing at Tara and whispered softly, 'I am good.'

'Well then, enjoy your time with the latest entrant to Elone.'

The expert walked back towards the chamber and the door shut behind her. Tioni sat there in the waiting room with a new life form quivering in her arms. Suddenly, all the preparations that she had made for this moment seemed inadequate. She wondered whether all clarents felt uncertain and unsure. Holding Tara gingerly, Tioni took her first steps carefully and walked towards the elevator. She exited the building and stepped on to the road. Standing at the shuttle stop, she held the small bundle close to her. The city was bathed in the first rays of the morning sunshine. Tara had automatically shut her eyes when they had stepped out. She lay quietly in Tioni's arms. The street was empty; the stillness and quiet of dawn was all around. Tioni waited for the shuttle, and wondered how Tara would change her life. The instruction manual about handling creations had made it out to be a simple job but the expert said that it would require work and time. Was she up to it?

The shuttle arrived. Sleek, the deep brown colour of wood, the shuttles traversed the energy corridors that were powered by energy harnessed from the sun, which was multiplied in units far away from the city.

No one was aboard the shuttle at that early hour. Tioni swiped her tag and the shuttle zoomed in the direction of her apartment.

The Council—the highest decision-making group—had been summoned for an emergency meeting and all seven members had been asked to be present. This had not occurred in the last ten zacs. The Council members usually decided matters through their tags. However, the unprecedented event that had occurred last night required their presence.

Enmeshed between tall, graceful buildings that were connected through criss-crossing skywalks, the Council building was medium-sized, yellowish in colour and stood in a small square surrounded by a few trees. The main room where the Council met had a round table and was draped in sombre colours. It was bathed in sunlight that was streaming through its transparent roof.

Crati sat on her designated chair at the round table. She had long black hair, which she wore on top of her head in a bun, an earnest face and a melodious voice. She was the current head of the Council, as per the rotation plan. The Council's rules were simple. The oldest resident was the permanent member, and the only one who could veto a decision. The leadership of the Council rotated amongst the other six members every five zacs. A member was nominated for thirty zacs. When a vacancy arose, a new member was nominated with the consensus of the remaining members.

Sitting around the table, the members waited for Crati to

open the meeting. She cleared her throat and announced, 'The Council is meeting because, as you all know, someone was taken last night. This incident is significant not only because this is the first person who has been taken in the last hundreds of zacs, but also because of another reason.'

The others looked slightly confused. Only Ultur, the oldest resident on the Council, sat still, her back straight.

Ultur had deep red straight hair, which hung below her shoulders. She was of medium height and a stout build. She had dark brown eyes that sparkled with the wisdom and knowledge of a long life, but, presently, they seemed to have lost their shine. Her eyes were blank and looked swollen, as if she had shed tears.

Crati cleared her throat, once more, and looked towards Ultur, but as per the norms of the Council no one interfered or advised the head unless explicitly asked. When Ultur didn't say anything, Crati continued, 'I am sorry to inform you that the one taken is Seeni, the creation of Ultur, and we have reasons to believe that her taking was not an accident.'

A collective sigh went around the table. They all knew Seeni. Charming and intelligent, she had been involved in the teaching programmes at the Irana Hub which was the highest education and research centre in Elone.

'What do you mean it was not an accident? How else could this have happened?' Ultur asked, her voice breaking a little.

Crati replied slowly, 'Our preliminary report indicates that Seeni was injected with Vish. There was an imperceptible prick on the side of her neck. She was found, as we all know, lying near the Fence. Detailed investigations are underway and we will know more by the end of this vihan. Since we have destroyed all stores of Vish many zacs ago, there is a view that those on the other side of the Fence might be responsible.'

'That is not possible!'

'It is unheard of!'

'There must be some mistake…'

'Why would they do it?'

'They would not breach the peace. It serves both sides!'

The exclamations came from around the table. Ultur was the only one who remained silent.

Crati waited, hoping Ultur would say something. She did not know how to deal with such a situation. No one in her memory had ever been taken. The event itself was catastrophic, but the suggestion that it was not an accident made it all the more unreal. When Crati had seen the report, she had been astounded. No act of aggression had happened since the Fence had come up. Clash-ii had occurred hundreds of zacs ago. At that time, many had been taken on both the sides. Ultur was one of the few who had survived Clash-ii. Crati hoped that she would help her make sense of the situation, but Ultur remained silent.

'So, what do we do now? We need a response,' Gela, one of the members, stated the obvious. The members looked at Crati, who, in turn, glanced at Ultur. She was staring at the screen before her, deep in thought.

'We will meet again when the final report comes. Let us receive confirmation whether the assumption regarding what happened is correct. We will decide our response then,' Crati announced. The meeting was seemingly over, but the members remained seated, uncertain and unsure. After a while, everyone walked out, one by one. Only Ultur and Crati remained in the sun-bathed room.

'How are you so sure that Vish was the cause?' Ultur broke her silence.

'Ultur, that is what the preliminary report mentions. As I said before, we decommissioned Vish more than fifty zacs ago. But we also know that it is not the case on the other side.'

'Hmm... I think your decision to wait for the final report is correct,' Ultur said and left. Crati noticed that her shoulders sagged and her gait was slow. She wondered if the shock would make Ultur need some replacements.

After she exited the Council building, Ultur decided to walk back to her apartment. The road seemed long, endless and empty, much like her life. She felt a near forgotten ache enclose her being. The house would be empty too. Midway, Ultur changed her course and walked towards the Fence instead. Thoughts of Seeni swirled around in her mind. Seeni would never come back home and call out to her. Seeni was gone. She was taken.

A long time had elapsed since Ultur had dealt with the finality of taking. The last time was during Clash-ii and that had happened many zacs ago. Elone had changed since Clash-ii. It now had big cities, with tall and elegant buildings, numerous trees and parks. Sky-hugging walkways formed a delicate mesh among the buildings. The roads were broad and shuttles crisscrossed the cities through energy corridors. A sense of grace and languid beauty suffused Elone's cities.

Crossing the skywalks and roads, Ultur finally reached the Fence. A pathway ran parallel to the Fence and it was lined with myriad vegetation. Thick patches of green were interspersed with colourful flowers and patterned leaves. She walked to the spot where it was claimed that Seeni had been found lying. Ultur gazed at the opaque space that was the Fence. It had not been breached since it had been created after Clash-ii. Ultur still had trouble believing that those on the other side of the Fence had taken Seeni, her creation. Ultur shook her head and began walking the path along the Fence. There was a sense of impending catastrophe. Ultur remembered things others did not.

Iwe was in a state of shock. She sat in her apartment and stared at the darkness outside. Iwe had never known of anyone being taken. And, now, Seeni had been taken. The full implication of that statement was just dawning on her. She could never speak to Seeni again, never see her or tag her. It was unbelievable. How was such a thing even possible? In the last vihan only, Seeni had tagged her about an interesting module at the Irana Hub. Now, Iwe could never ask Seeni for any further details.

Iwe thought of Tioni and sent her an urgent tag. She might know about Seeni. Iwe lay down on her bed and stared at the ceiling. Her flowing robe was wrapped comfortably around her. It would adjust to the temperature for a restful night. Her short copper hair framed her round face. Iwe felt as if there was a strange hole in her mind—something she did not know how to mend.

What had happened to Seeni? What would they do with her now? Suddenly, Iwe wanted to know what they did with someone who had been taken. Seeni, with her dark red long hair, elegant manner and sharp questions, what had happened to her? Her mind was in a spin. She fell asleep with these strange thoughts twirling inside her head.

When she woke up, the city was still engulfed by darkness. Her tag was overflowing and some of the older messages were now flashing on the screen in a wall. Iwe had not embedded the tag inside her. At times, she needed to shut it down. There were times when she craved silence and respite from the incessant conversations on the tag channels. The entire day the buzz on the tag had been about Seeni. The Council had sent out a message about her being taken. However, no one seemed to know what had exactly happened to her. There was still no word from Tioni. Iwe tried to enter Tioni's apartment workstation through the tag, but could not.

Iwe got worried. Seeni had been taken and Tioni was not reachable. The gamut of feelings sweeping through her was entirely new. Seeni—she wanted to talk to her, hear her voice. Iwe shut her eyes once again wondering when and how the hole inside her head would mend.

The land stretched all around the double-storeyed building. In the distance, the silhouette of mountains adorned the skyline. It was time for the harvest. Promly sat at the workstation and began to schedule it. The air sweeping in through the open windows was sweet and pregnant with the smell of ripe Amar crop. Over the last many zacs, Promly had become fond of this smell. Farming—it had never been on her horizon but now, it had become something she enjoyed immensely. She finalized the schedule and put the system on ready mode, to be activated at first light the next morning.

Stepping out into the open air, Promly stretched and felt a deep weariness in her limbs. She would go for a check-up after the harvest. It had been nearly forty zacs since her last round of replacements. Maybe some organs needed to be changed. In the fading sunlight, her ash hair glinted. Cut in a neat short style, it framed her long face like the hood of a cape. Promly was tall, slim and carried an air of authority about her. On the farm she normally wore short blouses with knee length pants, unlike the tunics and trousers she wore when in the city.

In the shed, on the other side of the main building, Promly could see the row of toboks neatly lined up. Each tobok was equipped with enhancements to execute the harvest-related work assigned to it. When the programme was activated, they would roll out and start working the farm.

Promly walked back inside the house. The screen on the wall was abuzz with the incident involving Seeni. Shock, incredulity, outrage and fear were being expressed. Promly could see that Ultur had been trying to reach her repeatedly through the tag. What had happened to the bright and energetic Seeni was indeed tragic. When she had first met Ultur, Promly had been a budding informatics expert and Seeni, just an infant. As she grew, Seeni exhibited excellence in computational ideas. It was Promly who encouraged her to join the Nividum, their main informatics hub. Seeni had followed that path and proved to be exceptionally good.

Two zacs ago, Seeni had travelled to Promly's farm, nestled in the hills, to meet her. They had walked through the farm together and talked. Seeni told her that she had left her assignment with the Nividum and had started associating with the Irana Hub. Promly had been sorely disappointed with her move.

Promly had tried to understand what had prompted Seeni's sudden change of path. As they had watched the three moons set over the undulating farm, Promly had asked, 'Why Seeni?

You are wasting your talent in the Irana Hub. What do you want to do there?'

'Promly, you headed the Nividum for countless zacs, why did you take up farming?' Instead of answering her question, Seeni had asked her one.

Promly had kept quiet. Seeni had always been inquisitive. Even when she was growing up, she had innumerable questions which would pop up on Promly's tag with unwavering regularity.

There was another series of innumerable tags from Ultur. Promly switched the channel to Ultur's house and they saw each other for the first time since Seeni had been taken.

Ultur was sitting on the sofa. The lights were dim and a sense of despair hung around her colourful apartment. The vibrant draperies hung in Ultur's apartment seemed to mirror Seeni.

Ultur began without any preamble, 'Promly, I had forgotten how painful it is when someone is taken. All of a sudden I am back at Clash-ii, when so many I knew were taken. You can't even begin to understand the sense of loss and abandonment that engulfs one when someone close to them is taken. The finality is unbearable. You came nearly fifty zacs after Clash-ii. By then, being taken had become a remote possibility.'

Promly sat in silence. What Ultur was saying was true. No one known to Promly had ever been taken. She probably did not understand the pain.

'Where is Onip these days?' Ultur asked, cutting across the silence.

Promly was taken aback. She had not thought of or heard from her clarent for many zacs. Like most residents of Elone, once she completed sixteen zacs, she had moved out of her clarent's home. There were some like Ultur and Seeni who continued to live together, but they were exceptions.

'She is in a city somewhere near the ocean. Why?' replied Promly.

'I was simply asking. Anyway, do you know what the Council is saying about Seeni?'

'Let us switch to our encrypted channel if you want to talk about it,' Promly advised.

They switched to their secure channel and Ultur continued, 'Crati announced that Seeni was taken by Vish that came from the other side! Promly, how is that possible? We have been at peace. Why would they do this now? And Seeni, why her? Do you think there has been some mistake?'

Promly did not interrupt Ultur. She let all the questions pour out of her. She sat in silence as a tear trickled down Ultur's face.

'Promly, if it is confirmed that the other side is indeed involved, then you know what you have to do,' Ultur said with a note of finality.

Outside, the breeze was blowing and the fragrance of the night flowers mixed with that of ripe Amar pervaded the room.

'Has the analysis report confirmed what Crati said?' Promly asked gently. Ultur's distress was upsetting.

'Not yet. The final report will come in about a vihan.'

'Let us wait till then, Ultur. By then the harvest will also be over and I can come to the city. We can work on this together.'

'How can you think of the harvest right now? That is not your main work, Promly, I hope you remember that,' Ultur said before breaking off the secure line abruptly.

Promly stood up and pressed the button to close the windows and dim the lights. When she became the head of the Nividum, Promly had moved into the apartment complex where Ultur lived. Ultur had been a part of the Council even then. Promly's technical skills and Ultur's ability to rally a group had helped them collaborate and work together, even in matters before the Council. They even had the access codes to each other's apartments. Promly understood Ultur's anguish, but the harvest of Amar was due.

It was time to sleep. This event was going to cause many sleepless nights in Elone, she was sure of that.

As soon as Iwe woke up, she checked her tag. There was no response from Tioni. Iwe tried to enter Tioni's apartment workstation again, but it was evident that her system was shut, which was unusual. The discussion about Seeni had already been replaced with other routine things in the maze of conversations on the tag. Everyone seemed to be awaiting the verdict of the Council on the cause.

Outside, it was a bright day. A brisk breeze was blowing throughout the city, cooling and refreshing. Iwe scrolled to the Vault. It was quiet as visitors had not yet started streaming in. Iwe managed the Vault, the store of their heritage. Since their arrival on Elone, material saved either physically or virtually could be found in the Vault. New materials were regularly sent to the Vault by the residents of Elone. Iwe's job was to collate the material and data, and add new materials under their proper classifications. She enjoyed her job.

As Iwe dressed, music flowed through her apartment. Seeni had shared this particular piece of music with her some time ago. It was exquisite and quite unlike anything Iwe had ever heard before. When she asked about it, Seeni's reply had been enigmatic, 'Iwe, it comes from a source about which I will tell you when the right time comes.'

Iwe thought about that reply and wondered. There had been many times she had found some of the things Seeni said incomprehensible, but she had never dwelt on them, until now.

Seeni had started visiting the Vault about five zacs ago. As part of the Nividum, she had access to all the materials of the Vault on her tag, yet she chose to come in person and often spent long periods ensconced in there. Iwe was slightly intimidated by her in the beginning. Seeni would ask for material that took a lot of effort to find. One day, Seeni had walked into Iwe's chamber and asked, 'Have you been through the Chronicle?'

'No,' Iwe had replied.

'What a shame, Iwe! You are manager at the Vault and you have not seen them? Don't you want to know where all this material came from? What happened in our past? The Chronicle details our journey since we arrived on Elone, you will learn about yourself when you go through them.'

Iwe had remained quiet. She had studied the story of their past while she was completing her education.

She knew that Elone was a beautiful place. It had large lakes and oceans, hills and mountain slopes covered with trees. They had lived here for thousands of zacs. She also knew that they had come to Elone from another planet called Earth, which had been destroyed. There had been a time, before the Fence had come up after Clash-ii, when they had struggled against 'them' on the other side. However, since the Fence, there had been peace. Iwe had learnt all this.

But, beyond that, the past did not interest her. She had never felt the need to know more. She appreciated music, enjoyed her job and liked to travel to the hills and the lakes. Water gliding was her favourite sport. For Iwe, this was enough.

'Not really, Seeni. We are here, that is all that matters to me. Why do you make such an effort to know everything, I don't understand.'

Seeni had merely sighed and left the room and Iwe had immediately forgotten about the conversation.

But, two zacs ago, Seeni had quit the Nividum and joined the Irana Hub. Her visits to the Vault became more frequent. Each time they met, she would ask Iwe, 'Started processing the Chronicle yet?'

Tired of shaking her head, one day Iwe began to process the Chronicle. Processing was easier than reading. She simply hooked her tag to the Chronicle document and let her brain directly process the matter. It rested the eyes and was faster than reading. However, the Chronicle did not hold Iwe's interest. At the slightest excuse, she would drop the processing and move on to something else. She had started with Chronicle-ii and was still somewhere in the middle when Seeni was taken.

Exiting her apartment, Iwe took a shuttle to the Vault. When the Vault came into view, Iwe was, as always, struck by its enormity. A large structure, gracefully built with flowing lines, it dominated the scene completely. It had arched roofs that let in the sunlight. Divided into various sections, dotted with workstations, the Vault attracted many visitors from far and wide.

Iwe's chamber was on the top floor of the building. She entered and began working. The day raced by and as the light faded from her room in the late evening, she tried to reach

Tioni once again, but her system was still shut. Iwe had arrived more than fifty zacs after Seeni, and about twenty-five zacs after Tioni.

Tioni had first come to the Vault as a visitor. She had visited regularly for a while, before she was given access on her tag to the material in the Vault—as per regulations.

Iwe wondered again why she was inaccessible.

The Chronicle-ii was open in her system, but Iwe did not feel like processing. With Seeni gone, there was no one to push her anymore. She switched to the 'documents-received' channel.

As she scrolled the list, a music document from Seeni, that she had sent three days ago, came up. Iwe felt a sudden sense of deep sadness. This was the last piece of music Seeni would ever send her. How difficult it was to accept this strange finality. Iwe saw the music had been sent to Tioni too. It surprised Iwe as Tioni was far removed from things like music.

Iwe played the piece. A lilting melody flowed through the room. Like the earlier pieces Seeni had shared, it was superb. Iwe shut her eyes and let the music drench her with its sweetness.

Tara was crying. But, her cries, floating around the house, sounded melodious to Tioni's ears. She went to the small bed on which Tara lay and looked at her. Since creations had not happened for so long, it had been difficult to find things suited for Tara's use. Tara continued to cry. The instruction manual said that whenever the creation cried, Tioni was to pick her up, rest her against her shoulder and slowly pat her. Tioni cautiously did that. Tara was so tiny. At times, Tioni thought she would slip through her hands and fall. She had processed the instruction manual many times so that she would make no mistakes.

With Tara held against her shoulder, Tioni paced the room. After a while, Tara stopped whimpering and rested quietly. Stopping by the window, Tioni gazed out. It was late evening. The sun was setting in a clear sky. Shuttles floated by in their respective energy corridors.

The warmth of Tara's little form permeated Tioni's entire body. It was a strange sensation, entirely new—the touch of another being against her. Over the last three days, Tioni had shut out the rest of Elone. There was only Tara and her. Every day with her brought a new discovery, a new sensation. She wondered once again whether all clarents felt the same.

Tara drifted off to sleep and Tioni gently laid her on the small bed. With the system switched off, there was complete silence inside the house. Her tag, workstation, and the screen on the wall were all lifeless and still. For a moment, Tioni thought of reconnecting, but then decided against it. She would spend some more exclusive time with Tara, before relinking to the system.

Tioni sank into a reclining chair by the window and watched as the night reclaimed the sky. This hour of the day was something Seeni liked too. She recalled Seeni's surprise when she had decided to apply for a creation. They had known each other since Tioni had done some replacements for Seeni. Seeni had questioned her incessantly about her desire to become a clarent. For Tioni, becoming a clarent had gained importance as the zacs had gone by. She was an expert at replacements;

people came to her from all over Elone for treatment. The idea to go for a creation had begun as the desire to observe all the organs, which she routinely replaced, since their beginning.

This seed of desire had crystallized into the idea of becoming a clarent. Tioni had mulled over it. When she had approached the Creation Facility for permission, she was told that she would have to wait while they brushed up the creation process. As the zacs had gone by, the seed of desire had taken deep root inside her. It had ceased to have any connection with studying the organs; rather, it had become an organic need within her.

As her eyes drooped, Tioni wondered why Seeni had not visited her and Tara yet. Seeni knew about Tara's imminent arrival as well as about Tioni's decision to delink from the system for some time.

Sleep had just begun to claim Tioni when Tara started to cry again. Tioni got up wearily from the chair, picked Tara up and began to pace the room. Outside, the night was dark and silent.

Ultur sat quietly at the table staring at Seeni's empty chair. Nearly five days had passed, but not a word had emerged about the reason behind her taking. Ultur had not stepped outside since her visit to the Fence. The finality of Seeni's departure had coiled around her entire being. The forgotten pain of loss had engulfed her. Tears rolled down her cheeks.

Ultur had been sure that Promly would come to the city immediately. But, to her surprise, the harvest seemed more important to Promly. Ultur wiped her tears and rested her head on her arms on the table.

Could it be true that 'they' had done it? If yes, then the question was, why? Was the peace and tranquility of all these past zacs going to be shattered again?

The questions arising from Seeni's taking circled in Ultur's head incessantly. There was simply no respite from them.

The sensor at her door vibrated, which caught Ultur by surprise. Visits to apartments were rare and were never undertaken without first confirming on the tag. Ultur did not recognize the person standing outside. Even though she looked familiar, Ultur could not place her. Through her tag, Ultur asked wearily, 'Who is it?'

Outside the door, Iwe read the question on the door's screen. She felt awkward. Why had she come? Iwe had never met Ultur, but she knew that unlike other clarents and their creations, Seeni and Ultur used to live together. Ultur would be feeling the loss much more than her. It was probably this thought that had brought Iwe here.

'It is Iwe. I manage the Vault. I knew Seeni,' Iwe spoke into the screen. Immediately, the door swung open. Inside, the colours splashed around the large room mesmerized Iwe. The walls were adorned with vibrant tapestries and vivid pictures. However, surrounded by a riot of colour, Ultur sat at a table, alone, colourless and wan.

Iwe sat across the table from her and searched for words. She did not know what to say. Ultur also continued to sit silently.

'Seeni sent me something a few days ago. Can I send it to your system, Ultur?' Iwe broke the heavy silence.

'What is it?' Ultur asked, surprised.

'A piece of music. It is very melodious.'

Ultur was taken aback. Seeni had an interest in music? She did not even know about this.

'How did you know her, Iwe?'

Iwe told Ultur about Seeni's visits to the Vault and how she had encouraged her to go through the Chronicle. As Iwe spoke, she felt tears rolling down her cheeks. Ultur watched her, unblinking. Grieving for those who had gone was not something people of Elone understood. Was the time coming when they would have to relearn it?

When Iwe stopped speaking, she dried her eyes. She felt a sense of relief as if the hole in her head had mended to a certain degree. She looked around the room again. The apartment was much larger than hers. An intricate and graceful piece of tapestry hung on the opposite wall. It reminded her of Seeni. Iwe could visualize Seeni in this room. It matched her sense of dress, her long dark red hair and the elegance with which she had carried herself. But, at present, despite the kaleidoscope of colours, the room had a sad and melancholic feeling pervading through it. Iwe thought her burnt red tunic was out of place in the mood.

'You can send me the music. I would be happy to listen to it,' Ultur said after a while.

Iwe sent her the piece. Silence fell over them again. Iwe had a question but she didn't know how to ask Ultur. She opened her mouth but hesitated. Finally, she couldn't stop herself and the words tumbled out, 'What happened to Seeni? No one seems to know.'

'Even I am waiting for the final word from the Council,' replied Ultur.

Iwe understood it was time for her to leave. She got up and walked towards the door.

'When I find out anything about Seeni, I will let you know,' Ultur said from the table. Iwe nodded and shut the door behind her.

The music was now on Ultur's system. She played it and the sweet melody floated throughout the room. As the notes went higher, Ultur was startled. She had never heard many of the instruments that were being played. She listened to the piece repeatedly but she could not identify the instruments. The system too did not yield any information on the instruments or about the music. It clearly had not been composed on Elone.

Ultur tagged Iwe, 'Where did Seeni get this piece from?'

Iwe replied immediately, 'I don't know. I asked her, but Seeni said she would tell me when the time was right.'

Ultur was shaken out of her stupor. The music continued to play in the background, while Ultur wondered whether the music was the key to understanding what had happened to Seeni.

After visiting Ultur, Iwe felt much better. She took a shuttle back to the Vault. After an extraordinary event like Seeni's taking, it had seemed things would never return to normal. But they apparently had. The shuttle was crowded and the walkways were abuzz with commuters. It seemed that barring a few, like Ultur, Iwe and maybe Tioni, life had moved on for everyone else.

Even the Vault had more visitors than usual. Once she was relatively free, Iwe tried to tag Tioni again, but drew a blank. Restless, Iwe decided to return to the Chronicle. She wondered why Seeni always insisted that she should read them. She realized she would know only when she had gone through them.

Chronicle-ii, Page nz[23]

For us, it was like starting all over again, like at the time of the Great Escape from Earth. Rebuilding was not easy. Our numbers had dwindled dramatically; there were not enough of us to build the cities and towns again. After Clash-ii, we had two priorities: shore up our numbers and work out an arrangement with the other side to foreclose the possibility of another clash. The repeated conflicts and skirmishes did not allow us the opportunity to settle down and create a world of our own.

Creation facilities were set up, and systematically, with complete records, creations began. Everyone became a clarent and could have as many creations as they wanted. While this process was underway, dialogue was on with the other side. Their situation was the same, and they too were looking for a permanent solution to the clashes. That was when Nanti on our side came up with the blueprint for the Fence. It was to provide a respite from the relentless strife and conflict that had plagued the two sides since our arrival on Elone.

The Fence is an electronic shield that extends till the Mesosphere of Elone. It creates an opaque barrier behind which we can live believing we are the only ones on the planet. Impenetrable, it can only be disintegrated by a simultaneous command from both the sides or if it is blasted with a nanoelectric surge. It provides a rational, workable and enduring solution to the conflict. We have to share the planet because we all arrived here together after the Great Escape, but with the Fence, we can do it in an insulated manner. The Fence provides a shield in whose shadow we can each evolve and grow.

Once the Fence came up, we concentrated on increasing our numbers. The Council decided by a Decree that clarents could only give preferences related to the physical attributes and appearance of the creation. No modifications were to be allowed to the creations' mental abilities. This Decree followed the practice that had originated on Earth and predated the Great Escape.

Over the zacs, we made major advances in replacements too. First, we found Nepo in subterranean Elone. The malleable material was ideal for organs. However, since Nepo was an exhaustible mineral, we worked to develop a renewable source. After researching for zacs, we developed Amar, which is now cultivated in large tracts on the foothills of the mountain ranges. The crop is reaped twice a year and then processed as organ raw material. Since we started using Amar, replacements last for about fifty zacs on an average. This better quality of replacements has ensured that creations are not as common as they used to be and have been on decline over the last few zacs.

Iwe stopped processing. She stood up and stretched. A mirror on the wall caught her reflection. She was tall and slim with small breasts and rounded hips. The burnt red tunic was looking rather nice on her. Her copper hair had grown till her shoulders, and her black eyes were shining brightly. Had her clarent asked for these features? It had been many zacs since Iwe had thought about her clarent. Like most others, she had moved out of her clarent's home after sixteen zacs.

Iwe turned from the mirror, the Chronicle was still open on her workstation. The Decree about creations mentioned something that predated the Great Escape. Earth—what was the story of that planet? Why did they need to abandon it? What had those people who had lived on Earth been like? How had they lived? She wondered, as she shut down the Vault system.

Iwe left the Vault and headed towards her apartment. The city was slowly slipping into the arms of a balmy evening. Lights flooded a circular building situated at the corner of the road. It was the Vayunum Iwe had attended. The Vayunums were the basic educational centres which were attended by everyone. However, only some of the people chose to move to the higher units, and even fewer to the Irana Hub. At her Vayunum, the instructor machines for the three students enrolled had been meticulous and rigorous. Iwe had specialized in documentation and had later joined the Vault.

As she waited for a shuttle, the shadows were lengthening as the city lights were brightening. Iwe wondered why she had never heard of the Great Escape prior to reading the Chronicle. Then, she recalled that at the Vayunum, the past was never mentioned.

The reaped Amar crop was in the processing pipeline and the ground had been programmed in preparation for the next sowing. Standing outside her house, Promly observed the bare fields which were dotted with the toboks at work. The mountain breeze ruffled her hair. Promly checked her tag. The Council was still silent about the reason behind Seeni's taking. This process was taking longer than Promly had anticipated. Since their last conversation nearly ten days ago, prior to the harvest, there had been no contact with Ultur. Promly decided that as soon as she reached the city, she would meet Ultur.

Promly went inside her house and switched on some music. Music always relaxed her. Any new music on the various tag channels invariably found its way into her collection.

She sat down to review her tag messages. Clepo had sent something. Promly opened it with anticipation.

It's moving closer to completion. We should be ready by the end of this zac.

Promly shut her eyes and leaned back in her chair as a cheerful composition played in the background. The long journey and quest was nearing an end. Promly let the music wash over her. The piece ended and another one started. The notes were lilting and soothing. It was unlike something she had ever heard before. The instruments and the tenor were completely different from the usual music pieces.

Promly checked the display. The title simply said 'Seeni'. She was not surprised. Only Seeni could have managed to find a way into her private collection and add a piece. The symphony had been added to Promly's collection two days before Seeni was taken. Promly had been so busy with the harvest that she had missed it. As the music continued to play, Promly wondered where Seeni had found such an exquisite and unique piece of music. As the crescendo rose in the room, Promly realized that the instruments were unknown and unheard of.

She tried to find the identity of the composer but the system did not yield any results. There was no information about the symphony anywhere.

Was this Seeni's way of telling her something? Promly sighed as the music played. Seeni, bright and energetic, why did it have to be you?

The small apartment was cluttered. Tara's arrival had played havoc with its neat and immaculate look. Tioni felt perpetually sleep deprived. Caring for Tara was proving to be overwhelming and very different from the simple process portrayed in the instruction manual. Once she rejoined work at the Remplazo, Tioni planned to get a tobok to help her out with Tara. Remplazo was a replacement centre where residents came for therapy and rejuvenation through organ replacement.

It was late afternoon and Tara was sleeping. Tioni was beginning to feel restless. Her days seemed to be passing by in a blur. All her activities were tailored to fit into Tara's schedule. As Tioni was trying to rearrange the room, the silence and weariness seemed to envelop her with a vengeance. It was time to link up with the system again. After tidying up and hurriedly eating two loaves of inola with korive sauce, Tioni finally reconnected to the system after more than a vihaan.

The Remplazo had sent her numerous reminders about the cases awaiting her attention. Tioni kept scrolling and then, she saw a message. *Seeni has been taken*. Tioni had a sinking feeling. She couldn't believe it. As she read further, the details started pouring in. She noticed that Iwe had been trying to reach her repeatedly.

Tara was wailing again. Automatically, Tioni got up, picked up Tara and began rocking her. Her mind was like a whirlwind.

What had happened to Seeni? Did this mean she would never see her, talk to her or meet her again?

It confused Tioni. She had never faced a situation like this before. Could she replace Seeni's organs to set things right? Then, with a jolt, she remembered learning long back that once a person had been taken, it was not possible to bring them back. Taking was such a rare phenomenon that nobody focused on it. It was something that used to happen in the distant past. However, now, it had happened to Seeni.

Tara had gone back to sleep. Tioni lowered her on to the bed and paced the room, unsettled and unnerved. Outside the window, a tree swayed in the late afternoon breeze. A pale sun bathed the quiet landscape. Everything looked the same, but Seeni no longer existed on Elone. Again, Tioni felt a tightening within her. She tagged Iwe and asked her to visit. Iwe responded immediately saying she was on her way.

As she waited for Iwe, Tioni found herself remembering Seeni with a clarity she had never experienced before. Like a vision, all the zacs they had known each other flashed before her.

Seeni was always full of questions even while replacements were being done. She wanted to know so many things. Tioni had been surprised at Seeni's sense of enquiry. It was not a common quality in the people of Elone. Seeni had pushed Tioni to start researching the Vault for information about the journey of replacement therapy and that was where she had met Iwe.

Tioni recalled the evening when they had sat on a rooftop café in the heart of the city. The last rays of the sun were falling on Seeni's beautiful hair lending them a deep shining red hue as Tioni had asked her, 'Why do you always have so many questions about everything, Seeni?'

'Don't you want to know, Tioni, since when we have been doing replacements? And what happened before that?'

'Not really, Seeni. Why does the past interest you so much?'

Seeni had looked at the vast expanse of the city spread out below. The air was clean and sweet as it swept across the rooftop.

'I know that one day Ultur decided that she wanted a

creation. So, she went to a Creation Facility and they took a cell from her body. She filled out a form, gave some specifications about my physical attributes and then left. When the time came, the facility called her and from an incubator they brought me out and handed me over to her. I had dark red hair and hazel eyes, just what she had desired. And just like that, I came to exist on Elone and I will continue to exist,' Seeni paused before continuing, 'However, I often think, where did that original cell come from? Where are the roots of our existence? You know I have read the Chronicle but it only speaks about us after the Great Escape. There is no mention of anything about what it was like on that planet called Earth. How did they live on that planet? Why did they leave? I even tried to find Earth but the entire galaxy seems to have vanished as if it was swallowed whole, lost in the innards of space. This silence, this impregnable wall that has been created across life on Earth is what intrigues me. We came from Earth but we know nothing about it. Doesn't it perturb you?'

Tioni had remained silent while Seeni had shared her thoughts. Tioni, on her part, had never contemplated about Earth or things like that ever before.

'But how does it matter to us, Seeni? And, why should it?' she asked.

Tioni remembered Seeni had been quiet as the setting sun enveloped them in a golden hue. Then, she had spoken softly, 'Because what happened on that planet has determined how we live today. It has decided who we are, what we value and what we find important. Have you ever heard of the word "passion", Tioni?'

Tioni had thought for a moment before answering, 'No. Not that I remember.'

'Neither had I. I discovered it in the Vault when I was processing some materials from Earth. I searched for it and realized that it is not mentioned in the Lexicon which contains all the words that have survived long enough to be remembered from the different languages that were spoken on Earth. You know what that means?' But, without waiting for Tioni to respond, Seeni had continued, 'It means that "passion" is not remembered at all on Elone. I had to look a lot to find out what it means. Simply put, it means "a powerful or compelling emotion". Have you ever felt something like that Tioni?'

Tioni did not understand where the conversation was going. There were many things that she liked or enjoyed doing such as her work, keeping her apartment tidy and going to cafés, but 'passion'? She did not understand what it meant.

'I don't understand, Seeni. We all feel something about the things we do. If we don't like them we don't do them and vice versa.'

'I know, Tioni. I first liked informatics so I joined the Nividum. Then, I decided to try my hand at the Irana Hub. But, having a passion for something? I am curious to know what that feels like.'

Silence had enveloped them once more. After a while, Seeni had declared, 'Look at me, Tioni, I exist and I will continue to do so. But, now, knowing about the roots of my existence has become my passion.'

Tioni was brought back to the present when her tag started buzzing, announcing Iwe's arrival at her door. Seeni's confident assertion 'I exist and I will continue to do so' seemed to reverberate in the air.

The door swung open and Iwe walked inside. Both Tioni and Iwe looked at each other. A sense of common loss hung over them but they did not know how to express it. Inside, Tara began to wail. Tioni turned and hurried back while Iwe stood rooted to her spot in the centre of the room, awestruck. Tioni returned with Tara in her arms and for the first time Iwe saw a creation in reality. The creature was incredibly small and looked helpless.

'Her name is Tara. Would you like to hold her?' Tioni asked.

Iwe couldn't gather her courage to hold out her arms. She stared dumbstruck at the sight of Tioni rocking her creation.

'When did she arrive, Tioni? Is this why your system has been shut off all this while? Did Seeni see her?'

The questions tumbled out of Iwe as she continued to stare at Tara who had stopped crying and seemed to be looking directly at Iwe with her blue eyes.

'Tara arrived the day Seeni was taken, and yes, I wanted to be exclusively with her that is why I had shut down my system. No, Seeni did not see her.'

To her own surprise, Tioni felt a tear roll down her cheek. She made a feed for Tara and, while Iwe watched in complete silence, she gently put her on the bed. Satiated, Tara lay on the bed and looked around.

Iwe approached the bed and observed the creation, her incredibly small limbs, perfect face and curly mop of hair. It was an astounding experience. Iwe stretched out her hand and touched Tara's cheek gently.

'Tell me, Iwe, what happened to Seeni?' Tioni's question broke the spell. Iwe came and sat down near Tioni.

'No one knows. We are all waiting for the Council to announce the details. Even Ultur doesn't know,' and then, as an afterthought, she added, 'I went to meet her.'

They sat in silence for a while as Tara kept them company with her gurgles. It was as if Seeni held a thread on which their silence hung, waiting to snap.

'Did you hear the music Seeni sent you?' Iwe asked.

Surprised, Tioni shook her head. She was not interested in music and Seeni knew that.

'She sent it to me a day before she was taken,' Iwe continued, 'It was copied to you as well. You must listen to it, Tioni. I have never heard such an exquisite piece of music. I passed it to Ultur too. Even she did not know where Seeni got it from.'

Tioni searched her tag and saw that there was indeed something from Seeni. She opened it on the screen.

Tioni, listen to this music. Does it not make you curious about where it came from? Once you hear it, go to your encrypted channel.

The message floated before them and Tioni could almost hear Seeni.

'Tioni, please go to your encrypted channel now,' Iwe urged.

Maybe the mysterious source of the music would finally be revealed. Iwe had been in a strange state since Seeni's taking—the source of the music, the material in the Chronicle, all these questions whispered in her head and confused her. Iwe wanted clarity. She wanted to return to her original pattern of life.

Tioni was silent for a while and then she played the music.

'I must do what Seeni asked. If she was around, I could have done it differently but not now.'

As the music played, the rhythm spread throughout the apartment. When it stopped, the room seemed to be drenched in serenity. Tara had fallen asleep. Once the last strains of the composition had faded away, Tioni accessed her encrypted channel and displayed Seeni's message on the screen so Iwe could read it too.

I am sure the music sounded good, even to someone like you who has no interest in such things. I have shared a few pieces with Iwe; she enjoyed them too. Iwe keeps on asking me where I got them from. Well, if you also want to know about the composer, just look for Maya. You can take Iwe's help as she is good with machines. You can start from the Irana Hub.

Tioni, where we come from is a determining factor in where we are going. It decides, in a way, how we live right now. The thread of the past links the present and the future. This is something I have recently understood. I will shortly be talking to Promly about this as well. When you find Maya, tell me. You both will enjoy meeting her, I am sure.

Tara, who had fallen asleep, whimpered in her sleep. Outside, the sky turned dark.

'Who is Maya? Did Seeni ever speak to you about her?' Iwe asked.

Tioni shook her head. She had questions of her own, 'Who is Promly? Have you heard of her, Iwe?'

'I don't know for sure. But, I remember that many zacs ago, someone named Promly headed the Nividum. Maybe she is the same one Seeni is talking about or maybe it is someone else,' Iwe replied and stood up, a little frustrated.

Seeni's message had not solved anything. Instead, it had added to the questions and confusion in her head. Iwe looked once more at Tara's sleeping form and was, again, struck with wonder at the tiny form breathing softly. Then, without saying anything more, she left.

The air was fresh and calmed Iwe to a certain extent. She

waited for a shuttle. One came rushing towards her but it was crowded so she let it go. She was not in the mood to be surrounded by others. She wanted some peace, some quiet. She waited for the next one wondering if she should tell Ultur about Maya. As she stepped into a relatively empty shuttle, she had made up her mind. She would find Maya and would take her along to meet Ultur.

It was a cloudy and gloomy day. Iwe sat at her workstation in the Vault and processed all the people associated with the Irana Hub. There was no mention of anyone called Maya. She scanned through data dating back nearly two hundred zacs but drew a blank. No one called Maya had ever seemed to have existed. The Irana Hub did not have music as a discipline either. Perplexed, Iwe read Seeni's message again, which Tioni had sent to her tag. She realized that she needed to visit the Irana Hub in person as the system had not revealed anything.

Iwe felt some trepidation going there. The Irana Hub was an exclusive institution, only a select few enrolled to excel in their chosen fields. She had never been inside. Gathering all her courage, Iwe left the Vault and took a shuttle to the Irana Hub.

Standing outside the Hub, Iwe marvelled at its sheer size. The Irana Hub was even bigger than the Vault. Rising as far out into the sky as the eyes could see, its different sections had different kinds of architecture. Some sections had rounded roofs, while some had slanted ones and others had flat roofs. The cream colour of the building looked somewhat muddy in the dark cloudy afternoon. The imposing building was surrounded by many trees and a small placid lake lay on one side.

Seeni had worked at the 'Developing Elone' section at the Hub. When Iwe pushed the button for that section at the massive entrance door, an elevator on one side of the door descended. Iwe stepped in and was swept up. Inside the elevator was a screen with many names. Iwe spotted the name Niosi. She remembered that Niosi had visited the Vault recently. Iwe pressed the button next to her name and a voice asked, 'Who is it?'

'I am Iwe, the Vault manager. I needed to ask you something. May I meet you?' It was a peculiar thing to do, visiting someone without tagging first. After some hesitation, the voice replied, 'Turn right when the doors open. You will see my name on the left-hand side.'

Iwe followed the directions. She felt a strange knot in the pit of her being. She realized she was trembling. Why did she feel as if she was doing something wrong? After all, she was only looking for someone Seeni had mentioned!

Niosi greeted her with a surprised smile. Iwe stood in front of her and blurted out the first thing that came to her mind, 'I knew Seeni. I just wanted to see where she worked.'

'Oh,' replied Niosi. Then, after a moment, added, 'Her space has been shut down till there is some clarity on what happened to her. No one can go in. But yes, she did work in this section. We used to see each other once in a while. But, Seeni always seemed busy in the systems area. She spent most of her time there.'

Iwe's head was spinning. Should she ask about Maya? She realized that she was still standing. As if reading her mind,

Niosi gestured at a vacant chair.

'Is there a music section here?' Iwe asked, still standing.

'Why don't you sit down? And no, the Irana Hub does not have a music section.'

Iwe had run out of questions. She smiled politely and left. She noticed that Niosi returned to her work even before the door could shut behind Iwe.

Outside, Iwe saw the display for the systems area in the distance and started walking down the long corridor towards it. Once she reached there, she realized that it was a secure area with limited access. Iwe swiped her tag at the door. As Vault manager she had access to many secure areas in Elone. Her tag worked for the systems area at the Irana Hub too.

Inside, the hall was nearly deserted. In one corner, Iwe could see someone sitting at a terminal. She also sat at a secluded terminal and entered into the system. Iwe searched for Seeni, but, the system no longer recognized her. She tried to retrace Seeni's journey in the system around the time she was taken. To Iwe's surprise, not only was Seeni not present in the system, but any work that she might have done had also been systematically erased. Iwe realized with a jolt that Seeni had ceased to exist in the system too.

Iwe switched to looking for Maya. She ran queries for music, instruments and looked at records going back hundreds of zacs. There was no person or musician by the name of Maya in the entire system. After spending a long time searching by using all techniques and skills at her command, Iwe was exhausted. In the system, neither Seeni nor Maya existed.

Afterwards, as she made her way home, Iwe felt tired and drained. Why was she running around chasing shadows that Seeni had scattered along the way? Seeni was gone. Did it matter now who created that music? What did that piece of music have anything to do with Seeni's taking? Iwe decided that this was her last effort to find answers. She sent Tioni a tag about her fruitless search and closed the issue. She decided that she would go for water gliding next vihan and try to finish processing the Chronicle.

Her return to the Remplazo was a tough transition for Tioni. Initially, after working for seemingly endless days, she used to enter her apartment late in the evenings with a sleeping Tara strapped to her back. She was exhausted all the time. It was then that she decided that it was about time she acquired a tobok to help take care of Tara. She got one shaped like a person, with a face, hands and legs and named it Hap. Hap tended to Tara at the Remplazo and later came home with her. While Tioni attended to the claimants for replacements, she continuously monitored Hap's system. She would also look in on Tara whenever she got time.

Tioni watched with tired eyes as Tara slept. Hap was emitting its soothing blue light and was alert to Tara's every need. Tioni was lying in the reclining chair by the window. She was slowly beginning to understand why creations had declined. Tioni felt constantly tied up and perpetually tired. By regulations, her creation would be with her for the next sixteen zacs, only then could Tara move out. Tioni sighed; maybe things would get better as Tara grew.

Feeling a bit rested, Tioni got up and prepared a meal. She emptied a mix of her favourite vegetable stew asipo in water, heated two loaves of inola to go with it. After eating, she checked her tag. Apart from many others, there was a tag from Iwe. She went through the details of Iwe's quest. Maya seemed to be an enigma, someone elusive, but she did not interest Tioni. It did not matter to her whether they found her or not. Seeni was gone and nothing could change that fact. Tioni was waiting for news on the cause of Seeni's taking.

The three moons were alight in the sky, despite it being the rainy season. The city was bathed in white light. The trees visible from the window seemed to be shrouded in a silvery cloth. The calante had passed with no rain but it was still humid. Tioni turned back from the window and dimmed the lights in the apartment. As her eyes became heavy, she remembered Seeni's explanation of the word 'passion'. So, the earthlings felt 'compelling emotions'. But, about what? And, why? She wondered what would have driven those inhabitants of faraway Earth to develop a passion for things…

The Council meeting was in progress. The room was cast in a gloomy light as dark clouds hid the sun outside. The skylight was grey and so was the mood in the room. Although everyone's presence had been requested, two of the members were attending through their tag channels. Crati looked around at the assembled members and announced that the verdict on Seeni's taking had come in.

'The channels for those who are not present need to be switched off. This matter should be discussed only within this room right now,' Ultur said with a note of finality.

Crati looked around the table; no one seemed to disagree with Ultur. The channels for the two absent members were switched off.

Crati began, 'It is confirmed that Seeni was indeed poisoned by Vish. And it can also be said with conviction that it came from the other side.'

'How can they be so sure of the latter?' Ultur asked. She seemed more composed and in command than the last meeting.

'The cause was Vish. That is confirmed. Since we no longer have any stores of Vish, it has to be from the other side,' Crati clarified.

The group around the table was quiet. The report had many ramifications. As the clouds floated across the sky, the room alternated between light and shadow which reflected the pervading mood. Around the table, each one of the members knew the inexorable change this catastrophic event would bring to life as they knew it on Elone.

'We need to keep this to ourselves for now. Let us discuss this again before deciding on what to do next,' Ultur stated.

'I agree. I propose to the members that we tell the population that Seeni was taken in a mishap,' Crati announced.

A murmur went around the table but no one spoke up against the idea. The meeting seemed to have finished, but none of the members stirred from their seats.

'We will find a way to deal with this as we have always done before. Let us meet again after some time,' Crati closed the meeting on a brave note.

The members trooped out of the Council building, each one lost in their own thoughts. No one spoke. Outside, the sun was hidden behind a dark cloud but its beams were giving the clouds a silver lining.

Ultur too had left immediately. She went back to her apartment. On the encrypted channel, she sent an emergency tag to Promly. While waiting for Promly's response, Ultur remembered the music. She knew there had to be some link. Maybe Seeni had stumbled across something. Ultur sent another tag to the laboratory that had possession of Seeni's remains.

I would like the brain-mapping of Seeni to be sent to me immediately. This direction comes from me as a member of the Council of Elone. She hoped that Seeni's brain-mapping would provide some clues regarding her activities in the period before her taking.

There was no response from Promly. Gradually, the tag channels began to carry the information about Seeni being taken in a mishap.

It was the norm. When something momentous or threatening happened, the members of the Council would ensure the residents remained ignorant about the same till the very end. The members believed that the Council was best equipped to manage the situation without creating unnecessary uproar. Even though, in the aftermath of any such event, it was often the residents who suffered the most.

Ultur played the music Seeni had found as she waited for Promly's response. Her silence was inexplicable. It made Ultur angry and uneasy. Whenever she thought of the enormity of the report on Seeni's taking, Ultur felt disoriented. A lazy afternoon was taking over the city when the laboratory came back with a reply.

During the tests on Seeni's form to determine the cause of her taking, the data in the brain got erased. Thus, the result of her brain-mapping is 'nil'.

Ultur stared in disbelief at the text as it flashed across the screen. At that moment, Promly joined her on their encrypted channel.

'Where have you been, Promly? I have been waiting for you for so long. Did you not receive the urgent missives I sent?'

'Something came up at the farm. What does the report say, Ultur? I know for a fact that whatever is being splashed across the system is not true.'

Ultur looked at Promly on the screen. She had a sheen of perspiration on her forehead, her ash hair was out of place and she seemed preoccupied. Promly was physically far away in the foothills, but Ultur felt that she was even further away. Like her image on the screen, Promly too appeared unreal.

'The report confirms that the cause was Vish, Promly, and so with conviction it has been said that it came from the other side.'

Since Promly remained quiet, Ultur continued, 'I also asked for Seeni's brain-mapping. They reported it as "nil".' Ultur waited for Promly to process the information. But Promly's image looked back at her, silent and expressionless.

After a spell of silence, Ultur became agitated and proclaimed, 'The Council would like you to take appropriate measures and report at the next meeting.'

Without waiting for Promly's response, Ultur switched off the channel. Promly did not try to restart it. The silence emanating from the blank channel was deafening. Ultur felt utterly isolated. The lilting music sent by Seeni was still playing in the background. Its melodious beat seemed to taunt her in a manner Ultur could not comprehend. This music was the key to what was happening, of that Ultur was certain. She also knew that this was not the time to think, but to act. She tagged Iwe asking her to drop by.

When Iwe saw the message, she wanted to ignore it. But she could not; Ultur was a prominent member of the Council after all. Iwe decided that she would visit Ultur and would tell her that she had put Seeni's taking behind her.

When Iwe entered Ultur's apartment, she was, once again, struck by the vivid colours on display. One of the compositions that Seeni had sent to her was playing in the background. On hearing it, Iwe was reminded of her failed mission to find Maya. She quickly told Ultur about the entire episode, eager to leave.

'Be it Maya or Promly, it is for the Council to look for these people and find out if they are of any significance, Ultur. I have done whatever I could,' Iwe declared. She stood up and moved towards the door, ready to leave the moment she found the right break in the conversation.

Ultur was pacing up and down the small room. Despite her medium frame, her presence filled the whole space.

'I know Promly, but who is Maya? I have never heard of her. Did you say that the Irana Hub has erased all traces of Seeni from the system?'

'Yes, Ultur, I tried many routes, but I came up with a blank every time. There are no traces of any music or musician called Maya either,' Iwe was waiting for the door to swing open as she had already pressed the exit button.

Ultur realized she needed her own allies in this crisis. Seeni had wanted to tell something related to Maya to Promly. There was obviously some connection. Ultur knew that finding Maya was imperative. It would help her understand what had happened, and how Promly was connected to all of it.

Ultur observed Iwe who was admiring the colourful tapestry on the wall. It was clear from the way Iwe was standing near the door that she wanted to leave. Her stance was disinterested and she seemed completely untouched by the unfolding events.

'Iwe, who else knows about this Maya?'

'Tioni knows. She works at a Remplazo. But she is very busy with her creation nowadays.'

The door was slowly swinging open and Iwe was trying to make her exit.

Someone had actually gone for a creation? Ultur was surprised. Their existence on Elone, as of now, did not need creations anymore. Creations had dwindled and then stopped, forgotten in a way. But all of this, the life as they knew it, could change exponentially and soon. The thought brought Ultur back into the moment.

'Sit down, Iwe. I want to speak to you,' she commanded. 'Understand that whatever I am going to tell you is meant only for you. If you discuss it with anyone else, as a member of the Council, I will put you in incarceration for a long spell.'

Iwe was taken aback. She did not want to get entangled into this any further. She stood at the open door and said firmly, 'I do not want to know anything, Ultur. It really is none of my concern.'

'It is, Iwe. Sit down and listen,' she said.

Ultur's voice held a command that Iwe could not disobey. She wanted to run, but found that her feet took her back inside and led her to the chair Ultur was indicating. She sat down. The door swung shut again. Iwe was dismayed, but she also knew that Ultur could not be disregarded.

'Seeni was taken not in an accident, but by administering

Vish that came from the other side. To understand why this occurred, I need to find Maya. I am convinced she is the key to what is happening.'

Iwe was silent. There was something ominous about what Ultur was saying. It reinforced her desire to leave as quickly as possible. She stood up again.

'But how does this concern me, Ultur? What happened to Seeni is sad, but I am done trying to solve this.'

'Sit down, Iwe. It concerns all of us because if the Vish came from the other side, it means that a clash or a conflict with them is imminent. I am sure you must have heard of the clashes and their consequences?'

Iwe nodded, 'Seeni encouraged me to read the Chronicle. I am still going through them. So, yes, I do know about the clashes,' Iwe sat down again.

Ultur realized that Iwe still did not grasp the enormity of what was happening. And then, she wondered whether Iwe was the right person to bring into this situation.

Iwe was sitting desultorily on the chair and glancing out of the window. She showed no interest in what Ultur was saying.

Ultur tried once more,'What happened to Seeni concerns the continuance of our existence as we know it on Elone, Iwe. If a clash occurs again, imagine what could happen. The destruction and losses that would ensue are unimaginable. The situation that we find ourselves in is grave. I need you, Iwe, to look for Maya. Find her and bring her to me.'

Iwe felt as if a weight had been put on her shoulders. She got up and walked towards the window. Seeni, the music, Maya, Vish, clashes—these words were swirling in her mind.

Why had she come to see Ultur after Seeni was taken?

She would not have been standing here if it was not for that one visit.

Iwe thought about turning around and leaving but Ultur's words about an impending clash kept her rooted to her spot in that colourful room.

How did all these events after Seeni add up? Seeni was taken by Vish which came from the other side. Somehow, a musician named Maya appeared to be involved and unless they uncovered the reasons behind all this, a clash with the ones on the other side of the Fence would occur.

Iwe felt that some important fact was missing from this information. She gazed out of the window and thought about it. As she watched the clouds playing hide-and-seek with the sun in the late afternoon, the gap dawned on her.

'But, who is on the other side, Ultur?'

'Don't you know? Were you never told during the zacs of your knowledge gathering? Did they not tell you at the Vayunum?' Ultur replied, shocked.

'No, Ultur. We were never told.'

Had they made an error in judgement? Had all the references been removed from the Vayunum instructors? Was this isolation from those on the other side of the Fence been an oversight on their part? Was it a mistake to continue living on their side of the Fence believing that the other side did not exist at all? Ultur wondered.

'Are they people like us or is it something else?' Iwe was asking again. Her face looked earnest now. This issue had managed to grab her attention. Iwe was looking questioningly at Ultur, her black eyes alert.

Ultur thought about the silent code she was breaking. But then, she realized that it needed to break, the unfolding events warranted it. How could they respond to this impending threat without acknowledging their existence on the other side? It was essential for their survival.

She took a deep breath and said, 'Iwe, they are a different species. They came from Earth too. They are called "men".'

Depletion

The night was spattered with stars. The three moons of Elone were mere slivers at this time of the calante. Through the telescope, it seemed as if Ime could reach out and touch the stars. Their twinkling lights, sometimes vanishing and at times bright, formed a canvas in which he remained lost for long periods. At his secluded post in the Aeona observatory, with the night sky and stars for company, nothing else seemed to exist for him.

Displayed on a large screen was all the work Ime had accomplished in the last calante. He turned away from it and walked out through a small corridor, towards the roof. The Aeona observatory was spread out like a dark mass below him. It was perched atop a hill with the reflectors and mirrors on the slope of the hill. A cool breeze was blowing and in the distance, the city lights twinkled. In the plain sky the stars seemed far away.

Somewhere, amidst the expanse of the darkness that enveloped them, there had to be a planet that could become their new home. Ime was certain of that. He tilted his head and looked up at the night sky. Many of the constellations could be seen without the telescope. Ime wanted to consult Valhan about some of the results of his work, but that would have to wait. Valhan had lexed him that he was travelling and would be back in the next calante.

Ime decided to go back to his apartment and sleep. He had spent many a sleepless night scanning the skies this past vihan. He summoned a travelor through his lex and walked back into the Aeona. Switching off all power, he moved to the elevator. The tobots working on various levels trooped back to their stands and fell silent as the Aeona shut down. The lex, a nano chip, was embedded in some part of the arm of every man. It was like an extension of the brain. It connected them to their main frame system and with each other.

By the time Ime reached the lower levels, the travelor was waiting for him. Made of a light metal and painted in vivid colours, the travelors had navigation panels in the doors. Inside, few seats were there. They glided across the city fuelled by energy stations that were scattered all over the cities. Ime got in and swiped his elbow, where his lex was embedded. The travelor began to glide towards his home.

The city was deserted in the early hours. Imposing grand buildings interspersed with smaller, plainer structures lined broad avenues. In a while, people would start stirring and a new day would start. Ime reached his block and walked through the gates to take an elevator to his apartment. The block had fourteen individual apartments, unlike the group houses. Each apartment was functional and was built in a manner as to let in a large amount of sunlight during the day. As he was moving towards his bed, Ime glanced at himself in the mirror hanging from one wall. He looked tired. His blue shirt and black pants were looking slightly unkempt, but he knew that as soon as he would hang them in the cupboard, they would be refreshed and would come back out in perfect condition.

Ime had a square face and dark brown eyes. His reddish hair had grown long again; he needed to cut it. Unlike many others, Ime preferred to keep his hair short. Long ago, their ancestors, who lived on the planet they had come from, mostly kept their hair short and Ime had decided to follow their practice. Changing into loose-fitting night clothes, Ime lay down on the bed and tried to recollect the name of the planet. It was invariably lost in the crowd of all the planets Ime visited through the telescope.

'Earth!'

That was it. That was the name of that distant and lost planet where it had all begun.

The day dawned bright and clear. While Ime continued to sleep, the city was bustling with life. The travelors were full of men going about their daily routines. Radul was sitting on his bed, having just woken up. He ran his hand through his dark brown shoulder-length hair. He was hungry and wondered what had been rustled up for breakfast. He lived in one of those big buildings called 'group houses' that housed a group of men. Each man had a room in the house. These group houses were managed by tobots that cooked and cleaned.

Radul's one window room was a mess. He was waiting for a tobot to come and clean it for him. His clothes were strewn on the floor and empty containers of enab rolled aimlessly amongst them. Kicking aside a few clothes, Radul stepped out and walked into the room where they normally ate. Blum and Saca were already there. The other three men who shared the group house with them had already eaten and left for the day. Radul picked up a bowl, poured the regular morning mix of parina, picked up a piece of the local bread craw and sprawled on a low chair.

'Radul, did you finally become a part of the Syned?' Blum asked.

'Yes, I did. It was a close finish. The Olders in the Syned wanted another of their kind, but we put in a lot of pressure and did not allow that to happen,' Radul explained, in between mouthfuls. He surveyed the eating room with his clear blue eyes. The furniture was old, although unlike many group houses, the paint on the wall was fresh. Radul had not finished his education and worked in a local tobot maintenance unit as a mechanic, but he was clear about what he wanted. He had to get out of this group house existence. Not being part of one of the designated professions, he could not live in an apartment. Once he learned that as a member of the Syned, he could move into his own apartment, he made it his mission to get that membership.

'What will you do in the Syned, Radul?' asked Blum, 'The Syned is supposed to lead us, but they don't do much, do they? They simply discuss endlessly without offering any solution. Have they done anything to replace these group houses with small apartments or increased the frequency of travelors to other cities? No. They are only concerned about themselves.'

Blum voiced a common feeling.

'That is what I want to change. We need to act and not simply talk,' Radul declared.

His entry into the Syned had not been easy. It was dominated by the Olders. Once in ten zacs, they rotated ten of their thirty members. Getting in the Syned was a tricky business; who proposed your name was significant. Radul had watched the rotation process closely last time. In the intervening zacs, he had identified and worked on getting closer to Patix, one of the important members, who Radul had known through his tobot maintenance work. By the time of the current rotation, he had laid the groundwork. Radul's name had been resisted by many on the Syned mainly because he brought nothing with him. He was not educated, he lived in a group house, was often intoxicated on enab and filled the lex highways with rubbish. Even though the issues against him were many, only one thing worked for him—he was a Younger. No other man of his cohort was trying for the Syned, and with Patix on his side, Radul had gained entry.

Since he had become a member of the Syned, Radul's ambitions had soared. In addition to the apartment, he now also wanted to change how the Syned worked. He had decided that as a new member, he would grab the attention of the Olders. He would find something important to bring before the Syned, something that would shake them out of their complacency, something that would make them sit up and notice him. It would not be about group houses or travelors—it would be something larger and more significant. Radul would propose something that would make Elone grow, change and expand.

Valhan watched the waves from the window. The room was medium-sized with cheerful pink walls, which were interspersed by long windows overlooking the sea. In the afternoon, the sea looked deep blue. The waves formed at a distance, and rushed towards the shore frothing white, before receding into the sea again. Valhan had come to Notus, an organ substitution centre, after nearly twenty zacs. There were a few of his organs that needed substitution. Valhan only came to this particular Notus whenever he needed a procedure. He liked being in the vicinity of the sea. His substitutions were scheduled for the next day. His lex had been loaded with all the information needed for the substitution. He shut his eyes and began to process it.

The material used for substitution has undergone further refinement since your last visit. Even though Nepo remains the base material from which organs are cultured, there have been additions of other materials that increase their usage time to about twenty-five zacs, from the earlier fifteen. After the substitution procedure is complete, you can return to regular activities after two days. If you have any questions...

Valhan opened his eyes. There was nothing new that needed his attention. Through the lex, he entered his work place at the Matsu—the organization that managed the minerals, natural resources and other reserves at Elone. Many documents were new, but nothing demanded his immediate intervention. Just as he was about to switch highways, the latest report about Nepo came in. The decline in the reserves of Nepo was confirmed. Every mine showed a drop in their reserves. It would last them only till the next ten to fifteen hundred zacs.

Valhan had first noted the trend nearly twenty zacs ago. He had studied and researched it thoroughly. It seemed that the decline in the reserves of Nepo would soon become a major challenge.

Nepo was the foundation of their existence. It ensured they

remained. A mineral available in abundance in subterranean Elone, it was easily malleable and with adequate processing, made for the ideal substance to forge organs for substitution. Simply put, it was the bedrock of life as they knew it. Continuous research and studies were conducted to refine Nepo, to improve its flexibility and usage.

Valhan moved out of the lex. He would discuss the decline in reserves of Nepo with Odep, when he met him after the procedure.

The door opened and the specialist dressed impeccably in the pale pink uniform of the Notus walked inside along with his tobot assistant. Shaped like a man, the tobot had long arms and short legs.

'How are you doing?' the specialist asked, as the tobot checked Valhan's parameters after hooking into a processor placed at the head of the bed.

'I am doing well. Are you changing many organs this time?' Valhan inquired.

'No, we'll change only what you need, maybe three organs. With the new improved materials, adaptation is excellent and the usage is rather long,' the specialist replied while looking at the screen he held in his hand.

'Do you have any other questions?' the specialist asked.

'When did you last have a nex here?'

The expert looked puzzled, 'Here? You mean at this Notus?' Valhan nodded.

'Well, we have never had one. In fact, I don't think there has been a nex on Elone for the last hundreds of zacs, since the last War. I can assure you that substitutions are absolutely safe. There is no danger of a nex.'

The question seemed to have confused the specialist

who quickly left the room. The tobot followed him, almost gliding on its short legs. Valhan lay quietly after they left. He, himself, could not understand why he had asked about a nex. He certainly had not been thinking about it. Was it because he was going in for substitutions? Or because the declining reserves of Nepo were playing on his mind? He turned to the sea again and tried to lose himself in the waves crashing against the shore.

Radul disembarked from the travelor and stood before the majestic building of the Syned. It had a gigantic arch in the foreground, behind which rose the towers and flat terraces of the Syned. He entered through the imposing doors and was taken aback by the grace and luxury of the interiors. This was his first meeting at the Syned and Radul was prepared to take it by storm. For the last vihan, he had been reviewing in his lex what he was going to say at this meeting.

He entered the main meeting room. Long, with a high ornate ceiling, it had a large rectangular table in the middle. Every member had a designated place. The furniture and furnishings were plush and opulent, royal blue in colour. Many of the members had already arrived and there was a quiet buzz. Despite the lex, with its ever busy highways, the members of the Syned always met in person after every four calantes. The members debated in a closed room after which the summary of their decisions was put on the lex highways.

As he looked around, Radul noticed that there was a definite sense of formality in the way the men were dressed.

Everyone's hair was in place, their attire was distinct and all the men had an air of importance about them, except him. Radul realized that he would have to upgrade his appearance and play by their rules to gain their acceptance.

Once everyone arrived, they took their seats around the table. When Patix entered, he looked towards Radul. With a clear look of disapproval, he nodded curtly and glanced away.

There was no formal chief of the Syned, but they followed the practice of one man conducting the meetings for ten zacs. Currently, Durk occupied that position. He began by welcoming the new members.

'It is always good when new members come into the Syned. They bring with them the idea of what the others think about us. I would like to introduce the rules to our new members. Firstly, you can speak and vote on issues only when you are present. There is no attendance through the lex. Secondly, all the deliberations in this room remain here. You are not at liberty to disclose the discussions; you can only share the decisions. Thirdly, members are required to be neat in appearance. They cannot be intoxicated and cannot raise their voices. Lastly, lex connections are lost in this room. They will restart as soon as you step out.'

The last instruction hit Radul like a physical blow. He tried to access his lex, but it was silent. The lex was like an extension of his brain and now that he was unable to access it, he felt strange, as if a part of him had shut down. Radul tried to recollect the issue that he had planned to bring up in the meeting, but he could not. His speech lay imprisoned in the lex. With the lex silent, his plan to shake up the Syned sank into oblivion.

'Well, if we start having personal travelors, the passages

will get clogged. There would have to be regulations…'

A discussion was going on while Radul struggled with the recall process. This overdependence on the lex had to change. He would not let the lex become the sole store of his memory. This would not happen again.

'One chair is empty. Who is not here?' Durk asked.

'Valhan is not present,' Patix informed him. He was small and stocky with thick black hair cropped close to his head. His beady eyes were a piercing grey and he always seemed to be looking intently for something. He was always dressed in a shade of beige. Patix turned towards Radul and asked, 'Radul, do you have something to say as a new member?'

'Not this time, but by the next meeting, I will definitely have something to say,' Radul replied awkwardly.

After some discussions, the meeting ended. The men walked out in groups. Radul was the last one to leave. As he stepped out of the main entrance, Patix accosted him on the steps.

'Where are you going?' he asked.

'To the tobot maintenance unit,' Radul replied.

'Walk with me around the Syned before that,' Patix said, firmly.

As they strolled around the building, Patix said, 'Radul, I supported your entry to the Syned because you were the only Younger who expressed an interest in matters of the Syned. You should prepare better, look better and learn to talk to others.'

Radul heard him in silence. His resolve to gain attention and acceptance within the Syned was strengthened by Patix's admonition.

'I know, Patix. I had prepared something, but it lay in the

lex and since it was shut within the Syned, I could not recall it. I have not had the lex silent for as long as I can remember. It was a very strange and uncomfortable feeling.'

Both of them were quiet as they walked.

'What do you do with your time? That is apart from drinking enab and messing with the lex highways,' Patix asked, breaking the silence.

Radul wanted to give a sharp retort, but restrained himself, 'Nothing much except work.'

Radul was getting restless. He was not used to so many questions. And he did not appreciate the manner in which Patix asked them.

'What about the time when you are not at work?' Patix persisted.

'I lie on the terrace of our group house most nights and gaze at the stars and the three moons,' Radul replied, exasperated, hoping Patix would realize his tone was irritating him. They had walked all around the building and would soon be at the entrance of the Syned once more.

'If that is what occupies most of your time, why don't you go to the Aeona and spend some time there? Ime manages the Aeona. Go and meet him. I will tell him that you will visit soon. Learn something about the galaxies,' Patix ordered again. Radul winced inwardly, his absurd response had landed him with a task! He knew that he would have to do what Patix was telling him to do.

'All right. I will go soon. Now, I take your leave,' Radul said, hurrying towards the exit, and made his way to the travelor's stop.

Radul knew that joining the Syned would bring some change to his existence but the fact that he would have to listen to others was something he had not factored in.

Ime unhooked from his processor and opened his eyes. All the data he had processed was displayed on the screen before him. He was confident, to a certain degree, that at least one of the two planets, that he had identified in a neighbouring galaxy, could sustain their species. He still needed to conduct more research though. Ime was waiting for Valhan, who would return after a few vihans.

Stargazing had attracted Ime when he was in the higher educational unit. He often visited the Koshum, which was the repository of all knowledge accumulated on Elone. He had met Valhan at the Koshum. Many times, they had sat on workstations in the same corner, never exchanging a word. Then, one day, Valhan had approached him and asked, 'What are you looking for here? Your dress tells me that you are enrolled in a higher educational unit. Not many learners come here.'

'I am interested in Earth, the planet we came from,' Ime had replied.

Valhan was a tall man, with a languid walk, well-cut deep brown hair, friendly hazel eyes, and a face that was gentle yet decisive. It was easy to speak to him.

'Why? What is it about Earth that interests you?' Valhan had countered.

'I want to know how it was different from Elone. Why was it destroyed? Could the same happen to Elone? Things like that. I also wonder if there are other planets where there are people like us. Maybe, from Earth they went elsewhere too,' Ime had answered, eager and animated.

That meeting had started a long string of conversations between them.

Gradually, Ime's interest in the stars and their existence grew and he decided to work at the Aeona. Valhan had encouraged him every step of the way. Then, about three zacs ago, Valhan invited Ime for lunch.

Valhan's apartment was airy with simple and functional furniture. One tobot was in attendance. The enab the tobot poured out for Ime was fine. For lunch, the tobot brought out freshly cooked vegetables, rice and kimpayo—bread made from the finest wheat.

'Since you have been at the Aeona for a while, Ime, I want to give you a task. Search the galaxies for a planet like Elone, a place where we could exist. Find us an alternate home,' Valhan stared out the window, into the distance, as he spoke.

Ime was silent; he didn't know what to say. The idea was interesting and alarming at the same time. After a moment, he said softly, 'Why? Is Elone in danger? Will we have to move from here like we did from Earth?'

'No, there is no danger. I am just curious. I merely want to know. We are a people on the move. We have been since we left Earth. We need to search for newer destinations on this journey.'

Ime realized then that Valhan was hiding something. He, however, did not pursue it further.

Since that conversation, Ime had begun searching in earnest. He had spent countless days shut in the Aeona without even returning to his apartment. He had studied planets, stars and their suns in the far-flung corners of the universe. The quest had been rigorous and exhausting. And now, finally, he had something to share with Valhan.

While Ime had been processing, he received Patix's lex about Radul's impending visit to the Aeona. Ime saw on the lex highway that Radul was one of the new members of the Syned. He opened Radul's identity data in the security system and found out everything about him.

He wondered why a man like him was on the Syned. But then, Ime shrugged away the thought. After all, the Syned was a group of eclectic people who were known to not do much.

He decided that he would put Radul through the standard visitor interface at the Aeona. He moved towards the telescope because night was falling and the stars were beckoning him.

The travelor dropped Valhan at the foot of the hills. It could have taken him all the way up to Odep's house but Valhan decided to walk. The narrow pathway meandered through the thickly wooded hills in a lazy manner. As he walked, Valhan could smell the woods. The breeze carried with it the waft of fresh leaves interspersed with the dank smell of wood and a whiff of flowers. Dry leaves crackled under his feet as he wound his way up. It was refreshing to visit Odep in the place he had made his home nearly ten zacs ago. The air seemed different and the shade under the numerous trees was welcoming. In the city, the air did not carry such fragrances and the vegetation was organized and neatly laid out.

Valhan reached the house nestled within a thicket of trees on the side of the hill. The door was wide open and he walked in. Dressed casually, Odep was reclining in a chair with his eyes closed. He was as tall as Valhan and seemed to be overflowing from the chair. His dark black hair had grown till his shoulders. He seemed to be a lot bulkier than the regular men of Elone. Valhan rapped his knuckles on the door and Odep opened his eyes which always seemed to smile. Like him, his eyes were also intelligent and kind.

'Valhan, why did you not tell me that you were coming to visit me? I was just about to step out for a stroll. You would have missed me, and would have had to wait,' Odep said, getting up from his chair.

'I did lex you, Odep,' replied Valhan, stepping inside.

'Ah, the lex! I took it out last zac. It must be lying somewhere in the house. Come, sit. Let me pour you a nice glass of enab. You walked up?'

Odep walked towards the other room as Valhan sank into a comfortable chair. The room was airy and gave the sense of being open to the elements. Valhan noticed that there was no screen or workstation inside the room. He remembered seeing a workstation when he had visited the last time. Odep was clearly no longer tuned into the system.

Valhan knew that Odep had constantly been doing strange things since he had hidden in the hills. But, removing the lex? It was unthinkable. It was an integral part of their being. How could Odep even think of separating it from himself?

Valhan watched as Odep brought two glasses and handed one to him. There was something markedly different about Odep. Valhan could not identify what it was, but he could discern a change.

'Yes, I did walk here but I can take a stroll with you if that is what you want. The woods are pleasant.'

'We will go later,' Odep said, sipping enab. 'You have come here after nearly three zacs, Valhan. Tell me what has been happening in that big city of yours.'

'Through the lex you can know what is happening anywhere, Odep.'

'We will talk about the lex later. You haven't come here to talk about why I have disconnected the lex, have you?' Odep smiled as he gestured towards the bottle of enab kept on the table.

Odep's plain speaking had taken him to great heights and then had brought him to the margins. An architect, Odep was one of the oldest and most distinguished men on Elone. He had built many of the buildings that crowned the skyline of Elone such as the Aeona, the Syned building, the Koshum, other smaller educational units and the graceful Notus that Valhan had stepped out of recently. Odep had been a part of the Syned for many zacs. He had pursued ideas and developed regulations and processes that had positively impacted their life on Elone. Valhan realized that in fact it had been Odep who had pushed for embedding the lex many zacs ago!

However, ten zacs ago, Odep had moved to the hills and disappeared into the woods. He had disengaged from everything—his work and his life. Many men, like Valhan, came to meet him initially, but their numbers dwindled as the zacs passed. Although he preferred to live on the margins, Odep always came up with solutions when confronted with pertinent issues. The Syned still reached out to him when faced with a challenge. And, Valhan still sought him out whenever a problem presented itself.

'Well, Odep, the reserves of Nepo are dipping—steadily. Although the decline is incremental, over time it will diminish.

Do you think I should bring it to the attention of the Syned at this time? What do you say?'

Odep sat silent and contemplative in his chair. He drained the glass in his hand with one quick gulp, placed it on the small table on the side and asked, 'You looked everywhere? In the seas, on the hills?'

'The reserves everywhere have been taken into consideration.'

Odep got up from his chair, smiled and said, 'Let us take a walk, Valhan. This room seems too small to discuss something on which our existence is based.'

They stepped out into the setting sun and took a small path that led deep into the woods.

While Valhan and Odep were walking into the woods, Radul was taking a travelor to the Aeona. He would lex Patix about the visit after it was over. As the travelor glided through the city, Radul noticed the pale slivers of the three moons for the first time in zacs. He had not looked at the night sky in ages. His reply to Patix was supposed to end that uncomfortable conversation but it had not turned out that way. He resolved he would deal with Patix and his sense of authority over time.

Much like the Syned, the Aeona building was grand too. As he stood before its solid doors, Radul wondered why he had never noticed these buildings before. He realized that he must have been too caught up in himself, the group house, enab and the lex highways. The world that lay outside his own had never caught his attention. The doors swung open and Radul entered.

In the security panel, Ime watched as Radul followed the tobot that lead him to the area where he was sitting. He noticed that Radul was tall and broad shouldered with electric blue eyes. Radul's careless walk, dishevelled look and insolent demeanour, all were typical of men who lived in group houses. Ime wondered if Valhan knew that someone like Radul was part of the Syned now.

As Radul neared his workstation, Ime stood up and said, 'Welcome to the Aeona, Radul. I have prepared for your introduction to the world beyond Elone. Please enter this chamber; your lex will connect to the appropriate highway. Be comfortable and enjoy your journey. A tobot is outside and will help if there is any problem,' Ime said while leading Radul towards the visitor interface.

Radul noticed that the tobots in the Aeona were taller than the regular ones. He entered a cubicle, while Ime returned to his workstation. The small cubicle had a reclining chair, with a glistening arched roof. A voice instructed him to connect his lex to the processor line. Radul did so and his journey of the cosmos began.

Outside, the three moons became brighter as the night sky became darker. The stars twinkled brilliantly as the city in the distance slowly surrendered itself to sleep.

After completing the visitor interface, Radul made his way to where Ime was working. He had the same bemused expression on his face as other visitors after a glimpse of the cosmos.

'I never knew so much existed beyond Elone!' Radul said as he looked around the Aeona. The three large screens that adorned the walls of the main laboratory in the Aeona were littered with countless calculations, the outcomes of which kept changing as the data processed continuously.

'Could I look at the actual sky through a telescope?'

Ime was a bit surprised but led him to the viewing chamber, without saying anything. Radul peered through the viewing pane of the telescope while Ime returned to his work.

'You stay here in the nights, Ime?'

Ime was startled to see that Radul was standing right behind him.

'Often I do. Today, I will. Is there anything else you want to see?' Ime asked. He wanted Radul to leave. He continued to peer into his workstation, his back towards Radul.

'I can see you have enab,' Radul said pointing towards the freezer in a corner, 'why don't we have a drink and then, I will go.'

Radul walked towards the freezer. Ime wanted to refuse Radul's suggestion, but Radul was Patix's guest and he could not afford to displease a member of the Syned.

'You go ahead. I don't drink enab when I am working and as it is, I have to complete a lot of work tonight,' Ime said, continuing his work, his back still to Radul.

Radul poured himself a glass of enab and stared at Ime's back hunched over some data. Ime's hair was neatly cut and his clothes well-fitting, though modest. Radul had checked Ime's basic details on the lex and that is why he knew that Ime had completed his studies at the higher educational unit and was now a manager at the Aeona. He knew Ime lived in an apartment and not in a group house. He was sure Ime had checked him out too, which explained why he had barely spoken to him all this while and was now sitting with his back to him. Radul's resolve hardened. He was going to change this behaviour of people towards him. That was why he had joined the Syned.

'Ime, what is it you do here at the Aeona?' Radul asked in an effort to start a conversation.

Ime turned around and faced him slowly.

Maybe after some conversation, Radul would leave. Radul was lounging in a chair opposite him. His hair was splayed across the back of the chair and the glass of enab was already empty. His pale yellow shirt hung over his shoulders and his trousers were loose.

'I keep a watch on the galaxies and planetary movements. It is my job to monitor frequencies, waves, ripples, or any other kind of movement in the cosmos. I also do research and study to keep myself updated. Keeping the equipment here up-to-date and in order is also one of my tasks,' Ime replied in a flat tone.

Radul nodded while pouring some more enab for himself.

A strange kind of silence hung in the space. While Ime wanted Radul to leave, Radul was thinking of something to say to keep the conversation going.

'How do you know Patix, Ime?' Radul asked, wanting to keep Ime talking. He wanted Ime to pay attention to him and not dismiss him. He was, after all, a member of the Syned.

'I collaborated with him on some research. It was a long time ago,' Ime sighed and replied. He realized that the man slouched in the chair, drinking copious amounts of enab was not going to give up easily.

'Does it bother you, Ime, that we have not had a single creation in the last many zacs?' Radul asked. Creations—he had decided to bring up this topic for his first meeting of the

Syned, but the lex rules had thwarted his idea.

Creations? Ime was taken aback. He had never thought about them nor did he know if what Radul was saying about them was correct. He immediately checked on the lex. The information was indeed true. 'Well, the Syned had put a moratorium on it hundreds of zacs ago. So…' he trailed off.

'Do you know why? Because men wanted to define the abilities of their creations!' Radul interjected. He had gleaned this information about creations from the lex highways. He continued in the same vein, 'Earlier, one could only put forth specifications regarding physical attributes but then men wanted to specify other attributes too. There were many debates and discussions after which this moratorium came into effect. And now, more than hundred zacs later, we have almost forgotten that we can create too,' Radul gulped down all the enab in his glass and poured himself another portion.

Ime sat quietly listening to him.

'But do you know, Ime, the gynake continue to create. Across that Fence, they create and grow in numbers, while we have been at the same level for countless zacs,' Radul was drawling.

The moment Radul brought up the topic of gynake, Ime lost interest in the conversation. There was a small minority in Elone, for whom the gynake were a rival in every sense of the word; the gynake clouded their every thought. Imaginary conflicts and competitions with them was a way of existence for these men. But the majority were like Ime—they lived knowing about the gynake on the other side, but never bothered about them.

'Well, Ime, let me tell you, this is going to change. This moratorium on creation is the first issue that I am going to bring before the Syned. I wanted to bring it up at the last meeting, but they shut off the lex and I couldn't remember what I was going to say. But, now I have it in my own brain...' Radul started rambling.

'Why do you think we need the moratorium to be removed? Simply because the gynake do not have it? Have you thought about it through the perspective of men? In fact, let me ask you, would you like to go in for a creation yourself?' Ime wanted to put an end to Radul's ramblings by a barrage of questions.

It did work and Radul fell silent. He had come upon something to grab the attention of the Syned, but he had not yet thought anything beyond bringing up the issue. As he sat there, pondering over Ime's questions, Radul's thoughts veered towards the gynake on the other side. He knew that their existence troubled him. Their presence lurked in the shadows of his mind. Why did the men have to share the planet with them?

'I don't know about all that, but I do wonder why no one worries that the gynake, who occupy half our planet, will outnumber us in a while,' Radul downed his third glass of enab in one go.

'We haven't had any clashes or skirmishes with them since the Fence came up. Then, why does their existence bother some of you so much?' Ime was taken aback with the vehemence that seemed to drip from Radul.

However, by then, Radul was too intoxicated to form a coherent reply. He smiled at Ime and reached out for the almost empty bottle of enab. Ime pushed the bottle away. He took Radul's arm and led him towards the exit. He put him in a travelor with the lex guiding it towards his group house.

As the travelor glided away and darkness enveloped Ime, he looked in the direction of the Fence. After many zacs, he actively thought about the gynake. Their existence on the planet did not overlap in any manner. In all the zacs since the last War, both the sides had learnt to share this planet and coexist in peace.

Ime walked back to his workstation. The conversation with Radul had somewhat unsettled him. For many zacs, Ime had been constantly searching for other planets where species from Earth might have gone. He believed that species, other than the men and the gynake, could have migrated to some other planet. However, over the zacs, Ime had found only an eerie silence echoing in the universe. Other than men and the gynake, no other species seemingly existed in the unending cosmos.

Valhan and Odep had climbed nearly to the top of the hill. Valhan could hear Odep's breath as it came heavy and fast from the climb.

'Let us sit on that ledge for a while and enjoy the sunset,' Odep said as he sat down.

They sat in silence while Odep's breathing became regular again. The setting sun was leaving a blazing orange glow on the landscape as it sank deeper into the horizon. At the opposite end, the three moons had begun to peep out, as if enquiring whether it was time for them to make their entrance.

'So, how long do you think the reserves of Nepo will last?' Odep asked.

'We still have reserves to last us for at least fifteen hundred zacs, but they are declining fast. Odep, we need to start looking for solutions now if we want to survive. We should not wait for the situation to become alarming. Are there some efforts going on that you know about?' Valhan asked.

'It is in the nature of men to actively search and invest in a better future, Valhan. We have been looking for substitutes for Nepo in the bosom of Elone and on the surface. However, nothing viable has been found yet. We have refined Nepo tremendously. I think we have to continue with our efforts,' Odep suggested.

'I think if we acknowledge that the reserves are dwindling, our search will gain momentum,' Valhan looked at Odep's silhouette in the setting sun. He then asked, 'Do you know where the reserves of Nepo exist in large quantities?'

The sun suddenly dipped below the horizon, the golden glow disappeared and the three moons shone brightly. In the distance, city lights dotted the terrain. A cool, gentle breeze was whispering through the woods.

'I know that the gynake have reserves on their side. They have no need for the mineral, but we cannot access the reserves, now or ever,' Odep replied quietly.

Valhan sat silently. How did Odep know so much about different things? He always wondered. He had so many questions. He wanted to ask him why he had come and hidden in these woods, why he did not design buildings anymore, why he had removed the lex—but he did not. He looked at Odep sitting next to him on the ledge. His kind eyes were looking into the distance. Valhan knew that there was a line that one could not cross with Odep. Odep shared things at his own pace.

Valhan decided to ask the most pressing of the questions, 'Why are they not using Nepo? Actually, when I saw the report of the reserves on their side of the planet I understood that they were not using it anymore but I could not guess why!'

Odep looked out in the direction of the Fence. They could not see it from where they sat but its imposing presence could still be felt. Somewhere, across the plains in the distance, beyond the slow meandering river, behind the city, the Fence was standing. It was a respite from the perpetual conflict, a harbinger of peace, an instrument that allowed coexistence.

'You know, Valhan, that the gynake came up with the idea of the Fence?' Without waiting for a response, Odep continued, 'The gynake are a formidable opponent. Like us, they also think about the future. They are adept at forward and lateral thinking. In this quest of finding alternative substitution materials, I think they have moved ahead of us. They have obviously developed a renewable material for substitutions, so they have stopped using or needing Nepo.'

'What do you think it is, Odep? This material? Can we not somehow get our hands on that technology? I am sure the Unumo is tracking what happens on the gynake side. The covert agency always does. I know who heads the Unumo, should I ask him? However, I would have to share the details of the dipping reserves,' Valhan was eager to find a quick-fix solution to the challenge facing them.

'I don't have any information about the nature of this material. Like you, I had merely observed that their reserves of Nepo had stabilized. The only reason for this could be that they had found a renewable source. You can talk to the head but I would suggest that you keep the decreasing Nepo situation out of the conversation. First, assess if they actually know what is being used on the other side,' Odep said as he got up from the ledge.

They began to retrace their steps towards his house. It was already getting dark and difficult to navigate through the woods.

They walked for a while in silence.

Then, Valhan ventured to ask Odep, 'Why have you taken out the lex?'

'I will answer your question the next time you visit. If I don't keep something back, you will not come for another three zacs,' he replied with a chuckle.

Both of them smiled in the gathering darkness. They knew that whenever Valhan would need to know or understand something, he would be back. It had always been this way, even before Odep had hidden in the hills. Odep was like a navigation tool they kept coming back to. The two men reached the house. In the enveloping darkness, the house, perched on the hillside with a solitary lamp burning inside, appeared lonesome.

'Valhan, I just want to say that whenever you deal with the gynake, do remember that we share this planet with them. Despite our clashes, we have a shared past from the time we lived on Earth. At one time, I am told, we called them "women". They still refer to themselves as that. Did you notice that "men" is a part of that term? We don't know much about those earlier times anymore. How or why we shared life on Earth? But I often wonder. Did we ever live together? Why did we diverge? They might be a different species but they are the only ones like us in the universe that we know of. We need to acknowledge this fact and always remember it.'

Odep held the door open for him as they entered his home.

The gaming lounge was dimly lit. There was complete silence across the various cubicles. In the occupied cubicles, men were busy playing. Gaming was a favourite activity amongst them and addiction to it was a common problem. Ensconced in comfortable chairs, with the lex connected to the gaming world, they could travel, play games, see stories play out and even create music.

When Radul was done with lex highways and enab, he would sometimes come to play. He always played 'Pathway'. It was a game that took the player on an endless journey through rivers, mountains, oceans and roads. The difficulty level of obstacles kept increasing as more time elapsed. Sitting in the lounge, Radul journeyed endlessly. He liked coming to the lounge. The silence it offered and the isolation of the cubicle gave him the feeling that he was in his own apartment.

Radul had just completed one leg of the journey on a winding mountain road and was processing the instructions associated with the next landscape when he spotted the word 'creation'. With a start, he opened his eyes. The game paused, and he looked around curiously to observe if someone had said something. There was silence all around as the men were lost to the gaming world.

He wondered why his mind had highlighted the word. He lounged back in the chair and stared at the ceiling which had an intricate design that was faintly visible in the blurry light.

'Would you like to go in for a creation yourself?' Ime's question reverberated in Radul's head as he stared at the ceiling.

Did he want a creation for himself? How would creations add to their lives? What did he hope to achieve with the debate that he had planned so meticulously? Radul realized that in spite of his research, he knew little about creations or their impact on their current lifestyle. Initially, it had seemed like an interesting idea to get attention, but now, as he thought more about it, he had more questions than answers.

As an ocean churned on the screen, Radul remembered the unease he had felt about the gynake while at the Aeona. He realized that he needed to know more about creations. He discarded the game and instead started searching the lex for information about creations. Each thread led him to the gateway of the Koshum. Radul understood that he would have to visit the Koshum because he couldn't access the data through the lex yet.

He left the gaming lounge and took a travelor towards the Koshum. It was late evening and the travelor was crowded. Radul stood in one corner and stared at the hazy city lights racing in the opposite direction as the travelor glided down the streets.

After some time, Radul alighted near the Koshum. He had to look up to take in its full height. Radul stood in front of it and observed its huge doors. The dark brown building leapt into the sky and spread over nearly two blocks. Since it was late evening, all the floors were not lit up. Radul felt a strange sense of trepidation. He had never been here before. He looked around and noticed, some distance away, the signage of Xint on a nondescript ordinary building. Radul was amused. The Xint was the organization that managed the finances of Elone but it resided in a plain building. Opposite the humble Xint, the structure of Etuis loomed high. It was indeed a sight to behold. It housed the main organizations of Elone. From the running of travelors, to promoting farming, marketing produce, the Matsu, managing Notuses—the Etuis was the hub. Domes and spires rose from it, and the colour of the building was a dull burnt red. In the lights of the evening, it looked regal and graceful. Radul recalled that Patix worked there. Somehow, remembering Patix and his own new-found place in the Syned removed his trepidation in a flash. With confident steps, Radul entered the Koshum.

He checked-in his identity and the elevator took Radul up to the reception area. A huge screen displayed various sections of the Koshum. Radul looked at the intricate display, at the various topics appearing and disappearing on the screen. Topography, geography, space, technological developments—there was so much knowledge in the world! It seemed as if all the numerous stars he had seen from the telescope at the Aeona were twinkling on the display. He scanned the display looking for a point to begin. Then he saw it. In one corner, it simply said 'Us'. He pressed the word and a flash informed him that the section was on the twentieth level. Radul took the elevator which opened into a large room with consoles, screens, workstations and more displays. The room was empty of men and tobots.

Radul sat at a workstation and began to search for information about the elusive phenomenon called 'creation'. After meandering through a maze of information, he came upon some relevant data about the topic. It had been added many zacs ago. Radul scanned it and then hooked on to process it. The night deepened, but Radul kept on processing.

Sunlight was pouring in through the window in front of the workstation when Radul opened his eyes. It had been one long night, full of startling discoveries. He rode down the elevator, his mind buzzing with all the new information, and stepped into the early morning sun to head home and formulate his next step.

The sun was bright. A cool breeze was blowing, laden with fragrances that seemed to change with each passing waft. The green expanse was interspersed with patches of exotic colours of blooming flowers. The Furawa garden incubator was always a riot of colour. One could design different patterns and fragrances of flowers on its systems and then generate the respective seeds. Most of the times, the flowers followed the design exactly, but at times, the patterns faltered too. The flowers designed at the Furawa were used to adorn public spaces, buildings and other far-flung areas.

Ime was hunched near the patch where his latest design was going to bloom. He came every vihan to watch the progress. Other than the stars that twinkled through the telescopes, his other interest was the wonder of seeing his designs sprout from the ground.

In a patch nearby, dark red triangular flowers with deep yellow stripes were swaying in the breeze. Ime walked across and observed them closely. A slightly tangy smell floated around the patch. The shade of a sprawling tree that occupied a large tract of the Furawa covered Ime as he knelt down. He found the flowers beautiful, and their fragrance delicate. He decided to find out whether their seeds were available so he could plant them in the Aeona.

Ime walked back to observe his own patch. The saplings had started to peek through the ground. They would take some more vihans to bloom. Satisfied with the progress, Ime took a leisurely stroll through the vibrant colours, patterns and intoxicating smells that changed at every turn, towards the gate of Furawa. The riot of colours at the Furawa was very different from the black and silver of the night sky that were his constant companions. On his lex, a message landed from Valhan.

I am back. Will come and see you at the Aeona later in the day.

Ime was glad. He had been waiting for Valhan's return so that he could share with him the results of his efforts. Ime had not lexed the information. He started walking faster. He wanted to get back as soon as possible and arrange all the data in readiness for Valhan's visit.

When he reached the Aeona, he found that things were somewhat in a mess. The main telescope had developed a malfunction and Ime spent the entire day along with two tobots to get it back on track. The long shadows of the evening were stretching outside, waiting to curl up with the advent of darkness when they finally managed to fix the problem. Ime returned to his workstation. All the relevant data about his discoveries was displayed on the screen. He began to arrange it in an orderly manner.

Ime had identified two planets as possible future homes for men. He had christened them Zeta and Tai. They emitted a yellowish light when he had seen them for the first time in the cosmos. Located in a neighbouring galaxy, they held the promise of sustainability of their kind of life. Every time he shut down the Aeona, Ime would try and catch a glimpse of the two planets in the cosmos. For Ime, they represented hope and potential. He often wondered if their ancestors had felt the same when they had first discovered Elone.

It had turned dark when Valhan finally walked in. Ime noticed that he was looking very relaxed. The vacation seemed to have done him a lot of good. After Valhan sat comfortably in a chair, Ime began to share his discovery.

Valhan and Ime pored over the calculations, moved among the telescopes and discussed at length about the new planets as the night stretched about them. Even as they spoke, Ime sensed that Valhan was preoccupied. His attention did not seem to be on the immense possibilities that Ime's painstaking research had opened up.

'Do you think either of these two planets have reserves of Nepo? Or something from which we can extract Nepo? Or something that could be a substitute for Nepo?' asked Valhan suddenly.

Valhan's question sent a shiver down Ime's spine.

Was this why Valhan had put him on this quest? Were the reserves of Nepo dwindling rapidly on Elone?

Ime had searched the universe for planets that had a hospitable atmosphere, water and suitable temperature to sustain life. He had not explored their mineral resources. Finding all the ingredients required to sustain life on one cosmic entity was a one-in-a-million chance.

'I have not looked at that aspect as yet, Valhan. My research was about primarily finding the basic requirements like a suitable atmosphere. If you want, I would start this quest for Nepo immediately.' Then he asked directly, 'Do we need to worry? Are the reserves down alarmingly?'

'We need to start looking for other reserves and intensify our efforts to find alternatives to Nepo. Ime, there is nothing to worry about at the moment, but we do need results. I want to bring it to the attention of the Syned, but not only as a problem, rather with a solution. Pour me some enab and let us eat something,' Valhan said, reclining on the chair.

While Ime was pouring enab and gathering loaves of craw with tibli sauce and vegetables, he heard from Radul.

Well, I have understood that I am not ready for a creation yet. Are you?

Ime gazed at the message for a while. Why was Radul asking these questions?

He took the tray to Valhan and told him about Radul's visit.

'How is someone like Radul on the Syned, Valhan? I cannot comprehend it. Patix promoting someone like him is inexplicable!'

Valhan began to eat silently.

Why had he not understood when Patix had asked him to support someone like Radul? The Unumo always took a person from outside and then trained him on the job. He had been asked to join himself long ago, but had refused. Valhan also remembered meeting Radul once. He recalled he had startling blue eyes; otherwise he was a typical group house man.

'What did Radul talk about while he was here?' Valhan asked.

'He spoke about creations and why the gynake still have them and we don't. Valhan, I get the impression that he is one of those men who still carry the existence of the gynake like a burden on their shoulders,' Ime replied between mouthfuls of craw dipped in sauce. He had not realized how hungry he was.

Valhan watched him. Ime's red hair was dishevelled and he looked tired, yet the earnest look that marked his bearing was intact.

'What do you think about them, Ime?'

'Them? The gynake?' asked Ime.

Valhan nodded.

'Well, I don't actively think about them. While I was in the knowledge unit, I had tried to discover how we had lived with them when we were on Earth, but there was no information available. It seems we have always been on the opposite sides of the Fence. Since we have been at peace, their existence doesn't bother me,' Ime stretched in his chair.

'Are you aware that they have found a substitute for Nepo? It seems to be a renewable source, Ime. We need to quickly discover something similar ourselves.'

Ime reflected on the information. It was a revelation that contained the seeds of potential conflict. Nepo could easily become the nucleus around which the two species would clash, once more. The potential of Zeta and Tai had taken on an entirely new dimension.

'Can we not ask them? Or maybe trade with them? There must be some channel that is still open for a dialogue? After all, we share this planet!'

Even as Ime said it, he could feel a sense of foreboding enveloping him.

The view from the oval window was of a vast, plain land. In the distance, the outline of mountains could be seen. Patix's office room was situated in one of the spires of the Etuis building. It was shaped like an airborne travelor, long with an oval window at one end.

Valhan stood near the window and looked out. Somewhere

beyond the vast land and across the mountains lay the Fence, the barrier to both conflict and opportunity.

While Patix sat at his workstation, immersed in something that needed his attention, Valhan thought about this visit, about what he was going to say and how he would say it. However, standing in Patix's room, the impending conversation did not seem that difficult. Patix and Valhan were markedly different in their approach to issues. Patix was a man on a mission, always trying to reach some distant goal. A sense of urgency and impatience permeated his bearing. On the other hand, Valhan was calm and collected. He planned and thought through matters. However, in spite of their differences, they had managed to work together and collaborate on many projects in the past.

'So, Valhan, where have you been?' Patix's question brought Valhan back from his reverie.

'You missed the last Syned meeting. You should be present for the next one. The new entrants will hopefully speak, and the proceedings will be interesting,' Patix joined him at the window and leaned against the window ledge. Daylight played with his taut profile, and highlighted the beige colour of his clothes. Even lounging in his own space, he seemed to be on edge.

'Patix, you have brought in Radul for the work of the Unumo, right?' Valhan had decided that being direct was the best way to bring the topic out in the open.

'Well, yes, in a way, you could say that. But, that is still a long way away. It could be one of the things he may be drafted for.'

Patix left the window and sat in the easy chair in one corner. He seemed quite comfortable discussing the Unumo.

'So, what is the Unumo doing these days? What is keeping it busy?' Valhan asked, still standing by the window.

'Do you want to ask me about the work of the Unumo, Valhan? Or perhaps there is something you want to tell me?' Patix stared at him, pointedly.

'I was wondering if there is any information about the material the gynake use for substitutions. Is it still Nepo? Or have they found an alternative? We have been experimenting in this area and would gain immensely by knowing if they are already on the same path. It would save us that much effort,' Valhan exhaled after saying what was on his mind.

Patix remained quiet. He swivelled slowly in his easy chair and ran a check across the lex and the Koshum. No information about the substitution materials used by the gynake was available. The Unumo had been trying to capture data about the renewable material being used on the other side, but they had not yet succeeded. He wondered who had tipped off Valhan about the same.

'Why are you interested in this area, Valhan? This is not your area of specialization at the Matsu,' Patix asked.

'I came across something on the lex about our recent failed efforts in finding a substitute, so I just decided to ask.' Even as he was saying it, Valhan knew that Patix would start looking at the Nepo reserves immediately.

'Well, this is a new area for us, Valhan. We have never thought about it before. Tell you what, we will try and get some information on this and share it with you.' Patix stood up and walked back to his workstation.

Their meeting was clearly over, but not this conversation. Valhan was sure that they would talk about the issue again, and soon.

'Observe Radul a little more before you decide on his role, Patix. He seems to have a deep angst against the gynake which is worrying,' Valhan remarked before leaving.

Even though Patix had not told Valhan anything, he knew one thing for certain—what Odep had said was right. The gynake were using a renewable substitute. Patix's silence had managed to convey as much.

After Valhan left, Patix sat at his workstation and started working frantically. He drew out statistics on substitutions, the number of Notus, and the developments in refining Nepo. As he processed the information, he saw that Valhan had been to a Notus in the last calante itself. The sun drew overhead as Patix sifted through the data that swirled around him. He switched gears and started to look into efforts that had been made to find alternatives to Nepo. He realized that men had been struggling for many zacs, but had not yet succeeded. There had been many promising starts but nothing concrete had come out of them. Efforts had focused on refining Nepo and its results. Patix switched to the Matsu and tried to find data on the consumption of Nepo and the quantity of its reserves. While he could access the information about consumption, the latter was secured.

Patix stopped and stood up. He had found the key to Valhan's questions. By the time he strode out of his room, it was late afternoon. He took an elevator to the basement of the Etuis building. He walked down the corridor that connected the basements of the Etuis and Kosham. As expected, it was deserted. At the opposite end, there was a door with no sign. Nondescript, it merged with the wall. Patix walked up to the door and stared into a spot on it. It slid open. As he walked inside, it shut immediately. Patix stood facing another innocuous looking door. He put both hands on the door and a number arrived on his lex. He punched it into the console and the door swung open to reveal Unumo's operational unit. After his last visit to a Notus, his parameters had been updated in the Unumo records.

The Unumo unit comprised a long room with many consoles and workstations. Two tobots were busy at their respective workstations. A soft humming emanated from the machines as they processed information from the bubbles. The bubbles were intelligent devices that floated all along the Fence. Sensitive and perceptive, they switched off if they sensed a probe from the other side. Hovering around unseen and unheard, they picked up noise and chatter from the channels on the other side which was then scrambled by the machines at the Unumo. Based on certain keywords, reports about the other side were prepared that wound up on Patix's screen.

Sitting before a console, Patix got to work. After a short while, he had accessed the data on Nepo reserves that Valhan had kept under secure access. As the data poured in and the machines calculated the patterns, the picture became clearer. Patix wondered why Valhan had not brought the declining trend to the attention of the Syned. It had become apparent quite a few zacs ago.

Patix stopped the processing and sat quietly. On the other side of the room, various screens flashed live images of important locations. Patix stared at the changing images. In a way, it was fortuitous that the decline in Nepo reserves was still under wraps. Patix could use the information for his plans.

For many zacs, the lack of vision in the Syned had troubled Patix. The Syned was supposed to foster the interests of men. It was supposed to improve their lives. However, it dwelt on mundane and unimportant issues. Nothing of substance was ever debated in their meetings. Patix wanted to wrest the leadership of the Syned and push for a plan that would alter the balance of power existing on Elone.

The peaceful coexistence with the others was a mere farce. They did not need peace with the gynake. The men needed the planet, all to themselves. This notion of half a planet with half the mountains, half the seas, half the minerals, half of everything infuriated him. He had lived in this half existence for countless zacs. He knew that now was the time to become whole and own Elone entirely. After the last War, when their numbers had dwindled and before a truce had been sought, many of the men had insisted furiously for a last push, but then it had been a matter of their survival. However, since the Fence had been put in place, they had strengthened their numbers, expanded their cities and grown exponentially, but still, only to half the capacity of Elone. For Patix and some others, there was never any doubt that Elone belonged to the men. They had always thought of the planet as their own. And now, it was time to reclaim it from the gynake.

The Fence was a symbol of peace to many, but to Patix, it was a constant reminder of their limit and he never understood how certain men had voluntarily accepted this limit. For many zacs, Patix had been trying to find a cogent reason to convince the men that this sharing of the planet must end. He had been trying to figure out a way that would compel the men to agree to breach the wall and break out of their limits.

Now, the reason had come to him. Nepo's depletion was the beginning. If dealt with properly, the decline in Nepo reserves could persuade them to take action. The more he thought about it, the more certain Patix became that he had found what he had been looking for—the cause to help push their limits.

He walked to a console that processed information from the bubbles. Patix scanned the reports that were being documented. He found that the term 'Seeni' was appearing again and again in the chatter. It seemed to be something or rather someone of importance amongst the gynake. He sat down and started processing the reports one more time.

The scenery outside the travelor window was passing by in a blur. The city had been left behind and had made way for trees, plantations and streams that were merging into a kaleidoscope of colours.

When Radul had agreed to meet Patix at the Point, he had not known it would be so far from the city. The lex had told him the distance and the time it would take him to get there, but the real journey seemed unending.

Presently, Radul was agreeing to Patix's orders without demur, but by the time the next Syned meeting would take place, this phase would be over.

Sitting by a window in the back, Radul shut his eyes and rehearsed the speech he planned to give at the next Syned meeting.

'When they begin, they are incredibly small, however, even in that miniature form, they carry the potential to be what you want them to be. They can be tall, short, fair, dark, blue-eyed or brown-eyed. They can also be the best in astronomy or mathematics or even proficient in cooking. How many of us sitting here even remember that they existed? Yes, I am talking about creations. But I have never seen one. And I know for a fact that there are many like me outside this Syned building. When I saw the image of a creation in the Koshum, I felt a strange sense of loss as if something very basic had been denied to me. And why? Because some time ago, the wise men of this Syned decided that until we reach consensus on what is allowed as input for a creation, we should not permit them. We have yet to reach a decision about the issue as nobody talks about it anymore and thus, the moratorium continues. So, I wish to bring this discussion back to the table. Is it time to revisit the moratorium on creations?'

Radul opened his eyes. He had memorized his speech to perfection. It was bound to hold the Syned's attention. However, what he planned to say about his own reaction when he saw a creation for the first time was not completely correct. He had stared at the image long and hard and had felt neither any connect to that image nor any desire to create one.

As he processed the creation procedure and the time they took to mature, the image of the helpless creature had lurked in his head throughout. He had found out that creations took nearly fifteen zacs before they could live on their own. He had also discovered that in earlier days, there had been centres where creations were nurtured, educated and brought up. Radul remembered hazily the centre where he had grown up. But, those centres were now shut. He realized that the established order would need to be re-engineered to start creations.

However, that was not the only reason why Radul had told Ime that he was not ready for a creation yet. In reality, he didn't know what he would input in a creation? He could not even begin to choose. He had thought about it fleetingly and then deeply. It was a crucial and difficult decision. For him, personally, creations seemed onerous and unnecessary, but debating about creations was one of the ways to bring the gynake back into the narrative at the Syned.

The travelor stopped and the other two passengers got off. In the momentary stillness, Radul saw a small habitation clustered around a lake. He could see outlines of manufacturing buildings in the distance.

The travelor took off again and the scene outside became a blur once more.

As the travelor sped up, the landscape changed and so did the sky. The afternoon sun gave way to dark clouds. Sheets of water lashed the empty travelor. Radul pressed his face to the window as the pelting rain gushed past in a swell of grey. Just as suddenly as it had started, the rain stopped and the sun came out again. Radul had already spent a long time in the travelor, yet, the journey did not seem to end. After a sharp turn, the travelor started slowing down.

The Point had arrived. Radul got off the travelor and stretched as he looked around. It appeared to be a place of interest for visitors. He could make that out from all the signs and structures. However, at the moment, it was deserted. In fact, after a closer look, it seemed as if no one had visited the place in a long while. Radul crossed over to an entrance arch. A slow breeze was blowing which added to the sense of dejection. Straight up ahead, Radul saw a large white structure. From where he stood, it seemed plain and round. The landscape was bare except for this white installation which stood out in the stark surroundings. No trees, shrubs or any other building provided relief to the bleak landscape, except this seemingly huge white orb. Radul had to tilt his head back to see it in its entirety.

Patix was observing Radul as he walked down the entrance road. He was pleased to see that Radul had cut his hair; it now hung just above the base of his neck. His pale green shirt fit him well and so did his dark blue trousers. Radul's entire bearing had altered for the better. His appearance would not put off the other members of the Syned anymore. As Radul neared him, Patix called out to him from behind the white structure, 'Come to this side, Radul. This is the front of the Point.'

Radul walked to the other side and saw that the installation was in fact half a sphere. On the rounded surface five steps were etched leading to a door. The topography of Elone was imprinted on the surface—the mountains, rivers, and the seas, all etched in pure white. The brightness of the installation was blinding in the late afternoon sunshine.

'Have you ever been here before? Do you even know what it represents?' Patix asked.

'No, I haven't. Although the deserted look suggests that no one has been here in a long time. Is that so?'

'Come, let us sit on those stools under the tree from where we can see it completely,' Patix led the way.

As they sat looking at the white structure bathed in sunlight, Radul thought it looked rather dreary. There was a sense of utter neglect all around it. Radul waited for Patix to start the conversation. He knew that there had to be a reason why Patix had made him travel all the way to this almost-forgotten structure.

Staring intently at the installation, Patix began, 'This is the memorial to mark the time when we arrived from Earth all those zacs ago. It was installed just after the last War. It is called the Point, but in reality, it is not the point where we landed. In fact, nobody knows where that exact location is.'

Radul looked at it again with interest.

'That is why it is built like half a sphere. It represents the half of Elone we inhabit,' Patix continued, while Radul stared intently at the memorial.

'Okay, but why are there five steps?' Radul observed the surroundings, wondering when the real reason for the meeting would be revealed.

Patix was working towards something, of that Radul was certain. And he was somewhere part of the plan, Radul sensed that too. He would have to be patient to understand Patix's motives.

'We do know that the spaceship that brought us here had a ladder with five steps which led to the ground. We came together with the gynake on the spaceship and then spread out.'

Then, after a pause, he asked, 'Radul, what do you think about the gynake?'

Radul looked at Patix who was staring at the memorial with his grey beady eyes. Longing, impatience and ambition were writ clearly on his countenance. Radul realized that Patix too thought about the gynake, and like him, their existence troubled him.

Radul went back to the night he had spent in the Koshum. It had given a form and image to so many things he had only heard about. The gynake, whenever talked about, were referred in the abstract. No images were associated with them. When he had seen an image of a gynake for the first time, he had been surprised to see that they were similar to men. Like them, they had two legs, two hands and they walked erect.

The only visible difference he could discern was that they had some sort of growth in their front that men did not have. They mostly kept their hair long and their dress was distinct. The gynake wore longer shirts, till their knees, teamed with loose pants or a flowing garment. Their dresses were colourful and had patterns, unlike the men. But it was their similarity that had caught Radul by surprise. He had tried to delve deeper but not many details were available about how they lived on their side or why they lived separated by the Fence when, in essence, they did not seem to be so different from men.

'I always thought they were a different species, Patix, but recently, I discovered that they don't look very different from us. They also seem to have a similar existence. They walk, eat, sleep and follow the sun's path, like us. I even tried to find out how we lived with them on Earth, Patix, but the Koshum only begins from when we arrived here. I know we came on common spaceships, but took up separate areas immediately. We have been in conflict ever since we arrived and it was only after the Fence came up that there has been some peace. I know that they occupy half our planet. I also know that they are going in for creations while we are not.'

Patix heard him out. It was clear that Radul had been investing in improving himself. If he continued on this path, he would make for an ideal candidate in the present circumstances.

'"Our" planet, Radul? Does Elone not belong to the gynake also?' he asked.

Radul took his time to formulate an appropriate response because he knew that this conversation was important. The setting itself indicated that.

'Elone is shared by both of us presently, but ultimately, it will either have to be theirs or ours. And Patix, the fact that they are increasing their numbers through creations and we are not is troubling to say the least. I want to bring up the moratorium on creations at the next meeting of the Syned. We need to remove the moratorium and start creations again to increase our numbers as well,' he replied. Then, added hesitatingly, 'Should I tell you how I plan to begin?' He wanted to see how Patix would react to the creation issue.

'What do you think the Syned will do, Radul? Do you think they would remove the moratorium? And even if they do, how will that make this planet ours?' Radul thought he had a glimpse of Patix's goal.

'Well, if we have enough numbers, we can just get rid of them in one push...I guess,' Radul wondered if Patix had a plan to follow up on. The sun was setting, casting an orange tinge on the white memorial.

Radul wished Patix would tell him what he wanted him to do. It was a long journey back to the city and it would get dark by the time he would reach home. However, he waited quietly for Patix to come to the point.

'But why do you think men would even go in for a push? They have even stopped visiting the Point. It was designed in such a manner so that it would constantly remind us of our half existence. But everyone has accepted things the way they are. Do you think that if we merely outnumber the gynake, men will agree to take action? No, Radul, no...not unless there is a concrete reason because no one on either side wants this truce to end,' Patix paused, as if to take a breath, but in reality, he wanted to gauge Radul's reaction. He then said decisively, 'If you think you would like to take this ahead then I could give you a reason.' Patix had thrown the bait; now, it all depended on Radul. How he reacted would decide whether he was the right choice or if Patix would have to look for someone else; someone who would become the face of this whole operation, someone who would be on stage, while Patix would be the one pulling all the strings, safely hidden in the background.

Radul looked at the desolate white structure bathed in a fading orange hue. Was he willing to get embroiled in all this? Did he want that half sphere to become whole? Was he prepared to take on the mantle that Patix was offering him? Radul remembered Ime sitting with his back to him, his own trepidation before entering the Koshum, his cramped group house—this could change everything. There was an ocean of opportunity in what Patix was asking.

'This planet belongs to us, Patix, the men. We need to turn this half globe,' he gestured to the memorial, 'into one whole. The gynake may outnumber us, but we can outmanoeuvre them. Why will men fight again, Patix? Tell me, and it will be my responsibility to rally the men. I can do it, I am sure, because I believe that Elone needs to grow and expand.'

In the deserted area, Radul's firm statement seemed to reverberate in an ominous manner. Patix observed Radul. His blue eyes sparkled and he appeared eager and alert. Patix realized that it was worth taking a chance on him.

'Our reserves of Nepo are dwindling, Radul. We need the reserves on their side to continue to exist. This is the big reason. But there is also an immediate trigger. There has been a nex on their side and they are saying that we have caused the nex through Vish. I know something is brewing on their side. This seems to be a battle call.'

Radul absorbed all the information. He had not been expecting this. What Patix had said about Nepo and its dwindling reserves sent a shiver down his spine. He felt alarmed. Nepo was the basis of their existence.

'Patix, are the reserves going to deplete soon?'

'No, Radul. But, they are dwindling and will eventually run out. The gynake, on the other hand, have large reserves on their side and they don't even need them. They use a renewable material for substitutions. I believe they have given a war cry by blaming a nex on us.'

Someone had been nexed! That was unheard of. Radul could not comprehend how such a thing could have happened. He thought about everything Patix had shared. If the issue was of Nepo, men could be galvanized. This reason was laden with potential. However, he was still unsure about the nex. It was like bringing an extinct idea back to life, something far removed from the reality of their existence.

'Did we cause the nex?' Radul asked.

Patix got up and beckoned Radul to follow him. They began to walk towards the exit. Patix cast one last look at the half globe as its forlorn shadow lengthened across that desolate place. At last, his plan of expanding their reach beyond the Fence was moving into a decisive phase. The man walking beside him would play a crucial role in this transition. Patix had to ensure that he used him appropriately.

'Does it matter whether we caused the nex or not? When you live on opposite sides of a fence, it doesn't matter what is, but what one "thinks" it is.'

Search

Seeni walked into the room and sat on the chair opposite Iwe's workstation. She usually never did that. Generally, she breezed in and out, leaving questions or information trailing in her wake. Seeni looked elegant and charming, as usual. Her long hair was tied loosely; her tunic patterned in myriad colours matched a long flowing pink skirt. Yet, something about her demeanour was different.

'So how is processing the Chronicle going? Do you find it interesting?' Seeni asked.

Iwe leaned back in her chair and replied, 'I am going through it. I began with Chronicle-ii as you know. Some things are new, but most, I already know. Overall, it's interesting.'

The screen before Iwe was buzzing with activity and she wanted to get back to it. So, she asked Seeni, 'Are you looking for something in particular at the Vault today?'

Outside the glass panes, the sun was setting. Its golden rays cast a glow on Seeni, as she sat in the chair. She merely smiled in a mysterious manner at Iwe.

'Did you like the music I sent you, Iwe?'

'Yes, I liked it very much. It is melodious and captivating. Where is it from, Seeni? Who composed it?'

Seeni got up from the chair and moved towards the exit,

leaving behind the glow from the setting sun on the chair.

'I think you are looking for the composer, aren't you? Maya. Did you find her?' When Iwe didn't say anything, Seeni whispered softly, 'Come, I will take you to her.' Seeni turned towards the door.

Iwe got up from her seat and ran after her but Seeni had already disappeared around a bend in the corridor. When Iwe reached the bend, nobody was there. Iwe stood at the edge of the empty corridor, feeling lost and defeated.

She awoke with a start. The feeling of being lost floated into her reality. She lay in the darkness thinking about the dream. It had seemed so vivid and real. The quest for Maya, thrust on her by Ultur, was chasing her in every dimension.

Iwe turned on her side. Looking for Maya seemed to be a pointless mission. Iwe had even entered the Irana Hub system and had trawled it for days looking for Maya or her music but there was nothing. She had come up against a blank wall, with nowhere to go. Iwe wanted to give up, but Ultur's firm belief that Maya was the key to knowing why the men had attacked Seeni made her continue searching.

Iwe was slipping back into sleep. She decided that she would inform Ultur that she did not know where to look for the elusive Maya anymore.

It was raining heavily. The day was grey and dark, lending a pall of gloom to the already deserted streets. A shuttle was winding its way down a corridor in the distance and seemed to struggle with the rain pouring down with full force. A gust of wind swept across the landscape like a triumphant army proclaiming its ownership.

Outside, the wind howled and water cascaded in thick sheets. But inside, Ultur's colourful apartment was shrouded in silence. From where Ultur sat, the movement outside seemed like a dance of the elements. She watched the seemingly silent performance, while the screen on the wall buzzed with incessant chatter. Her tag was overflowing with messages, but she had only looked at the ones sent by Iwe. As yet, there had been no breakthrough in the search for Maya.

Ultur was also searching. She had looked through channels, open as well as encrypted, old and new, but she had not come across anyone called Maya. She had even logged on to the Vault and hunted for Maya extensively. The only reference to the word 'Maya' had come up in the Lexicon which defined the word 'maya' as an 'illusion'. Ultur had wondered whether Seeni had been pointing elsewhere, with her reference to Maya.

As the days passed, Ultur had somewhat learned to accept Seeni's loss. But what she could not accept was Seeni's complete disappearance from all the spaces she had occupied. Seeni's workstation at home and at work had been wiped clean. In the annals of Elone, it was as if Seeni had never existed.

The rain had almost stopped. Ultur walked over to the window and looked out at the dreary grey skies. She felt a deep weariness inside her; she probably needed some replacements and therapy. The road in front of her apartment building seemed long and endless, as it wound around the city's contours. It was empty and dark. What would it be like to know that it would all end somewhere? To know that existence was not continuous and endless? If she ceased to have any replacements, when would it all end?

Her tag, lying on the table, beeped, jolting Ultur from the strange train of thought.

It was Iwe. She told her the same thing she had been telling her for the last few vihans.

'No sign of anyone called Maya. I have looked in all the places I could think of.' Ultur threw the tag back on the table.

She wanted to get rid of the thoughts that had recently germinated in her mind. Why was she even thinking about ending her existence? Where had this thought come from? Was it because of Seeni's absence?

This thought was anathema to their existence. It had never crossed her mind before. Ultur tried to concentrate on the task at hand, which was to find Maya.

She tagged Tioni as she also knew about Maya and her music. In a flash, Tioni was on the screen in front of her. Her apartment seemed untidy and cluttered behind her.

'Tioni, do you have any idea who Maya is?' Ultur asked directly, without any preamble.

'Maya? Oh, you mean that musician. No, Ultur. Iwe tried to look for her but could not find her. You have also not found her? All I know is that she composes melodious music.'

It was clear from her responses that Iwe had not shared their conversation with Tioni.

While Ultur was framing a response, Tara came crawling and started bawling at Tioni's feet. Tioni picked her up and looked apologetically at Ultur. But Ultur was transfixed. She could not remember the last time she had seen a creation. Ultur forgot Maya, the music and all that was happening around her. She watched, spellbound, as Tioni tended to Tara.

After putting her down with her toys, Tioni returned to the conversation. As Tara played, she let out whoops and gurgles that floated through the screen into Ultur's silent home.

'Seeni had said to look for Maya in the Irana Hub. Since no one by that name is there or has ever been there, it seems that Maya probably had something to do with Seeni's work,' Tioni did not know how to speak about Seeni to Ultur. This was the best she could do.

'What is her name? When did she arrive? I did not know creations were still happening. It reminds me of the time I brought Seeni home. It was so much work,' Ultur was still staring at Tara. Incredible energy was emanating from that small creature; something that had been missing from their existence.

'Tara? Yes, she does need a lot of looking after. The instruction manual doesn't quite prepare one for it,' Tioni replied while looking at Tara.

Then, turning back to Ultur, she continued, 'You look worn out, Ultur. Why don't you come down to the Remplazo? Some replacements and a little therapy, and you will be fine,' Tioni suggested.

This remark brought Ultur back to her silent apartment that was trying valiantly to look colourful and bright.

'Why don't we ever think of alternatives to replacements, Tioni?' Ultur sighed.

'Alternatives? Well, Ultur, actually, research for alternatives is in progress. We are working towards a stage where the organs can regenerate within, and this need for external replacements would be over. But, it will still take many zacs. Anyway, you should come for replacements soon,' Tioni said.

'Yes, I will. Take good care of Tara.' With that, Tioni's image dissolved.

Creations, replacements, alternatives, Maya, Seeni—all

these thoughts were clogging Ultur's thinking. 'There is no alternative reality,' Ultur reminded herself. Her thoughts about ending replacements had no place on Elone. Remaining forever, existing eternally—that was what drove them. And, if that was the aim, it was imperative to know what the men were planning.

Ultur thought about what Tioni had said. Maybe through Maya, Seeni had been pointing to something related to her work. It was all so unclear and ambiguous. Ultur went and sat at Seeni's workstation. She did this often. The blank screen seemed to mock her. Seeni's clean, deactivated tag was lying nearby.

Ultur waved her hand in front of the blank screen and it sprang to life. The machine asked, 'Where do you want to go?'

Ultur just sat there. There was a strange comfort in sitting in the place Seeni had occupied constantly whenever she was at home. After a pause, the machine asked again, 'Where do you want to go?'

Ultur continued to sit quietly and observe the rain dance outside the window. The rain was incessant, voluminous and buffeted by wind. Twice more the machine repeated the same question. But Ultur was lost in the rain and wind outside. Then, suddenly, she heard the machine say, 'Let me take you where you normally go.'

Ultur watched in fascination as the screen flashed the word 'patterns'. Thereafter, all the channels related to patterns appeared on the screen. Ultur scrolled down as the machine poured out everything on Elone that could fall under the category of patterns. While all the data on Seeni's work had been erased, this ability to recall—a small part of the machine's capability—had been missed. At last, Ultur had stumbled across something that had attracted Seeni's attention.

While running the programme to prepare the ground for the next sowing of Amar, Promly sat in a small room on an elevated perch in the middle of the farm. The room provided an all-round view of the farm. The toboks were busy in the fields around her. The system was working smoothly. Music was playing in the background. In the evening, Promly would take a round of the farm in her small shuttle.

A message from Clepo came in on the encrypted channel.

The information has been picked up. We had ensured that the noise was loud enough for them to hear. And about the rest, maybe you should schedule a visit.

When she had left the Nividum to become the head of their prime intelligence and research organization called Enodus, Promly had temporarily moved to the farm. She needed an occupation that could not even be remotely connected to Enodus and farming seemed like the best option.

She had changed her tag, her channels and all her coordinates. In a way, she had fallen off the radar. However, what was supposed to be a temporary measure became an enjoyable activity. The countryside with its unique sounds and distinctive smells captivated her. The continuous process of sowing, sprouting, growing and harvesting of the Amar crop kept her busy and Promly's forays into the city became rare.

Promly shared Clepo's message with Ultur. So, now, the men knew that they were suspected in Seeni's taking. When she had last spoken to Ultur several vihans ago, she had obliquely hinted at some action. But there had been no word from Ultur since she had abruptly switched off the channel after that fateful conversation. Maybe this news would bring her back.

After a long time, the Enodus had tried to send a message to the men. They had learnt to live with the men on the other side without rancour and with complete indifference. But the silence and the peace of these countless past zacs seemed to be under threat. Promly knew that the men would take this accusation as a sign of hostility. A backlash was inevitable. The men needed to be tracked closely, now more than ever. What Clepo had said was correct. Promly would have to go to the city soon and expedite the operation. The operation… whenever Promly thought about it, she felt a sense of both anticipation and apprehension.

If the women succeeded, then the men, their ridiculous bubbles, the stores of Vish, the Fence—everything would become meaningless.

The lake seemed to be trembling with ripples. The trees grouped along the opposite shore were wavering in the lake. Iwe strapped the water gliders to her feet and stepped on to the water. In a snap, she was gliding across the lake, her copper hair splaying in the wind. Leaving the shore behind, she glided towards the centre of the lake. As she sped up, she could feel the splash of cool water on her face. Iwe liked the combination of speed and wind involved in the sport. She often came to the large lake as it was ideal for water gliding and was a favourite water sporting hub.

Iwe gathered speed and the trees, the other gliders, even the world around her seemed to be lost in a haze of water and wind. After two rounds of the lake, Iwe slowed down and cruised to the centre. Other gliders near the shore of the lake shimmered like mere specks. Only a handful of gliders were speeding like her across the centre of the lake, wet and windblown. The ripples in the water became small waves near her feet, stretching out across the lake, creating different patterns.

Iwe shook her head and gathered speed again. She had come to the lake in order to escape the search for patterns that Ultur had tasked her with. She had gone through large amount of data on music patterns, fabric patterns, design patterns, replacement patterns, creation patterns—the list was endless. This was another fruitless search that had to be given up. Maya, the music, Seeni, her taking, Ultur's insistence—nothing mattered to Iwe anymore. She was only concerned with her work at the Vault and the activities she liked, like water gliding. She wanted to finish the Chronicle too, learn more about the elusive men, but this search for Maya gave her no respite.

She glided to the shore and sprawled on a bench in the shade of some trees. She was drenched and the passing breeze seemed cool. In Iwe's line of sight, a patch of dazzling yellow flowers was blooming. The faint fragrance from the flowers floated her way with the gentle breeze, calming her.

While Iwe was resting in the shade of the trees, Tioni was in her apartment tending to Tara. Tara had started crawling. As a result, Tioni's once impeccable apartment was now disorganized and in a mess. Most of her things were stacked up on higher shelves, so Tara's inquisitive hands couldn't reach them. Tioni instructed Hap to organize the apartment and then sat in the reclining chair near the window. Tara was on the floor, surrounded by small items Tioni had strewn around her. It was interesting to observe Tara's limbs grow and her focus improve. Tioni enjoyed trying to understand her unfinished words as she attempted to speak. Tara's curly hair had grown and hung around her face like spirals of a genome sequence, and her blue eyes were bright.

Tioni watched her from the reclining chair and remembered that she had not yet processed Tara's cell structure. It would help Tioni understand Tara's attributes better as she matured. After ensuring that Tara was busy, Tioni began to process her cell structure through her tag. She shut her eyes as the programme started to run and began to dissect each strand in Tara's genes. After a short while, Tioni felt a blip. For a moment, the processor seemed to go blank. Tioni opened her eyes to check on Tara instinctively.

Standing precariously, Tara was taking her first steps towards the window where Tioni sat. Her feet moved slowly and she landed on the floor with a thump. But she got up again, swaying on her feet, and put one step in front of the other until she reached the reclining chair. Clutching the edge of the chair, Tara looked up at Tioni and smiled. It was fascinating to observe all the changes happening in her limbs as she began walking. Tioni started capturing the images on her tag, forgetting everything else.

Promly was in the city after a long gap. She noticed that even though the city breeze was cool, it lacked the fragrance of the farm breeze. The tall buildings blocked out the sun and the crowds in the shuttles were overwhelming to say the least. She watched the city race by from a window high up in the Irana Hub. Turning from the window, Promly switched her attention to the information that was scrolling on the screen. Various reports from the Enodus were flashing, but nothing seemed out of the ordinary.

Promly activated the encrypted channel between her and Ultur. Despite Promly informing her about the action taken with the men, they had not exchanged a word. Promly focused on the screen again. The encrypted channel came alive and Ultur was sitting in front of her. She looked tired, her hair hanging limply by her side. The dark colours of her dress reflected the pall of gloom hovering over her apartment. All the colours were still there, but they had lost their lustre.

'When did you come to the city, Promly? Are you ready to present a detailed report on the steps taken by Enodus to the Council? Should I call for a meeting?' Ultur's questions were uttered in a flat unemotional tone.

'Just wait for a few more days. I will let you know when things are ready. Why don't you come to Irana Hub? We haven't met since Seeni—'

'Promly, do you know a musician called Maya? Did Seeni mention her to you?' Ultur ignored Promly's offer.

When she heard the question, Promly remembered the music Seeni had sent her. Maya—the name did not ring a bell. She made a mental note to ask Clepo to find her.

'No, Ultur, I don't know any Maya. But was Seeni interested in music? I never knew about it,' Promly wanted Ultur to keep talking. This silent mourning that had overtaken Ultur needed to be broken.

'And I never knew you loved farming so much, Promly.'

The connection was abruptly switched off. Promly realized that the chasm between Ultur and her was getting deeper.

She sighed and got back to her workstation. There were more pressing matters seeking her attention. Who was Maya? Promly had just sent a message to Clepo when a report flashing on the screen caught her attention. She processed it till the end after which she walked over to the window and looked out into the distance where the Fence stood. Things had started churning on the other side of the Fence. It was an important development. Their reserves of Nepo were dwindling. The men were in the throes of a crisis. Matters were converging in an extremely opportune manner. Promly was certain that the men would respond as per her expectations. This also meant that the project had to move as per plan. There could be no mistakes, no delays. She returned to the workstation and waited to hear back from Clepo.

After switching off the encrypted channel, Ultur set out towards the Fence. It had become an involuntary walk that took her across the broad avenues of the city, through sprawling blooming gardens and tall buildings that seemed to be lost in the mists of the sky. Ultur traversed the walkway wondering all the while about what patterns Seeni could have discovered. There had been no breakthroughs regarding that lead either.

She descended near the Fence and walked the pathway towards the spot where Seeni had been found. Colourful flowers were blooming and leaves seemed to be waving to her in the breeze. It was deceptively serene and quiet. On the other side lived the men who had supposedly taken Seeni.

Ultur stood near the spot and stared at the opaque area that denoted the Fence. It had served its purpose well. It had made them forget about the men. Everything had been running smoothly. Then, why had this happened? Why with her Seeni?

Ultur had started coming to the Fence to find some solutions, but after every visit, she walked back with more questions. Why did they have to share their world with the men? Just because they had come together on a spaceship all those zacs ago? Why did they have to share Earth in the first place? They were two distinct species competing for the same resources, then, what had tied them together? Were they going to end the clash that had been suspended the last time, once and for all? Who would win if that did happen?

Ultur shut her eyes. The vision was too daunting.

When she opened her eyes again, the opaque space of the Fence seemed to mock her with its silence and serenity. Ultur turned around and started the long walk back to her apartment. She had gone only a little distance when she started feeling tired. Maybe Tioni had been right. She needed to go in for some replacements and therapy. Ultur slowly walked towards a shuttle stop and tagged a shuttle.

What would happen if she stopped taking replacements? The thought stealthily crept into her mind again.

The shuttle arrived and Ultur boarded it. She looked around at her co-passengers wondering if anyone sitting in the shuttle had ever thought about ending their existence. Maybe, sometimes?

We arrived on Elone from Earth in zac 01. Not much is known about the journey or the Great Escape that brought us here. Earth was a dying planet, getting colder, flooded and uninhabitable with passing time. No one remembers where the spaceship carrying us landed exactly. We fanned out and occupied a large part of the planet. The main focus in the beginning was to build cities, harness energy, grow as well as manufacture food and create. There were only a few of us and the challenges of the new terrain led to many losses. Replacements were still being developed, so creations were a priority...

As Iwe processed the beginning of Chronicle-i, she could sense a tag coming in. Tioni had sent her a clip of Tara walking on her own. Iwe watched in fascination as Tara took her first halting steps. Thereafter, Tara was walking around the apartment without faltering. Iwe stopped the Chronicle processing and tagged Tioni. She was at the Remplazo and looked drawn and her brown uniform tunic was somewhat dishevelled after a long haul at the replacement table. Tara and Hap were with her, waiting to head home.

'It was great to see Tara walking. She is growing so well.' Then after a pause, Iwe remarked, 'Tioni, I was processing about when we first arrived on Elone. After our arrival, we focused on creations, but that focus faded over zacs. Tara has happened after countless zacs. And till Seeni, no one had been taken for hundreds of zacs. Both these incredible events happened together. Isn't it amazing?'

'Yes, Iwe, they did happen together and as a result Seeni never got to meet Tara.' Tioni was clearing her workstation and continued, 'Why are you even delving into the past, Iwe? Seeni had declared that finding the roots of existence was her "passion", and now she does not even exist anymore!' she said it in a matter of fact manner as she was still trying to come to terms with Seeni's absence.

'Have you read the Chronicle?' Iwe asked, breaking the silence that had descended across the channel.

'No, I have not. Why do you ask?'

'I admit that I had started processing them because Seeni had insisted that I should know about the past. But now, they have begun to interest me. Do you know the Chronicle barely mentions the men in reference to the clashes? There is no detail about them. It is like we have mastered the art of believing that they do not exist. But the fact is that they do, and according to me, this deliberate forgetting is not the best of ideas.' Iwe had been reflecting on this as she processed the Chronicle.

Tioni sat down with a sigh. She was tired and in no mood to discuss these issues.

'Iwe, I have the cell structure from which Tara was created. I want to process it to analyse the attributes she will develop as she grows. Seeni and I had thought we would explore the structure together. Now, since Seeni is not around, I was thinking if you would like to join me?'

Iwe hid her disappointment about Tioni's lack of reaction regarding her discovery and stated flatly, 'Sure, that sounds interesting.'

Tioni began to process the structure through her tag. The screen before Iwe went dark for a moment and then Tara's cell structure began to be broken into its individual strands. In different parts of the city, Tioni and Iwe watched with eagerness. Suddenly, the processing stopped and the screen went blank.

'There seems to be some problem, Iwe. The same thing happened the last time I tried to process Tara's cell structure.'

The screen was still blank, but Iwe could hear Tioni.

Hello, Seeni. Where have you been? I have been waiting for you since years. I mean, for some part of your zac.

The words appeared swiftly on the screen.

'Who is this? Why is she talking to Seeni, Tioni?'

'Iwe, is this someone at your end?'

Both of them asked at the same time.

Seeni, you said that you would analyse the cell structure of Tioni's kid. I have been waiting for you here for a long time. Do you want to transform to audio? I mean, do you want to talk?

The words were tumbling on to the screen in rapid succession.

Iwe and Tioni read the words, perplexed and confused. It was strange to realize that someone on Elone did not know about Seeni! The different language also puzzled them.

'Seeni, are you there? Why are you not answering me?' said a metallic sounding voice coming through the system.

Iwe searched the system for the identity of the voice or for a source from which the messages were coming. There was no recognition. Iwe tried to generate the image of the voice, but she did not succeed.

Finally, Iwe decided to reply, 'Seeni has been taken. Who is this?'

The voice did not respond for some time. It seemed like the person had exited the system.

'Who are you?' the voice asked suddenly. It was loud and commanding. Iwe was rattled by the resonance of the sound. Tara started whimpering at Tioni's end.

'Is that Tioni's kid crying? Oh, it's been ages since I heard that sound. Tioni, is this you? Where is Seeni?'

The programme that was analysing Tara's cell structure stopped and Tioni appeared on the screen again. She was holding Tara. Iwe and Tioni looked at each other in utter confusion. Why was this unknown person not able to identify them from the system?

Iwe spoke again, 'I am Iwe. I am the manager at the Vault. As I said before, Seeni has been taken. Who are you? Somehow the system is unable to recognize you.'

'I know you. You are Seeni's friend. Taken? That cannot be. It doesn't happen here. Has she gone somewhere? When will she be back? I have been waiting for her.'

'She is not coming back. She has been taken. They say it was a mishap.' There was a mix of anger and pain in Tioni's voice. Iwe was slightly taken aback. She had not understood the impact of Seeni's taking on Tioni. With the passage of time, it had stopped bothering Iwe. Her concern, now, was the men on the other side.

'Seeni died! What are you saying? It doesn't happen here now, does it? You don't die anymore. What happened to her?' and the voice fell silent. The only sound that floated in Iwe's room was that of Tara's gurgles.

Iwe watched as Tioni rocked Tara in a mechanical manner. She then placed Tara on a chair and began to wind up with Hap in attendance. They were both waiting for the voice to say something. Some of the words being used by the voice were incomprehensible. Iwe was filing them so she could look them up later.

'Iwe, is the kid still around? I think I can hear it,' the voice broke the silence once more.

'I am Tioni and who you hear is Tara. Now, we would like to know who you are and how do you know Seeni? She never mentioned that she had shared our plan to go through Tara's origin cell with anyone else. Also, how can you not recognize

Iwe and me from the system?' Tioni could no longer contain her impatience. This mystery game had gone too far.

'You both know me. Seeni told me that you loved my music. I am Maya. I am very sad to hear about Seeni's death. I wonder how you two are coping with it since this is not a common occurrence for you. And how is her mother doing? Ultur—that is her name, right?' The voice spoke slowly.

At that moment, someone walked into Tioni's cubicle. She immediately switched off the channel. Iwe continued to stare at the blank screen, trying to comprehend what was happening. She had seen someone enter Tioni's cubicle and understood her immediate reaction.

'Are you there?' Iwe asked the blank screen but only darkness stared back at her and her room remained silent.

Maya.

Iwe couldn't believe that Maya was communicating with them through the system. She spoke a language that Iwe was not familiar with. She was apparently inside the system, yet the system did not recognize her. Where did Maya live? Why did no one know about her?

All these questions whirled around in her head. Iwe also felt a sense of exhilaration. The mystery composer had been found. Should she tell Ultur? But what would she tell her? She had to find out more about Maya.

Iwe kept sitting at her workstation for a long time, waiting for some sound to emanate from the system. However, there was only a quiet hum. She also tried to access the voice, recognize it, locate it, but all her efforts were in vain.

Late evening had descended over the city. A cool breeze was blowing and the three moons were glowing in the corner of the evening sky. The lights of the Vayunum that was located at the corner were slowly coming on. Iwe couldn't believe that Maya—the elusive musician—did exist. There was no doubt about it now. She had accessed their system. She knew about Tara and Ultur.

Ultur…maybe Ultur had been right. Maya probably did hold the key to Seeni's taking and maybe she could tell them more about the men. Iwe felt a sense of calm pervading her being as things started sorting in her mind. At least the seemingly never-ending quest had ended.

Outside Tioni's window, it was pitch dark. The stars were shining feebly and the three moons were in hiding. Tara was sleeping in the other room. A serene blue light flowing out from Hap bathed the room in its glow.

Iwe and Tioni had been trying to find Maya ever since she so mysteriously appeared and then disappeared. They had opened and processed Tara's origin cell many times. Sitting at Tioni's workstation, they tried again. Tara's origin cell structure opened and Maya's voice said in its metallic tone, 'Hello'. It was a strange word. Neither of them had ever heard it before.

'How are you doing? Sorry for disappearing like that. I just needed some time to mourn Seeni. That is why I cut the conversation short last time. I miss her. I am sure you do too,' Maya said.

'Who are you? Do you have a face or a body?' Iwe interjected.

'Me? Well, how do I describe myself? Let me tell you the way I told Seeni when we first found each other many years ago. Sorry, I meant when I met her sometime in the last zac. I am a woman's consciousness; your ancestor from Earth,' Maya's metallic voice resonated in Tioni's small apartment.

'Where do you live?' Iwe asked impatiently.

Since they had last encountered Maya, Iwe had been wondering if Maya was a programme created by Seeni. It seemed to be the most logical conclusion. However, its exquisite compositions defied any logic.

'I live in this gargantuan enmeshed system that runs your world.'

Before either of them could ask her anything else, she spoke once again, 'Now, I have a question. What mishap killed Seeni? Or what took her? What happened to her?'

'We don't know. We thought you would be able to tell us something about it. Actually, the Council has reports that those on the other side of the Fence had attacked her with Vish. Ultur is sure that you would be the key to understanding what happened to her,' Iwe replied, relief flooding through her.

At last the issue was out in the open. There was no other way to confront Maya. Tioni, on the other hand, was stunned. The other side had attacked Seeni! The idea itself was absurd as well as alarming. She looked at Iwe. Iwe had stated the information with confidence. It must be correct.

A thick silence enveloped them. A sliver of blue from Hap was spilling into the room. Tioni was restless. She went and sat in her reclining chair, near the window. Outside, the city had long gone to sleep. Lights in most of the buildings had been turned off.

'Who told you about Vish being the cause?' Tioni asked Iwe.

'Ultur. There is also some talk of an impending clash. It's all so very confusing, Tioni. Do you even know who is on the other side? They are another species called "men". They came with us from Earth. We have fought with them twice already. If they attacked Seeni, then it is a serious matter. Ultur thinks Maya is linked in some way to Seeni's taking. That is why I have been searching for Maya,' the words tumbled out of Iwe's mouth and hung in Tioni's silent home.

'Iwe, what you are saying is unbelievable,' Tioni said, after a while. She did not know what to say. She too had never heard of 'men'. It seemed that the other side had suddenly come out into the open; as if a curtain had parted and the stage was finally visible. But why would they attack them? It was absurd.

'I am also confused, Tioni. Let us wait for some time. Once we know what role Maya has played in Seeni's taking, I will inform Ultur. Then my work is done in this matter. Maya, are you around?' Iwe persisted.

'I am here. Where will I go? I was wondering why would the men kill Seeni? And contrary to what you believe, I don't know anything about it. Seeni and I used to chat about a lot of things. She always wanted to know about the way things were. She was full of questions and had an unending interest in life on Earth. Of course, she also liked my music...'

Iwe lost interest in the conversation. Finding Maya had not solved the mystery. The more Maya spoke about Seeni, the more Iwe became convinced that Maya was nothing but a programme in the system which created exquisite music. Her statements about her being from the past seemed facetious and pretentious.

'Are you a programme, Maya? Because you are obviously not a person,' Iwe declared.

Tioni got up from the reclining chair. Maya's statements about Seeni's interest in Earth had caught her attention. She knew that Seeni always wanted to delve into the past and Maya claimed to be a link to that long-forgotten time.

'Maya, did you tell Seeni about "passion"? How did she find you? When did you come into our system? And how? Who are you?' she asked, the questions rushing out of her. If only she could reach out and grasp Maya!

However, the faint hum of the system was the only reply she got. Tioni waited for a while before calling out again, 'Maya?'

'She left, Tioni. Don't get carried away. It is just some mischievous programme,' Iwe tried to convince her.

Tioni sat near the workstation in the dark room with the pool of blue light spread around. Iwe sat by her side. Maya would find them again. That was certain.

The Council meeting was still a calante away. Ultur sat at Seeni's workstation and tried to find Maya. She agreed with Iwe. Maya was simply a programme, injected into the system by the men.

'A woman's consciousness'—there was something ominous in the description. What was it even supposed to mean? The men seemed to be taking the battle to a different level altogether. From the fight for space and resources that had scarred Elone twice already, they seemed to have moved to playing some nebulous yet lethal game. And her creation, the inquisitive Seeni, had somehow stumbled on to this game. She had probably found the reason why the game had begun, and where it was supposed to end. So, she had been taken.

As the puzzle seemed to fall into place, Ultur's attempts to access Maya became more intense. However, the search was proving futile. Ultur had also accessed Tara's origin cell and waited for a long while. She had entered Tioni's system and the Vault, deploying all the search techniques at her disposal, but Maya remained elusive.

Hunched over Seeni's workstation, Ultur had been trawling the system for Maya since morning. She was tired and exhausted, and so went and lay down on the couch.

What was going to happen to their world as they knew it?

Promly, as head of Enodus, should have been dealing with this situation. However, Ultur hesitated telling her. Promly's move to the Enodus had changed the equation between them. Her move to the foothills to cultivate Amar had further deepened the wedge. Ultur had never given it much thought before, but Seeni's taking had brought the deep chasm between them out into the open. Ultur would consult Promly only if she failed to find any answers. She tagged Iwe to locate the origin of any strange, unaccounted for programme in the system and waited for her response.

Iwe was still at the Vault when she saw Ultur's tag. After telling Ultur about Maya, she had withdrawn from the situation. She was not going to search for elusive patterns or people anymore, much less strange programmes. It was up to the Council to take over this matter. Iwe read Ultur's message and deleted it. She was convinced that Maya was some programme in the system that Seeni had discovered and probably tweaked to say the things that she did. Who knew the facts? More importantly, it did not seem to matter since the programme only produced music and spoke a different language. It did not appear to be sinister.

It had become dark outside and Iwe began to shut down the systems of the Vault. While the processors shut down, she recalled some of the strange words Maya had used. She had managed to find the meaning of most of them. Consciousness, or as Maya had said, 'a woman's consciousness,' had been the most interesting one.

The lights dimmed and the Vault became dark. Iwe stepped out and walked towards the shuttle stop. In the corner, the lights of the Vayunum were still blazing. A huge tree stood on the side of the road, like a sulking hulk in the darkness, still and quiet in the dark night.

As she waited, Iwe wondered about 'consciousness'. Did Maya's statement mean that the consciousness of men was different? Who were they, the creatures, who lived on the other side of the Fence? Why did they know so little about the men when they shared the planet with them? Did men have a different awareness and perception about things?

The shuttle stopped in front of her and the door slid open. Iwe stood rooted to the spot. The door shut and the shuttle sped away. Iwe turned and went back to the Vault.

As Iwe was returning to her workstation, Tioni was putting Tara to bed. Afterwards, Tioni sat at her workstation. Ever since Maya had spoken to them, she would open Tara's origin cell every night and wait for Maya to talk to her again. Unlike Iwe, Tioni was not sure who or what Maya represented. The only thing she was certain about was that Seeni had interacted with Maya. If Maya had been linked to the men, she would have known about Seeni being taken. Before Tioni came to any conclusion, she wanted to ask Maya many questions. Tioni wanted to know when Seeni had connected with Maya. Which past did Maya claim to belong to? How long ago? What did Maya know about a woman's consciousness? Had Seeni been so interested in Earth because of Maya? Was Seeni taken because of her? Once Tioni knew answers to these questions, only then would she make up her mind about Maya.

As the night lengthened, Tioni sat in her reclining chair, waiting for Maya. She often slept there as the stars moving across the sky relaxed her. As she saw the glowing orbs in the sky, she recalled the last time Seeni and she had met. They had discussed Tara's imminent arrival. Tioni had been planning, preparing and going through the manuals, full of anxiety and eagerness. Tioni tried to remember if Seeni had said anything important or had mentioned Maya.

The glow from the screen of the workstation created a pool of light around it. The cell structure was open.

Tioni softly called out, 'Maya, are you there? I want to talk to you.'

The hum of the system was clearly discernible in the silence of the night.

'Tioni, creations happened very differently on Earth. It was a process we cannot even imagine in our world,' Seeni's statement suddenly rang in her ears. She had said this the last time they had met. Caught up in the preparations for Tara's arrival, Tioni had not paid attention. But now, Seeni's statement rung out loud and clear in her mind as sleep began claiming her. In a trice, she was wide awake. She wanted to know everything.

'Maya, please come back. Tell me what you know,' Tioni was beseeching the darkness.

A gentle breeze was blowing across a sleeping city. The three full moons seemed to smile in understanding as they bathed the world in their silvery sheen.

Clepo sat in a chair near the workstation, lost in thought. Promly was standing by the window tapping her fingers on the ledge.

'No, Promly, no one called Maya has ever been known on Elone. I have checked all the records that exist since we came here. There is no record of anyone called Maya. Who is she?'

Promly watched Clepo's heavy hair swing from side to side as she shook her head vigorously.

'She is some sort of musician. Her music doesn't belong to this world. The instruments, the tenor and sound are not found on Elone. Seeni had access to her or, should I say, Maya had access to Seeni.'

'Then it must be some programme that has gone wrong. We will try and find it.' Then, after a pause, she added, 'When do you want to visit the site?'

On hearing Clepo's question, Promly forgot about the music. She felt a familiar tingle of anticipation.

Down below in the streets, things were going about as usual. People were milling around the roads, shuttles were passing by and the tree at the far end of the road was flowering. From the height of her window, it looked more like watching a game being played out. And now, the game was nearing its end.

'I will go after the Council meeting, Clepo. You keep a close watch on the work assigned to you. Also, I want to find this Maya—person, programme or illusion—whatever it is, I want it found. Nothing can remain hidden once the Enodus starts looking for it, right?' Promly said.

Clepo stood up and moved towards the door. She hovered near it uncertainly. She was in awe of Promly. In fact, all of them at the Enodus were. Promly had visualized the whole plan. She had been working on it single-mindedly, taking hard decisions along the way.

Promly saw Clepo standing hesitantly near the door.

'What is it, Clepo?'

'What do you think will happen at the Council meeting?'

'Nothing is going to happen. It would be business as usual. Leave all these things to me. You just concentrate on finding Maya for me. Put a unit on it. It is surprising how many people know of her, yet no one knows who or what she is.'

'Since your call was the most appealing and insistent, I decided to respond to it. Tioni, why do you stay awake and call out to me every night? Your calls tug at me in the same way someone used to pull at my heartstrings so very long ago.'

Tioni awoke with a start. She was sure she was dreaming.

A pool of light was emanating from the workstation. Outside, the three moons were glistening. But all was quiet and still.

'Maya, are you there?' she whispered in the silence of the night.

'Yes. So many people are looking for me relentlessly these days. But, I can't be found like that, Tioni. I am a consciousness. You simply have to be aware of me and reach out to me.'

Tioni came and sat at her workstation. Her eyes were still heavy with sleep, but her mind was alert. She wanted to ask so many things, but did not want Maya to disappear again. She chose the common thread between them, 'Maya, how did you get to know Seeni?'

'She was looking for her roots and since our roots lie in

our consciousness, we met,' Maya's metallic voice was booming in the dark.

'When did you meet? I mean how long ago, Maya? And, why did Seeni never tell me about you?' Tioni persisted.

'Did you ever ask her why she was seeking knowledge about the past so passionately? She didn't tell you because probably she felt that you would not consider conversing with a consciousness. Or, like your friend Iwe, you would also suspect my existence in every manner.'

So, Seeni had learnt the word 'passion' from Maya! Tioni wanted to ask Maya about creations and so many other things. However, she needed to order her own thoughts before talking to her.

'Why don't you come here tomorrow? I will call Iwe also. She doesn't suspect you, she is just sceptical because we have never come across a phenomenon like you before. You can tell Iwe and me more about the past that you belong to and what it was like to be a woman then.' Tioni realized that it would be better if Iwe was also present. She responded to situations differently. Together, they would be able to understand Maya better.

The system was humming. Tioni wondered if Maya had left. She waited for Maya to respond.

'You want to hear about the past, about me? Seeni was in the middle of what I like to call Maya's story. But, it has to be heard with an open mind and with no prejudices.'

Was that a smile Tioni could discern in the now-familiar voice?

'Yes, we do want to hear about your story. But before you leave today, tell me Maya, did you compose all the music you gave Seeni? It is simply breathtaking. It is so different from anything we have ever heard in all these zacs.'

'Tioni, music always belongs to a time, but sometimes, it becomes timeless. I am a musician, and yes, I have composed all the music you have heard. I will meet you again tomorrow.'

This time the quiet hum of the system told Tioni that Maya had gone.

It was late evening and Tara was asleep under the watchful eye of Hap. The three moons were riding up the dark sky slowly as the stars appeared to keep them company. Tioni was waiting after a long day at work for Iwe to arrive. Maya's story—she wondered again why Seeni had never mentioned it to her. This was the tragedy of someone being taken—one could never ask them anything again. She wondered how people earlier had lived with this gap on a regular basis.

Iwe walked in and Tioni noticed that her short hair was dishevelled and she had an unconvinced look on her face.

'Strong wind outside, Iwe?' Tioni asked to lighten the mood.

'Yes. Is she here?' answered Iwe.

'Not yet. I was waiting for you to arrive before I called out to her.'

Iwe sat down on the chair next to the workstation. She seemed uneasy.

'What if Maya is a programme introduced by the men into our system, Tioni? We could be playing into their hands. I understand much more about them and our clashes now. We have ignored them, living as if they do not exist for perhaps too long. But they do exist and have always been present right across the Fence. They are the species that has repeatedly fought with us to capture Elone for themselves!'

'Even if that is the case, Iwe, we must engage with Maya to try and understand what the men are trying.'

Silence fell on the room. Tioni got up from her perch near the window. It was time to try and reach out to Maya. There was no knowing how long Maya's story was going to be.

'Are you both there?' Maya's metallic tone burst across the room before Tioni could call out to her.

'Yes. I was just going to try and reach you. We are both eager to hear from you, Maya,' Tioni said.

'Maya, have you told your story to the men too? Do you have any contact with them?' Iwe interjected.

'The men? I don't know if they who live on the other side of the Fence know the story. It's not mine, yours or theirs. It's ours. This story is about both men and women.'

The words hung in the room, like vapour that was thick and hazy, confusing the two women sitting huddled together near the workstation.

'Maya, why don't you tell us what you told Seeni? It would be a good place to start,' Tioni said.

'If you want to know something, you must know what to ask. Seeni knew how to ask the right questions. I am not a storyteller.'

Tioni realized that Maya was not easy to talk to.

'You said you were from the past. From which past—were you there during Clash-i?' Iwe asked.

Now that Maya had admitted that the story had something to do with men, Iwe was more convinced than ever that Maya was a programme introduced to confuse them.

'Iwe, do you know where all the women before you on Elone came from?' Maya asked.

'Yes, Earth—a planet far away that was destroyed.'

'Well, I too came from Earth.'

A silence fell on the room again. It was broken by a wail from Tara. Hap attended to her and she fell asleep again. Tioni sensed that Maya was not forthcoming. The course of the conversation had to change.

'Maya, what is your passion?' Tioni broke the silence.

'It is interesting that you use that word, Tioni. You heard it from Seeni, I believe? I told her about it. It has fallen into disuse in your world. When time is not a precious limited resource, passions fall by the wayside. My passion is music. In fact, on Earth, music and Aryan were my only two passions.'

'We know what music is but what is "aryan"?' Iwe asked.

Maya's statement about time had caught her attention.

'And why do you say that time is a resource and a limited one at that? It flows and exists perennially,' Iwe continued.

'Well, Iwe, tell me, what do you think are resources for you?' Maya's voice was patient.

'I think all the knowledge that exists on our side of Elone, Amar, water, trees, flowers, all of us, we are resources. Time flows and exists along with us. It doesn't have any independent existence,' Iwe had never thought about such things earlier. Maya was a rather interesting programme.

Tioni, on the other hand, was getting restless as the exchange was not moving forward.

'Maya, we are here to hear from you, not exchange questions and answers,' she interjected.

'Tioni, the only way you learn and understand from a consciousness is if you let it question you too,' Maya's laughter floated around the room, tinkling and light, quite unlike her metallic voice.

'You said earlier that you also came from Earth. Then, when and why did you enter our system? Are you the only one or are there others like you too?' Iwe was now keen to hear what she had to say.

'Maya, do you remember what Earth was like? What is aryan, your other passion? Is it as good as your music?' Tioni put forth her questions as well.

Somehow Maya's laugh had lightened the atmosphere in the room. The night had deepened outside, but the blue light coming from Tara's room and the light emitted by the system bathed the room in a serene glow. It was easy to forget that Maya was not there in person. She seemed as real as both of them in that warm glow.

In her city abode, Promly was sitting in the darkness processing inputs from the Enodus. They had still not found any trace of Maya. Promly stopped the processing. She got up and put korive sauce and vegetables between two loaves of inola, poured herself a rich, red wine, and reclined on the couch. As she began to eat, the now-familiar thoughts flowed around in her head.

What was this mystery of Maya? How come no trace of anything—programme, person, intrusion—had come up despite the thorough search?

Promly tagged up the music that Seeni had sent and began to play it. As the notes flowed in the night, Promly began to process the instruments used in the melody. A few were immediately recognizable, but most were unknown because they had never been heard on Elone. The system drew a blank, again. Then, Promly entered the Vault and processed all the instruments in all the available records but she came out empty-handed. Promly knew the music needed to be traced. It proved that Maya existed. She finished her meal, and continued to process the reports regarding the search for Maya once more. The lights dimmed further but she persisted. Maya had some link with the men, she was sure of it. They had probably orchestrated the music. But, what was their plan and why had they chosen music?

In the chatter that Enodus had picked up, Seeni's taking and the declining reserves of Nepo were prominent. They also found out that there was going to be an important meeting of the Syned soon. In all this, where did this music and Maya fit in? How had Seeni come across it?

Promly tried to break down the music to discover any hidden messages or secret code. As she waited for the analysis to flow in, reports on the operation made their way to her.

As she perused the details, Promly felt a familiar surge of excitement. Their operation was nearing its conclusion. One well-planned push and everything would change. When she was drawing up her plans, she was sure that Ultur would work with her, but their present interactions were under stress. Promly would have to work alone and reach out to Ultur only when the need arose.

The music analysis finally came in. No patterns, no codes, no messages were hidden in that beautiful piece of sound. It was pure lilting music which, somehow, did not belong to their world.

Promly had dedicated one tobok in the Enodus to continue searching for the origin of the music. The rest were busy with the operation. She was clear that no strange melody or its mystery composer was going to come in her way.

The music began to play again and Promly fell asleep listening to the melody. In the window, the first rays of sunlight made an appearance. Maya's music continued to play as dawn broke in a world that did not recognize it, but was still enthralled by it.

'I loved music from the beginning. It was something that brought light into my life. Music gave my life meaning,' Maya said.

'How did you meet Seeni?' Iwe interjected.

'We need to structure this conversation instead of asking random questions. Only then will we learn about you, Maya, and what you represent,' Tioni declared.

She wanted to know about Earth, while Iwe wanted to know more about Maya's existence on Elone.

Maya's tinkling laughter rang out in the room again.

'You don't really know how a gang of girls chats, do you? You cannot set rules for a consciousness, Tioni. It simply is. You either engage with it or ignore it.'

Silence fell as Iwe and Tioni waited for Maya to say something. After a while, she said, 'As I said before, Seeni was looking for her roots. She would spend long hours sifting through all the data on Earth that exists in your Vault, Iwe. I identified her as someone who actually had a sense of curiosity. After ages, I felt like reaching out to someone. I followed her on your system, and one day when she was streaming some sounds at the Irana Hub, I inserted some of my music at the end of her track. She instantly realized that it was different. Thereafter, she began to look for music, different patterns in the music I had put in her system, and distinct sounds. She searched extensively and when I felt she was ready, I called out to her, like I did with you girls, the other day. Seeni, the one with a questioning and curious mind, accepted my existence without a murmur. I miss her,' Maya said simply.

Her statements echoed around Tioni, as Seeni seemed to flash past in the blue darkness.

Iwe sat there thinking Seeni must have discovered something other than music. She had noticed that the programme had admitted tracking Seeni.

'Did Seeni ever tell you something she knew about the men? Did she discuss anything about them at all?' Iwe asked.

'No, Iwe. She did not tell me about the men, in fact, it was I who told her about them. But I spoke not about those who live on the other side of the Fence, but of the men who lived on Earth.'

'That is what we want to know, Maya. We want to know about Earth and what you know about it that we don't,' Tioni was almost pleading now.

'Tell you what, girls? Why don't you start processing? I will relate Maya's story to you and it will roll out like a film before you. No questions, no interruptions. Is that a deal?'

Many of the words Maya used did not make sense to Iwe and Tioni, but they understood what she was trying to say. Iwe activated her tag so that all the words that they could not comprehend would be slotted and their meaning looked up instantly.

Now, since Iwe knew more about men and was aware of

their existence, she wanted to know why they had attacked Seeni.

Tioni, on the other hand, hoped that maybe Maya's story would tell her why Seeni spoke about things the way she did. If she learnt something important about their past, it would probably interest Tara when she grew up. With their eyes shut, both began to process the input.

Maya's Story

The music of the orchestra rose to a crescendo and like a wave receding from the shore, it died down slowly. As the last notes floated over the packed audience, the applause rose like a rushing wave. Tired but exhilarated, Maya turned around and bowed to the audience. On various devices across the world where people were watching the show, she appeared beautiful with her expressive eyes shining bright and her full lips parted in happiness. The sweat on her brow shimmered like a crown.

Maya looked out at the dark auditorium and wondered if he had found the time to come. She banished the thought from her mind and enjoyed the moment. When the curtains came down, she turned and, without stopping to greet anyone, walked towards the dressing room, like always. After a performance, she needed some space and a little quiet. The Trin band on her arm was signalling that Ria wanted to speak to her. Maya shut her eyes. She let the fatigue, thrill and the simple joy of doing a job well wash over her.

When Maya eventually walked out of the dressing room, the place wore a deserted look. People had left; the instruments had been packed away and stored safely for the next performance. Maya strolled on to the stage and surveyed the empty theatre. Despite the dark hush, an anticipation for the next show permeated the hall; she loved that feeling. Then, she stepped down and walked through the empty aisles towards the exit.

As Maya stepped outside, she was immediately struck by the blistering heat. At 11 p.m., in the so-called autumn month of October, such hot temperature had become normal. Her Trin band sent a message to her car and it drove up to the steps. Maya got in and pressed the 'home' button. The car began to navigate towards her home. Maya leaned back in her seat and watched the city go by. Small, self-driven cars sped over the roads which were devoid of pedestrians because of the sweltering heat. The weather had become extreme, to say the least. From this furnace, in no time they would move to a winter that was popularly called 'The Freeze' by the media. Winter was long-drawn and extremely cold; the temperature was getting worse. The aura of spring and the melancholy of autumn were unseen and forgotten.

Ria was beeping her again. Maya took the call.

'Are you on your way home? I am going out, Mom, and I won't be back till the day after. When is dad coming back from his trip this time?'

Ria's impatient voice, as it amplified in the car's speakers, managed to take away the soothing effect of the performance for Maya. Ria was nearing thirty, but in 2185, thirty was the new teenage!

The neon signs along the highway were flashing their new mantra, 'Ninety is the new Fifty'. Bright billboards were advertising age extension formulae and interventions. Defeating the tyranny of numbers was the continuing rage. Very soon they would have to start counting age differently and the long-held associations with numbers would acquire a different meaning.

'Yes, I am on my way home. I will

see you day after. About dad, I think he would come back sometime next week. Ria, please eat something before you leave,' Maya said and shut the call.

Once the car turned off the main avenue and on to the side streets towards her locality, the bright lights receded and the stars were visible. The super-speed trains, cutting across the sky, blocked them at certain points, but when they passed, the stars shone bright.

Maya wondered what he was doing at this moment. Was he studying the stars or was he sleeping? She wanted to reach out to him, but hesitated as she always did.

When Maya reached home, it was dark and quiet. She alighted near the porch and the car made its way towards the garage. She had forgotten to alert the house panel of her arrival; if she had, the lights would already be turned on, the food would be warm and the temperature cool. As Maya entered the house, the lights and the temperature adjusted as per her specifications automatically. Help also activated and began preparing her meal. She deactivated Help as she was not hungry.

On the days of her performances, Maya did not practise music during the night.

Instead, she lay down in her bed and watched the night sky through the glass windows. The star-studded sky was losing its sheen. Increasingly, fewer and fewer stars were visible, although she could still see the Great Bear and Orion clearly. The stars and the constellations remained constant; it was only on Earth that things were changing exponentially.

Sometimes, the pace of change in their lives was simply exhausting. Seven decades ago, the changes that they had thought would be attained in fifty years happened in ten. When Maya had been a teenager, life expectancy was about a hundred years or maybe even less. People now routinely lived to about double of that. When life had started being extended, there had been endless debates on the ethics surrounding it, what it meant for humanity and the future. However, the world took to it soon enough and extending one's life became a routine part of existence. Death remained, but it could be delayed, and their time on Earth stretched.

Time gave them the opportunity to learn more, explore more, pursue passions and love more. Maya smiled in the darkness when she thought about it. Yes, her long life had given her time to do all that. Yet, she wanted more—always.

The days had become cooler. The trees had started to become bare, the few birds that had remained around the city were returning home earlier and soon, 'The Freeze' would overtake them.

Sitting in a small room at the back of the house, surrounded by windows, Maya was absorbed in her music. Her Trin band signalled that there was an interesting debate taking place on the waves. Maya stopped her practice. These discussions fascinated her. Humanity's obsession with talking about things endlessly and from all possible perspectives was engaging to say the least. The end result was almost always the same—they embraced the latest upgrade in the market. Maya tuned in to the latest one on 'structured babies'.

'It is a human right to be able to have the kind and number of babies one wants. No one can tell me it's wrong to desire a baby with certain qualities, characteristics and abilities,' someone was saying.

'Suppose I want a baby with no specifications. I want it as it was in the olden days. I want a surprise package.

Will I have the right?' A male voice was asking.

Maya smiled when she heard the question. When Ria's father and she had decided to have a child so many years ago, she too, had some choice in how to structure her child. Even though the kind of detailing that was possible now was not available then, a menu had been given to them. However, they had decided to go in for a 'surprise package'—to have Ria in the ancient way, to let nature take its course.

'Why would you want that? Can you even imagine not knowing what your child will be like?' Someone interjected, horrified.

Maya remembered the joy of watching Ria grow up. She neither had an ear for music like her mother nor a love for sports like her father. She was impatient, hot-headed and lazy, but she grew up and became an expert in her chosen field of bio-infotech and was quite passionate about her work. 'Because it is an enjoyable voyage of discovery. There is a thrill in nurturing a child that you do not know everything about in advance,' Maya joined the conversation as she often did.

'That is nonsense. Even structured babies have their own unique characteristics. We can fix their looks, their health, their abilities, tastes and other small details but they still grow up into their own person.'

'Well, then, I guess it all boils down to personal choice,' Maya conceded.

'But will I be allowed to have a "surprise package" baby some years down the line? There is so much pressure to structure the baby nowadays,' the male voice said, sounding really concerned.

'You guys are debating a dead topic. Now, since human cloning has taken off, we need to discuss how exciting it would be to have a baby that is an absolute replica. Someone who would be just like me, looks like me and has my abilities! That is what I call living forever. That is real immortality, not these stupid life extensions they keep talking about!'

Maya lost interest in the conversation; life extension, cloning, immortality—all these were oft repeated themes in their lives and talking about them endlessly was no longer engaging. She switched off from the wave. Standing near the window, she looked out at 'The Freeze' that was creeping in and embracing the city in the fading sunlight. Drops of dew frozen on the brown leaves looked like small chandeliers waiting to light up in the dark. The grass on the sidewalk had faded and icicles were forming on it. It would soon be cold, really cold. Suddenly and with an intensity that surprised even her, Maya missed him. So, she sent him a small message.

Aryan was busy at his workstation when Maya's message beeped on his phone. He picked it up and read: *How are you?*

She had reached out to him after a long time. The past few months had been hectic. Aryan was sure he had achieved a major breakthrough but it needed some minor validations before he could announce it. He stretched in his chair, and swivelled it around. Through the glass panels of the observatory, he could see the stars gazing back at him. They were his true friends, twinkling in the distance, constant and always ready to be explored and discovered.

He ran his hand through his salt-and-pepper hair. He had let his thick unruly hair take their natural course, like he did with many other things. This pursuit of meddling with nature that had become the prime motivator for most of humanity troubled him no end.

Maya; how she loved running her fingers through his hair. As he thought of her, Aryan felt a sense of serene joy. He stood up and moved towards the telescope. Soon, he was lost in the stars that seemed so near and palpable. With the longest solar eclipse due on 16 July 2186, the next year, there was a lot he needed to get done. As the stars came closer to him, everything on Earth receded into the background.

Winter or 'The Freeze' came with a ferocity that enveloped the entire city. The sun was reduced to a dying ember in the sky. With every passing year, the winter was becoming more severe. All the prophecies about climate change, which had been debated endlessly in the last two centuries, had started to come true in the last fifty years. The previous winter had seen many people freeze to death, all over the globe, in one night when the temperature had suddenly plummeted. It was mandated that all work during the stark winter months be done from home and movement outside was restricted. Supplies were stocked for the duration of 'The Freeze' and everyone waited with bated breath for the thaw, which arrived later and later, each year.

In the enforced solitariness of the bleak winter months, Maya composed most of her music. She collaborated with other musicians and released it on the waves. The three of them, Maya, her husband and Ria, would be ensconced in their respective rooms at home, working while connected to a world that was, in a sense, hibernating.

It had been snowing for the last two days. It was dreary, cold and forbidding outside. Maya was busy with a new composition when Ria knocked and entered her room. Maya stopped composing and patted the seat next to her. Ria lay down and put her head in Maya's lap. Instinctively, Maya began to stroke her hair. Ria's long silky amber coloured hair fell over the side of the couch as they both watched the bleak snow-covered landscape outside.

'Mom, do you know, in the bio-infotech area, there is a lot of talk of "merger" these days? They say that humans will not survive this constant "wintering" of the planet, so, they are coming up with the "merger".'

'What is that? I haven't heard of it,' Maya responded.

In her head, her latest tune was playing. Ria often came and discussed the bizarre ideas that her area of work threw up with Maya.

'Remember how, in the twenty-first century, they tried hard to achieve "singularity"? They had tried to put consciousness on the machines. Even though they were unsuccessful, that idea remained, like so many others. Mom, what is it about ideas that once they emerge, they never disappear or wither away? They just keep circulating, waiting to be picked up, brushed up again and acted upon once more.'

'What about this "merger", Ria?' Maya was suddenly very interested in the conversation. Any idea that explored life beyond its real and imagined boundaries always excited her.

'First, you tell me why ideas don't die? And I know you are really listening to me now because you have stopped stroking my hair and your eyes are animated,' Ria chuckled. To Maya, her tinkling laugh sounded like sweet music as it filled the room.

'Ideas are born from the union of reason, observation, imagination and quest. The basis of these ingredients may change, but since these concepts are never-ending, the ideas also remain.'

'Interesting thought. Well, merger is the same thing, Mom. It is based on the same belief. You would be able to transfer your consciousness to a machine and live forever. Quite horrible, if you ask me. What do you do with consciousness if there is no physical body to relate to? They are saying that they will soon start looking for volunteers before turning it into a commercial venture.'

'Who will look after the machines if everyone transfers their consciousness to them, Ria?' Maya asked.

Ria sat up. She walked to the window and watched the feeble light outside.

'If these winters continue to grow longer and more severe, only the machines will survive, Mom. What we need now is another planet. Earth is nearing the end of its days, as predicted a while back. If you ask me, the solution is not merger, but moving to another planet.'

Another planet? Maya knew that finding another planet had been Aryan's dream and quest for the last many years. Nothing mattered to him more than finding a planet where humans could survive. That was his passion, his only real desire.

'Mom? Where do you keep getting lost? Did dad have dinner?'

'Yes. Let me know about the developments regarding merger. You never know, I might volunteer to test it out!'

'Don't be crazy, Mom! It's stupid and frightening. Why would you even want to live in a machine forever?'

'Life is beautiful, Ria, but cruelly short. That is why there is such a quest for longevity. Immortality seems to be the eternally unattainable fruit of living.'

'Don't philosophize this, Mom. Merger is not some music that you create that will live on the waves forever. This is you, your mind, your consciousness. Imagine, my mother with her beautiful music and vibrant mind becomes a machine. How would I relate to it? It is unacceptable. Don't even think about it,' Ria said firmly.

There was some logic in what Ria was saying. Maya realized that she had not thought it through. She would discuss it with Aryan, when they met. It had been a long time since they had last seen each other. The silence from his end only meant one thing—he was completely engrossed in his quest.

'These are exciting times, Ria. So much is happening everywhere. I feel as if we are on the cusp of some major leap in the process of life. Humans are now being cloned, they are merging with machines, planning to move to a new planet...imagine not being there to see it all!' Maya said.

The thaw had begun slowly. The tips of brown trees, stripped bare of leaves, had begun to emerge from the snow that had covered them for months. In a few weeks, the trees would be laden with small shoots and then the flowering would begin in earnest. Even nature had adapted and knew it had to hurry through its course.

Aryan was waiting for Maya. He had called her to the astronomy tower because he wanted her to be the first one to see it. After a long rejuvenating shower, he strolled outside in the gallery surrounding the tower with a cup of steaming coffee in his hands. From the height of the astronomy tower, everything below looked like a model. He felt like he could reach out and touch the clouds floating in the sky. The sun was setting, leaving an orange tinge behind. By the time Maya would come, the light would be perfect for viewing.

Maya—she brought music to his life, she never left the spaces of his mind, and she loved life and him.

Aryan came back to the workstation and put on one of Maya's compositions. For him, the celestial music that reverberated silently in the beautiful cosmos was all-encompassing. The rhythm and symphony of the universe was what he understood. From the world around him, it was only Maya's music that connected with him. The music played on and Aryan turned on his workstation. He tuned in to various news channels, something he had not done for a long time. He realized that cloning was the latest flavour in town. After many hiccups, human cloning had finally begun. Once it took off, clones would alter their world as they knew it.

Aryan switched off the chatter. These leaps into an unknown future rattled him. He had never understood why Maya revelled in these changes. She looked forward to them and the supposed opportunity they presented. She had a husband and a child, yet, she embraced change with great joy. He, on the other hand, was on his own, had been through a string of relationships, had no child and no ties of substance, yet, he found the leaps and turns frightening. Aryan delved far and wide in the unknown universe, he spent his days and nights in the company of unreachable stars but he was grounded. He found change and uncertainty difficult to deal with. And Maya never seemed to understand this about him.

The elevator opened and Maya entered the tower. Aryan's heart skipped a beat. Whenever he saw her after a long gap, there was something about Maya that made him feel that way. This had not changed since they had entered each other's lives many years ago. They had met in the corridors of the university and had occasionally exchanged greetings. Then, one day, Aryan had invited her for coffee and since then she had occupied a certain space in his mind...always.

Maya was wearing a colourful outfit. Her hair was tied back, her eyes were bright and she was smiling. Her countenance was always happy, as if life was just opening its curtains for her.

Maya saw Aryan as he stood beside his telescope. His salt-and-pepper hair was unruly but short, just the way she liked it. He was one of the few in their time who let greying take its natural course. Aryan stubbornly held on to things, wanting to believe that change was a mirage. Cloistered with the stars and planets, the changing world around him disturbed him.

Aryan smiled at Maya and his ordinary face lit up. As she walked into his arms, she heard the strains of her latest composition. A small patch of salt-and-pepper hair was peeping out of his pale yellow shirt. Maya snuggled into his arms and felt at peace.

'Maya, I want to show you something. Come here to the telescope's viewfinder.'

Maya found her nose pressed against the glass pane and she was peering at the world that fascinated Aryan. There were numerous glowing objects scattered in the darkening piece of sky that Aryan was showing her. Whenever Maya looked into Aryan's world through the telescope, she sensed a cosmic symphony that seemed to envelop all those things floating around in the universe.

'Do you see that big planet? The one which has a bluish tinge? It is located on the far left?' Aryan asked.

'Yes, I do, Aryan,' Maya said, turning back towards him. He was standing right behind her with his hands on the telescope, embracing her. He gently turned her head back to the viewfinder.

'That, Maya, is the future home of humanity. It is a planet in another galaxy.

It is light years away from us, but it can support life as we know it. It has a huge sun that is bigger and brighter than our own. It also has three moons, as beautiful as our own. Its terrain is also much like ours. There is water, mountains and air that we can breathe in. The only major difference is time. The planet takes about eight of our years to complete one revolution around its sun. That means the days and nights are longer. I believe the seasons too run much longer than ours. On that planet, Maya, time takes on another meaning. We can build a new world on it, Maya. It is right there, tucked away in the cosmos, awaiting us,' Aryan said, without stopping to take a breath.

They both looked at the bluish speck through the telescope. It seemed like a beacon that beckoned across the galaxies.

'Maya, this is what I have been working towards all my life. I am going to go public with this in a while. So, I thought you should be the first to see it.'

Maya felt her vision blur as she stared at that distant planet. Tears rolled down her cheeks as the moment overwhelmed her. Through the glass pane, the planet seemed so far away, it almost felt unreal.

When she turned around this time,

it was to kiss Aryan. He returned her salty teary kiss, only briefly. He never kissed her long and hard. Hand in hand, they walked away from the telescope. Her composition was still playing softly in the background.

'I think you should give it a name before you present it to the world, Aryan. It is your discovery. By the way, when do you think we would be able to visit it because I would love to go,' Maya said as she reclined in the large sofa in one corner of the room. This was always her perch when she visited Aryan at the astronomy tower.

Aryan's full-throated laughter reverberated in the room. His face completely transformed when he laughed. A naughty, childish innocence took over his otherwise serious countenance.

'Maya, it will take a long time before we can figure out the technology that is needed for humans to travel such long distances and stay alive. People who actually live long enough to go there can name it, whenever they reach. I am simply going to call it Earth's clone, let us say, E-lone. What I want people to remember is that I found it for all of us.'

Aryan came and lay down next to her.

They remained there, entwined, staring at the glittering stars through the skylight. Maya ran her fingers through his hair.

'I am tired, Maya. It has been an exhausting journey to this point. Sometimes, I wonder what I will do now. What do you do once you achieve your dream? One never thinks about that,' said Aryan.

Maya raised her head and rested it on her elbow. She looked at him as he lay next to her. Seeing him from so close gave her great happiness. But as was his habit, Aryan pulled her on to his shoulder.

'You just find another dream, Aryan. That is what life is all about,' Maya sat back up as she spoke. Her hair clip fell off, and her shoulder-length hair hung, framing her face. She looked earnest and animated, 'Aryan, do you know they are looking for volunteers for the "merger" project? They will be able to transfer our consciousness to machines. It will come through in a few decades. We will be old by then, about to die maybe, despite all the life extension programmes going on. So, I was thinking why don't we both volunteer and merge? Then we would be able to observe humans moving to E-lone and maybe we could go with them. Just imagine, Aryan, this could be your next dream.' Maya's expressive face was alight with her thoughts as she spoke.

'Why should I wait for decades to merge? I would like to do that right now,' Aryan said as he pulled Maya back into his arms.

Aryan kissed her softly and swiftly, repeatedly. With the flick of a button on the wall, the lights dimmed. They threw off their clothes and embraced each other in the soft light. Maya lay with her back towards Aryan and played with his long fingers. He cupped her breast gently from behind and fondled her the way she liked it. She turned to face him. Aryan whispered, 'Stroke my body with your hands. I like your touch. I missed your touch.'

Maya moved her hands down the length and breadth of his body and found him erect and ready.

Maya felt her own arousal as Aryan bent over her and took her nipple in his mouth gently. Pleasure surged through her and she held onto him tightly. Aryan held her close in his arms.

They were entangled and enmeshed with each other; lips to lips, chest to chest, thigh to thigh and toes to toes. Aryan entered her and she let out a moan. The spaces between them had ceased to exist, and an eternal symphony played out under the skylight.

The momentum grew; Aryan paused, gathered his forces as they played the game of ascending and then descending again at the right point, only to ascend again. It seemed as if they were floating and about to land in a high release of exhilaration.

Then, it happened. Both of them climaxed together. The primordial programming came to its predetermined conclusion. Maya looked at Aryan as he lay next to her with his eyes closed. He opened his eyes slowly and smiled, pulling her back into his arms so that her head was, once again, resting on his shoulder. Embracing each other, they relaxed in the afterglow of the happiness they had experienced together.

As they lay in each other's arms, exhausted but happy, Maya asked, 'Will you at least think about the merger project?'

Aryan remained silent. He shut his eyes wondering how Maya was always ready to reinvent, to move ahead, leave things behind. He wanted to dwell in the moment that they had just experienced together, but she had already moved far ahead.

'Aryan, you spent most of your life looking for the future home for humanity. Now, don't you want to see it yourself, some day in the future? How can you not have the urge? Look at me; I am ready to leave everyone close to me behind.'

Maya wondered if Aryan would ever feel this urge to live more, to experience some more. Would he ever be able to extricate himself from the confines of the universe and feel the pulse of life on the ground?

'Maya, I will think about it. I have been so busy these last few months that I haven't kept abreast with all the developments on this. And, as you say, we still have many years to decide about that. Anyway, I heard today that human cloning has started! Maya, men and women would no longer make love. What a loss! Imagine Maya, not knowing the absolute beauty and joy of what we just shared.'

Maya laughed and ran her hand through his hair.

'Aryan, you always think about such things. If men and women stop needing each other for procreation, think of what the world would be like. All the conflict and rage that has simmered through the ages between men and women would end.'

'Hmmm,' Aryan was feeling drowsy.

'You should hear Ria talk about this.'

She paused to look at Aryan. His eyes were closed and his long lashes were clearly visible.

'You know Aryan, the world has changed so much. Even here, in this insulated astronomy tower, you can't escape this reality. As technology has become the prime mover, its neutrality towards men and women has transformed the dynamics between us. As traditional gender constructs have crumbled, the conflicts and debates have intensified. Men and women have been engaged in an evolutionary dialectic that is rooted in biology. Change biology and all conflict will cease.'

'How wrong you can be sometimes, Maya. Now let's sleep for a while. Stroke my back, the way I like it,' Aryan said, turning over.

Iwe stood up with a start. What she had just processed was beyond something she could even imagine, think or dream in her world. It was startling, disturbing and at some level, disgusting. Could there ever have been such an interaction with those creatures on the other side of the Fence? It was probably a bizarre rumour that the men were trying to spread. Iwe was shaking her head as she stood in the darkness. She felt strange and disoriented. Maya's story seemed like a fantasy that had no basis.

'I don't want to know anymore, Maya,' said Iwe, 'the creatures you describe may look somewhat like those on the other side of the Fence, but they were obviously a different species that died on Earth.' She stood near the dark window and tried to feel the familiarity of the night as it enveloped the city around her.

A man had found Elone? Why had she never been told that by anyone? And if that was the case, why did the men bring them to Elone too? The whole story smacked of a plot.

Tioni sat there transfixed. Iwe's abrupt movement had stopped the input. Men and women had shared such a dramatic physically intense activity. It was unimaginable. What was it that had compelled them to do something like that? The physical form seemed to provide some strange joy to both of them as they indulged in that activity. It seemed alien, new and incomprehensible.

Tioni continued to sit near the screen. The story did not throw light on how creations had happened on Earth. Even if it was a fantasy, Tioni thought Maya's story was fascinating.

'Maya? How did creations happen then? Who is this "dad" that Ria keeps referring to? Where is she now? Your creation?'

The silent hum of the machine was the only answer.

'Maya, don't leave. Please complete your story,' Tioni persisted.

'I haven't gone anywhere. Iwe's abrupt exit made me lose the thread of my story. Well, creations happened when a man and a woman made love at a time when the woman's body was fertile. Physical intimacy led to procreation. Sometimes, fertilizations also occurred outside, but women always carried the baby for nine months and gave birth through a painful, laborious process. "Dad" was one of the terms kids used to refer to the man who was their father. Men and women needed each other to create, Tioni. We were dependant on each other for procreation since the dawn of time. Somewhere along the way, it changed. So, now Tara is created from a cell provided only by you and is nurtured in an incubator. She is handed over to you when she is fully formed. On the other side, men can do the same. You do not need each other for reproduction any more. The basis for civilization has changed.'

Tioni absorbed all this information. Many questions were brewing in her head.

'Where is Ria? And the man she called dad?' Tioni asked again.

Before Maya could reply, Iwe suddenly came and sat near the workstation.

'This "love" between those men and women, what did it even mean? I checked the Lexicon, it defines "love" as "a deep feeling for someone or something". What was it, Maya?'

Maya's tinkling laughter dissipated the stress that had accumulated in the room. Outside, the night was disappearing and a faint light was embracing the city.

'It is ironic, girls. Millions of light years away, in a world that does not even use the word anymore, the meaning of love still puzzles humanity. Love is whatever it is to the person who feels it. It can be exhilarating and uplifting. It can also hurt and cause pain. But for me, it is energy—positive energy. It never disappears even when it is up against a non-receptor, it simply transforms to fuel different dimensions of life.'

'Maya, Aryan was wrong. Even though we all use the name he gave this planet, "Elone", no one knows who discovered it,' Iwe pointed out.

Tioni was a little surprised. The things about Maya's story that struck Iwe were different and quite distinct from the ones that impacted her.

'Yes, Iwe, he was wrong about some things and I was wrong about some others,' sighed Maya. Her voice was fading into the distance; she seemed to be retreating into the dark caverns of the system again.

'What were you wrong about, Maya?' Iwe tried to stop her from leaving.

'When men and women stopped needing each other for procreation, the conflict did not stop. It sprouted wings and escalated, beyond our wildest imagination. It took a form that none of us could foresee. Look at where things are in this day and age!'

Alternatives

The thick blanket of snow outside was spotless, serene and seemingly endless. The majestic mountain range curved in the horizon and was dazzling with the sun dancing off its pristine white slopes. In that forbidding landscape, the Gazer building stood out like a beacon. Built high on the top of a mountain, in the shape of a thin rectangle, the building seemed to reach out to the clear skies above. Solitary and purposeful, it housed the highest-altitude telescope in Elone. Inside the building, there was a different world altogether. Flowers bloomed on various levels and their colours and fragrances floated around the warm environs. The foliage blooming inside enlivened the building that was surrounded by snow-clad mountains.

Tobots inhabited the floors, working and maintaining the facility. Ime had arrived three vihans ago. Presently, other than him, only two other men occupied the huge building.

Sitting at a workstation on the top floor of the building, Ime could sense the delicate fragrance coming from pink flowers planted nearby. He had also brought seedlings of the red triangular flowers from the Furawa and planted them in the Gazer. The quest Valhan had set him on required work at the Gazer telescope for a few calantes.

Ime's euphoria of discovering Zeta and Tai as two possible future homes had been replaced by the need to find out whether either of the two planets had reserves of Nepo or a substance that could replace Nepo. Last vihan, a small probe had returned with soil and atmospheric data from both the planets.

In the night sky, Zeta and Tai displayed a yellowish tinge as the light from a nearby star reflected off them. Absorbed in his search for Nepo, Ime had not yet processed the already accumulated data on the two planets; he still had to map their environments completely. Ime had observed some anomaly in his data regarding Nepo. One of the more advanced tobots was working on it, but had reached no conclusion.

Across the Fence, a substitute for Nepo already existed, but they couldn't lay their hands on it—neither through stealth nor through negotiation. As Ime pored over the current data streaming in, he wondered if this complete disengagement from their neighbours was the correct strategy.

Outside, fluffy snowflakes swirled and twisted on their way down. Ime realized he had been working since early morning. He got up, stretched and decided to take a ride in the rondural around the mountain on which Gazer was located.

A rondural was the only way to go down the Gazer and the mountains and reach the plains, from where transport was available to go back to the city. Ime rode it often to see the view as well as to get away from all the data that was constantly pouring in.

He took the elevator till the embarkation floor and stepped into a waiting rondural. He sat down on a small bench and strapped himself securely before setting the rondural in motion. He circled all the way down with his nose pressed to the pane. The transparent spherical capsule floated around the building slowly and gracefully, as if performing a dance with the falling snowflakes.

As he was floating down through the landscape, Ime entered the Furawa through his lex so as to assess the progress of his saplings. The flowers he had designed were set to bloom in the next vihan. However, there was an override as a message came in from Valhan that Odep would visit Gazer the next day and he would join them the day after.

Ime was surprised. The Gazer building was hardly a place people visited. Unlike the Aeona, few knew about its existence. 'Odep'—the name was certainly familiar, but Ime could not place him. He ran Odep through the lex and as images floated past, he remembered. Odep was the great architect, a member of the Syned, and a problem-solver. But now he lived tucked away somewhere in the hills, away from the limelight. Why was he coming to the Gazer? Earlier, Patix had forced Radul on him and now Valhan was sending someone too?

The rondural had reached the top again and docked. It was always freezing at that height. Ime hurried into the building and returned to his workstation. In the snow-filled sky, nothing was visible. As per the forecast, it was going to be a clear night. Maybe then he would find some hope for Elone on those distant planets that emitted a mysterious yellowish light that flickered across the universe.

Radul had been waiting for a sign from Patix ever since their meeting at the Point. However, there was no word from him.

The days passed in silence. It seemed as if the meeting at the Point had never happened. Radul sat at his favourite place in the Koshum and stared out of the window. He was now a frequent visitor there. Since the meeting at the Point, he had been trying to learn more about Nepo. If Nepo was going to be the basis on which the entire battle against the gynake was to be fought, Radul wanted to be well-prepared. He had also started looking at other things, randomly trawling through information, facts and figures that never attracted him earlier.

His search took him to information about life on Earth, the details of the last two Wars, the decision-making of the Syned over several zacs and how substitutions had ultimately beaten nex. As his knowledge grew, Radul understood where Patix wanted to go. The look on Patix's face as he had watched the memorial was etched in Radul's mind.

For days, Radul had kept a vigil on the highways to see if the issue about a nex on the other side came up. However, nothing even remotely connected to the same had appeared. Radul had never known of a nex. Someone ceases to be—it was unthinkable. It was something he could not even imagine. Were men actually capable of causing a nex on the other side? Why would they do so? If they did, how did they do so?

When no answers came to him, Radul returned his attention to the work at hand. Nepo—the 'wonder' mineral used to manufacture substitute organs. He knew that efforts of many men had gone into refining it, making it better, long-lasting and suitable. So, how had they not managed to find a renewable substitute yet? When he had looked at data for Nepo reserves, he had found that the data was not readily accessible. This information was only available to long-standing members of the Syned. He wondered about Patix and the others in the

Syned—were they going to lead them? Were they capable of changing anything?

Radul got up and walked towards the large window on the opposite side of the hall. The sky outside was dark. From the twentieth floor of the Koshum, lights twinkled like stars in the city below. Radul stared in the direction of the Fence.

What were the gynake doing about Nepo? They must be facing the same decline since they had been living on the planet for the same duration. In fact, if they were not there, all the reserves of Nepo would be available for the men.

As he stood there, Radul wondered why he was even waiting to hear from Patix. All the ingredients for a battle cry were in his possession; all he needed to do was work out a plan. As Radul stared into nothingness, he decided to put the wheels in motion, on his own.

Odep had reached the Gazer building and was resting in the visitors' lounge. When he had stepped out of the rondural, Ime was struck by a sense that there was something different about him. He was tall, slim-shouldered, with short black hair, and was dressed in a fine jacket. Yet, there was something distinct about him that Ime could not identify immediately. While waiting for Odep to join him, Ime sat at his workstation and gleaned more information about him.

Not much was known about what he had been doing since his retirement into the hills. It seemed that he did absolutely nothing. He had built such grand buildings in the past, had pushed so many ideas in the Syned, and had been instrumental in setting up certain regulations for the lex and highways. Then, why had he stepped back? Ime could not understand why Odep was resting in the middle of the day. Such rest was never required.

He debated in his mind whether he should share his current explorations with Odep or wait for Valhan.

Ime returned his attention to the data as the late-afternoon sun dipped in the horizon. He was lost in his research regarding the availability of Nepo on Zeta when he felt a slight tap on his shoulder. Odep was standing right behind him.

'You actually think Zeta or Tai would be able to support life as we know it?' Odep was smiling as he sat down near Ime.

Ime realized this was Odep's way of letting him know that there were no secrets between Valhan and him.

'That is what my initial assessment suggested. However, I must confess that since I have started working at the Gazer, I have come across contradictory data which I need to analyse further,' Ime explained.

'Do you know who discovered Elone all those centuries ago, while living on Earth?' Odep stood up and peered through the viewing panel of the telescope.

'No, I was never able to find that out. When I was undergoing my education in this area, I searched a lot, but I could not find any name. Do you know, Odep?' Ime asked eagerly.

'No, I don't either. Unfortunately, not much is known about that ancient past of ours,' Odep sounded wistful. He walked to the glass windows and began looking outside at the setting sun.

'Their instruments and equipment must have been much better than ours,' Ime wondered aloud.

Odep stood silently, looking through the glass pane. The disappearing sun was casting a pale glow on the glistening, snow-covered mountains all around.

'I don't think so, Ime. Their numerous discoveries did ensure that we did not have to reinvent. But we have built on their knowledge base and moved far ahead. They were strugglers compared to us. What spurred them on was the lack of time. That impetus is what we lack because time is no more finite for us. Do you think it was a man or a gynake that found Elone?'

'Would you like to see the data on Zeta and Tai?' Ime said abruptly as he did not know how to respond to Odep's questions.

'We can do so later,' Odep said. After a long pause, he asked, 'Ime, do you ever wonder what life was like when it was not infinite, going on forever?'

He turned away from the pane and sat in the chair opposite Ime's workstation.

'Well, I don't wonder because I don't know what living like that means. Can I get you something to eat?' he asked hurriedly and was relieved to see Odep nod his assent.

He quickly got up and took the escalator to the pantry. There he took his time selecting something to eat and pouring a glass of enab.

First Radul and now Odep—these men had the luxury of thinking and wondering about these strange unconnected issues because they did not do much. Ime decided he would open up the topic of Nepo again to end this odd irrelevant talk.

He returned to his workstation and placed the tray loaded with vegetables, tibli sauce and kimpayo in front of Odep.

'What should we do if Zeta or Tai have the potential to be future homes for us, but don't have reserves of Nepo?' Ime asked.

'Well, we can all go there and start living like our ancestors on Earth did… Live to actually feel the urges of a people racing against time,' Odep was smiling as he said it.

'You don't mean what you are saying, Odep. How can we live without Nepo? It is the basis of our existence,' Ime was puzzled.

'It has become the basis because we have made it so. Anyway, do you think either of those possible future homes have Nepo?'

Ime quickly opened his workstation and began to share his findings with Odep. As they discussed and pored over the data, the evening lengthened and it started snowing. Odep suddenly got up from his chair, walked over and stood by the glass wall of the room. The snowflakes would come swirling towards the glass and melt away. He watched them, intently. Ime sat quietly near his workstation, waiting patiently for Odep to return so that they could continue the research. It was clear to Ime that even though Odep seemingly did nothing, he knew a lot. His questions and insights surprised him. But then he had been one of the most talented men on Elone before he stepped out.

'Come here,' Odep beckoned Ime over to where he was standing, 'just see the snowflakes. They dance and frolic in such a beautiful manner.'

Ime went and stood next to Odep. The snowflakes were twirling in the reflected light and disappeared when they touched the pane. Nothing about the falling snow seemed different to Ime. The Gazer building remained snowbound perpetually. He saw snowfall every day. In fact, he was tired of staying in the dismal surroundings and was anxiously waiting to go back to the city. However, he stood patiently near the pane waiting for Odep to resume the task at hand.

'You don't find it fascinating, Ime?' Odep asked, his gaze not leaving the shimmering snowflakes.

'Not really. It snows all the time here. Anyway, why don't we get back to our discussion?' Ime suggested.

Odep let out a long sigh. He put both his hands on the pane and continued to look out. Ime leaned against the pane, unsure what to do. He looked at Odep's profile as he stood there. At that moment, Ime first noticed a strand of silver hair in Odep's head, gleaming in the lights. As his eyes followed the shining silvery strand, they fell upon the fine lines near the corner of Odep's eyes.

Ime turned around and walked back to his workstation, slightly confused. He flipped the pages on the screen, but his mind was elsewhere. He had never seen anyone like Odep on Elone. What was happening to him? He decided that he would talk to Valhan when he came in the next day. Ime concluded that Odep probably needed some substitutions and that too, fast.

Odep came back to where Ime was sitting and both of them delved into the data once again. Ime snuck a glance at Odep to see if he had made a mistake earlier. The side of Odep's head that was visible to him had no strands of white. Ime wondered if it had been a trick of the failing light.

'Ime, you have done some good work here. Although after our quick analysis, I think that between Zeta and Tai, it is Tai that might be more suitable to host life as we know it,' Odep declared after spending a few hours poring over the data.

Outside, the snow had stopped and an eerie darkness enveloped the building.

'What about Nepo? Do you think Tai has it or something

like it?' Ime asked.

'I cannot say. That would need some more data mining and analysis of the figures gathered from Tai. We can discuss it with Valhan when he comes in tomorrow,' Odep got up from the chair and stretched.

'I am going to sleep now. It's been a long day for me.'

Odep left and Ime watched him go. There was so much to discuss with Valhan when he came in the next morning. Ime got up and looked through the telescope one last time before leaving for the day. Both Zeta and Tai were emitting their yellowish light far away in the cosmos. It was interesting to think that Tai might support life at some time in the future. It would have cities, roads, seas, mountains, buildings and them.

After a while, Ime started shutting down all the data that had opened while Odep and he had been working. Once the shutdown was complete, he moved towards the escalator to go to his room. His lex was vibrating in his arm. He hadn't accessed it all the while he had been working with Odep. Ime began reading as the escalator moved down. One of the first messages to pop up was from Radul. He had entered it only a few moments ago. It was flashing on all the popular highways.

There are mutterings in the air that there has been a nex on the other side of the Fence and the gynake are blaming us for it. Isn't it strange and rather unbelievable?! First, THERE HAS ACTUALLY BEEN A NEX. It simply doesn't happen. And, second, why are they blaming us? What are the gynake up to? Will someone please answer?

Radul

Ime read the message with disbelief. He swiped his arm at the door of his room and it swung open.

What was Radul doing? Why was he manufacturing such

things? Or was it true? If yes, then, how did he even know about it? Why did Valhan not know?

Ime changed his clothes and fell on the bed, exhausted. He accessed the message again. But in that short span of time, someone had removed the originator of the message. It was now an unknown entry in the system. Even though the name of the originator had been removed, the message remained intact, available for all to see.

As Ime's eyes gave in to sleep, the traffic on the lex increased. Men were not only reading the message but also reacting to it. The floodgates had opened.

Valhan was sitting in the travelor that would take him to the Gazer building. It was a long journey from the city. Outside the window, the scene was green and lush. Trees were swaying in the breeze with golden rays of sunlight sparkling over their foliage.

His lex was constantly buzzing. Valhan was puzzled by the entry on the lex highway that was causing so much noise in the system. The message, that didn't state the name of the originator, was quite dramatic in its content and completely focused the attention of the men on the gynake, something that had happened after endless zacs. There was incessant chatter going on. Men were crying for 'war' as if it was the next glass of enab they were talking about. Valhan wondered if Patix's Unumo had something to do with it. Was it true? Had there been a nex?

As the landscape outside changed to dreary, Valhan

disengaged from the lex. There were bigger things to think about as well as tackle. He was sure that the buzz around the nex entry would disappear as other things would claim attention on the lex highways. Chunks of snow were now visible on either side of the travelor. As they made a sharp turn, the Gazer building leapt into view. This was Valhan's second visit to the Gazer after many zacs. It was magnificent, reaching tall and erect into the skies. Valhan watched mesmerized as the travelor drew closer to the spot from where he would board the rondural. For a moment, Valhan wondered how men, who had imagined and built such a stupendous structure, had not yet found a substitute for Nepo.

After a short walk, from the point where the travelor had dropped him, Valhan was sitting in the rondural, rotating up to the Gazer building. When it reached the top, the door swung open. Ime and Odep were waiting for him at the disembarkation station. Odep had cut his hair and the languid laziness that had enveloped him in his home was also absent.

'Did you read what Radul put on the lex? It is creating havoc among men,' Ime remarked as soon as they were inside the building.

'How do you know it was Radul?' Valhan asked, surprised.

'I saw the message with his identity at first but then, someone turned it anonymous. I am sure it came from Radul.'

They entered the Gazer Building's warm and colourful environs.

'What is on the lex?' Odep asked, a little confused.

Valhan explained and Ime felt a sense of relief knowing that Valhan was there. As the three of them walked towards the telescope room, Ime could clearly discern the silver streak in Odep's hair. It was there on the right side. A silver dash in the dark patch. Ime knew he would have to wait till Odep was not present to discuss this matter with Valhan.

The three men moved towards Ime's workstation and set down to work. The sun had dipped low by the time they took a break to discuss.

'Odep is of the view that Tai is more suitable to be inhabited, between the two,' Ime told Valhan.

'I agree with him. The temperature on Zeta tends to touch extreme conditions because of the orbit and distance from its sun. So, let us abandon Zeta and concentrate on Tai. First, we need to establish whether it has Nepo or something that could be refined into Nepo,' Valhan had decided on this plan of action while they had been studying the data.

'I am concentrating on that search and that is why I have extended my stay at the Gazer,' Ime said.

'We need quick answers, Ime. This lex message about the supposed nex suggests that something is brewing and it doesn't feel right. What is your view, Odep?' Valhan tried to draw Odep into the conversation. Odep, on the other hand, was reclining in his chair with his eyes closed.

He opened his eyes, smiled at the other two, stood up and strolled to the glass pane. It was snowing and soon a white blanket would descend from the sky, enveloping everything in view.

'Why are we looking for a new planet, Valhan?' Odep asked.

Valhan was a bit stunned as the answer was pretty obvious to him. Ime was watching Odep closely. From where he sat, Ime could clearly see the streak of silver in his hair.

'The reserves of Nepo will eventually run out. So we need to either find a substitute or a place where Nepo already exists. I think, in a way, we are looking for the second option since we have been unsuccessful in finding a substitute so far,' Valhan answered.

'Nepo and even its substitute exist right here on Elone. The gynake have both of them. So, why are you looking elsewhere in the galaxies?' Odep asked while still gazing out of the pane.

Valhan stared intently at Odep. Ever since he had withdrawn into the hills, he had started speaking in this confusing manner. Valhan felt he had to put in a lot of effort to even understand what he was trying to say.

'Are you agreeing with that message on the lex? Do you also believe it is time we confront them, occupy their half and annihilate them?' Valhan asked, as that seemed to be the logical outcome of Odep's question.

A heavy silence enveloped the room. Odep came back to his chair and sat down. Valhan was sitting upright, waiting for a response. Ime, on the other hand, was staring transfixed at the silver strand in Odep's hair. No one spoke and the thoughts expressed by Valhan floated in the room like a wisp of a cloud being tossed in the wind.

'Why is there a silver strand in your hair, Odep?' Ime blurted out. He, himself, was taken aback by his words. After a stunned silence, Odep's laughter rang across the room, loud and clear. He ran his hands through his hair, leaned towards the workstation and looked at his hair from side to side in his reflection on the screen.

'I think that is the only question to answer among all the others that are chasing us. Ime, I have a white strand of hair because I have stopped going in for substitutions. I have lines on the sides of my eyes. I feel tired frequently and need rest in the afternoons. I lose my breath when I walk up the mountainside near my home and,' he whispered conspiratorially, 'I have not one but two strands of white hair.' Odep chuckled softly.

'Ime, I am growing old and one day in the future I will be nexed. Valhan, don't look so shocked. This thought had come to me a long time ago, when I had finished designing a manufacturing unit near the hills. By that time, I had designed and constructed many buildings, done a lot of work for the Syned, made many regulations and discussed countless issues. One day, as I was sitting on the ledge—the same one on which we sat together, Valhan, when you visited last—watching the sun go down, it struck me. The whole universe has a cycle of creation and annihilation. It is an endless process. From where I sat and watched, the sun went down every day and the three moons arrived. Then, they left and the sun appeared. Each of them appeared and reappeared. Nothing stayed forever. It was just a thought, but as the zacs passed me by, it gnawed at me. Every time I went to a Notus, it seemed as if the universe was whispering something in my ears. The whispering grew louder, till it became so loud that I could not ignore it anymore. That was when I retreated to my hillside home in the hope that the silence would drown out the sound or provide some answers. The silence, however, spawned new questions. In those long days, when I did not have my work to occupy me, I searched for answers...in the Koshum, in the Syned documents, in all the places I could think of. But I realized that answers exist only for those questions that are asked and no one in all these zacs had ever asked this simple question—how would our lives change if our time became finite? If we knew that there was a certain nex in our future? We are a species that only thinks about existing forever. All our endeavours, thoughts and research are aimed in that one direction. We found Nepo and since then we have been focused on refining it, making it better and finding substitutes. And, now, that we know that Nepo is declining, we have started looking at other worlds where it might exist or thinking about waging a war with the gynake. Our only objective around which we have built our world is to live eternally. I am hungry, can we eat, Ime?' Odep changed the topic abruptly.

Valhan sat rooted to his chair while Ime, in response to the command, walked bemused towards the pantry. Odep wandered towards the window again and watched the darkness outside. It had finally stopped snowing.

'You cannot be serious, Odep,' said Valhan. 'You cannot stop substitutions and decide to be nexed. It is unthinkable. It has never happened on Elone before. Why are you doing this?' Valhan was babbling.

Odep remained silent. The door slid open and Ime entered with three bowls of rice mixed with vegetables and tibli sauce along with many loaves of kimpayo. He seemed to have loaded the tray without any thought. He poured out three glasses of enab and placed them on the table. Odep sat down and began to eat. The other two just watched him in silence. They felt that Odep did not belong to their world.

Valhan remembered the aura of difference he had sensed in Odep when he had met him last. He now realized that it stemmed from the fact that his body was deteriorating and he was letting it happen.

'Ime, book the first available Notus. We are taking Odep there in the morning.'

Odep sighed, 'Eat something, Valhan; you too, Ime. This is going to be a long night. Me and my white hair will try and answer all your questions.'

'I am not hungry,' Ime declared. He could not help staring at Odep. He seemed like a strange new star that had suddenly appeared in an otherwise familiar galaxy.

Valhan picked at his food and swirled the enab in its glass.

Wasn't it Odep who had told him to look for other habitable planets before the decline in Nepo reached alarming levels? Then why was he talking about all this now? Would there be a time when Odep would not be there to guide him, help him? Well, he would not let that happen.

'Ime, do you know what a nex is?' Odep asked.

'Yes. It is when a person ceases to exist. I am told that, theoretically, it could still happen to any of us, but it hasn't in a long while. In fact, no one I know has ever been nexed,' Ime replied.

'For us, nex is a mere concept now. A "maybe" or a "could be" event. We have, in a way, conquered it. Men like me, who have been around much longer, know very well that when we came to Elone, nexes happened and they happened often, especially in the two wars with the gynake. It was a reality at that time, an enemy that needed to be vanquished. And over time, we did beat it, on both sides of the Fence. Then, in an attempt to rebuild our numbers, we started with creations. But as nexes became rare, creations began to dwindle. We even put a moratorium on them which has been in operation for so many zacs. Do you know why no one has ever raised the issue of lifting this moratorium?' asked Odep. When both Ime and Valhan didn't say anything, Odep continued, 'Because we, men, as a species, have forgotten that we can also create.'

'Radul plans to bring up this issue of the moratorium in the Syned for reconsideration,' Ime interjected. He was happy that the conversation was once again about matters he could deal with.

'We forgot about creations because we live for perpetuity. We do not have nexes, so we do not need to create. We exist on this planet and we see ourselves as being here...forever. We are working towards making our bodies better, our minds more intelligent, but we are not thinking about creating another cohort of men. Whatever the reason given for the moratorium, its continuance is only because of the fact that we have forgotten the need for creation,' replied Odep.

'But what is wrong with the moratorium, Odep? Why do you think having nexes and more creations is a better way to live?' Valhan asked.

'I am not saying that it is a better way, Valhan. I am just saying that this was the way we lived in the past. All I am trying to understand is how the finiteness of life changes the way one lives. So, I delved into the past because ultimately it is our past that determines, to a large extent, where we stand today. I wanted to understand why existing eternally is our driving force today and what was our driving force in the past.'

He paused to take a breath and let his words sink in.

'The Koshum holds some basic information on how life was on Earth. Time was very limited for our ancestors and that was why they started to fight biology. They fought disease and other myriad causes of nex but they could never completely win the battle. We have carried it on, bettered it, and over time, conquered nex. It was the battle that was initiated in our past, in another galaxy, that has made us who we are today.'

Another pause and he continued, 'Limited time became a resource that had to be utilized well. Since they knew from the beginning that nex awaited them, the inhabitants of Earth lived their lives as an unending quest to savour every experience and gather as much knowledge as they could. To create, to invent, to excel, to break frontiers—that became the essence of a life well-lived. In a way, the prospect of nex—the happening that we have relegated to the conceptual level—shaped and determined the way life was lived on Earth. The idea that life was short and had to be maximized in every possible way was the driving force of that civilization. They tried to extend their life in many ways; succeeded in some, failed in others. As the natural conditions on their planet deteriorated, they searched the universe for an alternative home. They found Elone and came here. That is how we are sitting in this room, debating nex, Nepo and the gynake, in a room that is like a beacon of light in the surrounding darkness.'

Odep leaned back in his chair and closed his eyes. The tension in the room belied the picture of serenity he presented.

Ime got up and walked towards the telescope. It was familiar and known, like a refuge from all the strange things Odep was talking about. In the far distance, Zeta and Tai flickered in the sky, beckoning him with the promise of a new world.

Finally, after what felt like zacs, Valhan spoke up, 'So, are you trying to say that all the progress we have made is against what the universe had designed for us? How can it be, Odep? This,' Valhan stood up and spread his arms gesturing at the world around them, 'is how we live. It has been our way of life for countless zacs. No one has complained; we are not going through any unrest. Why do you think the way men lived in the past was the better way to live? Don't forget, they too tried to fight nex. Living eternally was a dream for them. For us, it is a reality.'

Valhan was pacing around the room.

Ime wanted to end this odd discussion and get back to the main issue. What Odep was suggesting was bizarre. Men getting nexed as a certainty was a positive thing? Nothing could be more absurd than that. Ime looked at Odep reclining in his chair. He seemed to be much older than any man he had ever seen. Ime felt a distaste brewing inside him.

'Odep, we, people of Elone, do not yearn for nex. We find ways to get around it. We have been doing so for countless zacs and we have managed to achieve great progress in that. Our challenge, today, is to find ways to defeat nex when confronted with declining reserves of Nepo. So, please do not confuse the issue,' Ime's voice contained a tone of authority and decisiveness that took Valhan by surprise.

Odep sighed, 'What I am trying to discover is what we have lost in this journey. This is not to say that the past was better or that we are doing something wrong. But, as a species, if we have gained unending life, we must have lost something. That is what I want to identify. That is why I have decided to make my time finite and see how I live differently. And I have realized that as my body gradually deteriorates, the desire to have a creation has started taking root inside me. That is why, Ime, I would support Radul's stand of opening the debate on the moratorium. We need to start talking about creations. We cannot let that fall out of our sight. I think the urge to create is something we have lost in our journey. As I said before, destruction and creation is a rhythm of the universe. Our way of life has brought a long pause in destruction so we have lost the urge to create. I guess there must be other things, other yearnings that we have lost as well. I want to understand that loss. Maybe there is something that is worth reviving, worth looking for. For me, creation, for one, is worth reviving.'

After listening to Odep, Valhan found himself agreeing with Ime. Odep, with all his knowledge and his brilliance, was on completely another track.

'Odep, for a moment, let us keep this thought of loss and gain aside. If we do not find Nepo reserves on Tai and we are unable to come up with a substitute readily, do you think it is time to go for a last push against the gynake?' Valhan was taken aback by his own question. He realized that this thought must have been lurking somewhere within his subconscious for it to have come out with such ease.

'Imagine, Valhan, our planet without the gynake on the other side of the Fence. How would it feel? If we nexed that species and were on our own on Elone?' Odep threw the idea before the other two and waited patiently for their responses.

Elone, their beautiful planet, would belong entirely to them. Valhan thought about Elone's serpentine rivers, the majestic mountains, the lush trees and the endless seas—it would all be theirs to enjoy. They would have access to the unused reserves of Nepo and would also get their hands on the substitute the gynake had developed. There would be no need to maintain the Fence and the Unumo. Men would be free to create, to exist and live without the spectre of the gynake hanging around them.

'It would be the right thing, Odep. This planet is ours and we should own it completely,' Valhan felt a strange sense of relief as the matter clarified in his mind.

Ime remained quiet and looked at the twinkling galaxies visible through the telescope. He had been tracking the stars and planets for so many zacs. Each time there seemed to be a semblance of a transmission or any sign of life from anywhere, he would get excited. But there had only been false signals. There was a thundering silence in the universe all around them, there seemed to be no signs of any kind of life present anywhere. As far as his knowledge went, they were alone—apart from the gynake—in this unending cosmos.

'All I know, Odep, is that if we vanquish and destroy the gynake, we will be all alone. And at least for me, it is a rather disconcerting idea. I think we should be exploring ways of sharing our respective knowledge rather than aiming to annihilate each other at regular intervals.'

Odep looked at both the men with their diametrically opposite views as they stood together, but were not looking at each other. Odep's questions had opened a wedge between Ime and Valhan that they, themselves, did not know existed.

'Remember, Valhan, I told you nearly the same thing on that ledge the other day. The gynake are the only similar species that we know of in this universe. We have lived with them across the Fence for a long time now. In fact, we lived with them on Earth, and we came to Elone together. There must have been something that tied us together. I think that is also lost to us now; lost to both of us. We have never stopped to look for that bond, never questioned the roots of the animosity that plagues us today. But the knowledge that we shared an intertwined existence is still with us. I agree with Ime—we should not lose them…not now, not ever. As for this planet, Valhan, it belongs to them as much as it does to us. We should acknowledge and accept this fact. Solutions to the problems of men need to be found in this framework.'

There was a continuous stream of data and information flowing in from the Unumo. Patix sat in his room high up in the Etuis and occasionally looked at the streaming data. The inputs from the other side of the Fence had remained unchanged, both in substance and in frequency. It seemed as if they were preparing for something.

However, the trajectory of the message put on the lex by Radul was more vital for Patix. He had been tracking the kind of responses, the channels and highways the message was garnering. It appeared as if the message had taken on a life of its own. It refused to go away or be overtaken. From the kind of cacophony it had generated, it seemed as if the men had been waiting for a trigger to pour out all their venom against the gynake.

Where had this angst been hidden all these zacs? Even Patix had been taken by surprise by the intense reactions. Suddenly, the men were unanimously calling for action. Some of them wanted the Fence to be pulled down and supremacy over the gynake to be imposed. Others wanted to wipe them out completely and own the planet. Patix was surprised, it took just a rumour—that the gynake were trying to accuse the men of a nex—for the men to get ready to annihilate them. He was confident that just a whisper of the declining reserves of Nepo would be enough to convert this anger on the lex into action.

The sun was shining in all its glory. Patix got up and looked down at the streets. As always, whenever he saw the miniature forms scuttling below, Patix felt a sense of power.

The rivalry between men and the gynake had not subsided in the endless zacs that had elapsed. It merely simmered and waited, ready to rear its ugly head at the smallest excuse. For a moment, Patix fleetingly wondered about the origin of the rivalry, but then he decided it was irrelevant how it had all begun. The important thing was that it existed and had to be used appropriately.

Patix looked in the direction of the Fence. The time had come to assess their strategy and take hard decisions. Patix knew Radul would be waiting to hear from him, but he had decided that he would let him work on his own for some time. It was important for Radul to feel and believe that he was leading this. Only then would he be able to convince the others. Patix, on his part, would take over at an appropriate time.

As he stood, contemplating, next to the window, his lex received a message from Valhan.

I am returning from a visit to the Gazer building. I will come and see you. By the way, the message about the nex, is it correct?

Gazer building? What was Valhan doing there? Anyway, he decided that they should meet. If he could convince Valhan about what he was thinking of achieving, it would go through the Syned without much opposition. Valhan would also be able to tackle Odep, if by any chance that recluse decided to come to the Syned meeting. Patix knew Odep would be asked to participate when such momentous things were to be discussed.

Radul had been tracking the message he had put on the lex. When his identity had been removed, he had understood that

Patix approved of the content, but had decided to hide the originator. The reaction to the message had astounded Radul. The fact that men felt so strongly about those creatures on the other side of the Fence was a revelation to him. There were some who spoke of moderation, but they were crushed and ridiculed.

Radul was in the gaming lounge playing a new game that had been introduced. It was called 'Down with Them'. It was a battle game with the gynake as the enemy. It had taken the gaming groups by storm. That small message, with its unsubstantiated suggestion, had unleashed a new beast among all of them.

As the game progressed with the slaying of many gynake, Radul realized he was unable to play with full concentration. He disconnected the lex and reclined in his chair.

How should he harness all this energy that had been released on Elone? Should he reach out to Patix about this?

Radul felt a sense of uncertainty as he sat staring at the faint designs on the ceiling of the gaming lounge. Everywhere men were discussing the message, but no one knew who had put it on the lex. Radul had to ensure that with his next step he would be acknowledged as the leader.

Disengaging from the console, Radul stepped out into the cool night. The three moons were shimmering behind a translucent cloud. As it had become his habit, he took a travelor to the Koshum. Picking up a bottle of enab from a dispenser, he went to his familiar perch in the section called 'Us'. He wanted to know when this angst against the gynake had begun. He thought that if he could find the source and trajectory of this feeling, he would be able to mould things better.

The veneer of the clouds had dissipated and the three moons were clearly visible by the time Radul took a break. He went to the window, opened it and let the cool breeze caress his face. It seemed as if the conflict between them was like the sky. It was ever-present. The Koshum told him about how they, the men and the gynake, had come here together but eventually, they had spread out. It also detailed how the gynake had tried to capture major chunks of Elone—that had been the reason for the first War. Then, a lull had followed after which the gynake had tried to occupy some land that had large quantities of Nepo which led to the second War. Finally, the Fence had come up. It seemed that the animosity and rivalry had existed long before they even came to Elone from that faraway planet—Earth.

Realizing that Earth was the clue to the whole mystery, Radul had looked for information about how the two species had lived on Earth. However, the Koshum had no answers. Radul had hit a dead end. There was no one he could ask. The men in his group house would not understand why he was wasting his time trying to find the origin of the conflict. And he did not want to reach out to Patix. He looked up at the clear sky and the twinkling stars that reminded him of Ime. He could probably ask him.

The day outside the Gazer building was glorious. Sunshine reflected off the snow all around; it was blinding to look outside. Inside, the telescope room was bathed in the golden rays of the reflected sunshine. The fragrance of flowers floated in the air, lending a cheerful disposition to the environs. After their long discussion a few nights ago, Ime, Valhan and Odep had behaved as if nothing had happened. They had worked with full concentration on the matter at hand. Ime had been following the cacophony on the lex highways, but he had not brought it up. They focused on exploring and investigating Tai, ignoring all the other issues that Odep had scattered before them.

Odep and Valhan were to leave that day. Ime was staying back to go through additional data and come up with a final assessment on the feasibility of Tai as a possible future home.

What is the origin of the conflict between us and the gynake? Do you know anything? What was life on Earth like, for both our species?

Radul's message had popped up on Ime's lex some time ago. Were men all over Elone struggling with these issues? How was it that someone like Radul was thinking so much? Ime could think of no reply. He knew nothing either. In fact, even the strange yet knowledgeable Odep was clueless about this matter. Ime wondered if men had ever tried to find out about all of this before. Probably the wars and the struggle to live on Elone had occupied them. Then, the peace since the Fence had come up must have pushed all these questions aside. Now since, in a way, the Fence had been breached, these questions had reared their heads once more.

The door opened and both Valhan and Odep walked in.

'Ime, I think we are heading in the right direction. You complete the last bit of analysis and we should be able to come to a conclusion. Odep and I will leave now. You can return to the city once your work is over,' Valhan said moving towards the elevator that would take them to the rondural station on the upper level.

Odep came to where Ime was sitting and put his hand on Ime's shoulder. Ime was startled. It was a strange gesture. He did not know how to respond, so he stood up.

'The silver strands in my hair are not something to be afraid of. They signal the passage of a long journey. They also mean that this journey will come to an end. I am beginning to understand that it is this knowledge that makes the whole journey worthwhile. You are welcome to visit me whenever you are free,' Odep said with a smile.

Ime merely nodded and went back to work. Odep and Valhan boarded the rondural and began the descent.

Facing each other, Odep and Valhan looked out at the magnificence of the snow-clad mountains. After a while, Odep turned towards Valhan and said, 'Valhan, you had asked me once why I removed the lex. The reason is simple. I wanted silence from the noise we generate on the lex highways. I did not want to know what was happening all around as it happened. I felt no need for it. Initially, I used to look at it every hour. Then, once in two hours, and slowly, I glanced at it only when I remembered or needed it.'

Valhan sighed, 'Odep, when will you go to a Notus? If you do not agree, I will have to bring it up at the Syned meeting so that the other members force you to go,' He was still looking outside. They had reached nearly the middle of the descent.

'If we sort the current problem in a manner that will allow both our species to continue to coexist, only then will I go to a Notus.'

'Is this what you are planning to do? Make the decisions of the Syned hinge on your ideas of existence? They will not be bothered, Odep. You have been nestling on that hill for so many zacs. Elone has moved on without you. I hope you know that,' Valhan was now looking at him directly in a beseeching manner.

'But I can see that you are bothered, Valhan. And, this "barter" that I am proposing is only to keep you on my side while you debate and decide in the Syned. Sometimes, I try to imagine the thoughts of the men who left Earth and came here. Why did they come with the gynake? Were they always at war with them? Were there any other species on Earth that were left behind and so have been lost to us forever? The galaxy in which Earth existed perished as well, I am sure you know that. Anything that was left behind on Earth was destroyed completely. It would have been a great loss, Valhan. That is why I insist that we should not lose the gynake, even if we remain hostile. Maybe they have the answers to some of these questions. Maybe they know something about our shared past. Imagine, if we lose them, we might lose our only chance to know.'

After a pause, he continued, 'It is only when we recognize and identify what we have lost, that we can appreciate what we have. Valhan, I have no ideas of existence that are different from yours. I have enjoyed the benefits of this long existence. I have done a lot of things and fructified many ideas. You can say that this decision to stop substitutions is also an idea that I am trying out. I find that losing the sense of endlessness that we have in our existence has made me experience life differently. The sunrise seems more beautiful, the wind sings a tune and the snowflakes dance. All these feelings that I simply never registered have taken on a new dimension. You can say it is the idea of loss that makes things seem so precious. It seems contradictory, but that is what it is.'

Both the men stayed silent for a while. Odep smiled, 'As

for Elone moving on without me… that is what change is all about. It was the same on Earth. It is we who have created a world where nothing changes, in the real sense, because its inhabitants do not change. Do you really think that by moving to Tai we will change our world? Of course, it can be argued that we do not need to change our world. I accept that. Nothing is intrinsically wrong with our world. We exist and will continue to do so. We will build big cities, fight wars, discover new things and maybe, one day also create new men. In this journey, some men, like me, would have strange ideas and might throw stones in your placid waters. Valhan, ideas move us along. Remember, it was someone in a faraway galaxy who had the idea that moving to another planet would help us survive. In all the time we have existed as a species, different ideas have been tossed around and tried out. Some churning is good, Valhan, it makes the journey more interesting.'

They had reached the bottom and were waiting for their respective travelors.

'So, now you are proposing that we should go back full circle and have an existence limited by time. Why? Because it makes us appreciate existence more. I think it is absurd,' Valhan said finally.

Odep let out a deep sigh, 'No, Valhan, there is no going back, I know that. As a species, the desire to exist forever seems to have become a part of our genome. But we can at least try and reclaim what we have lost along the way.'

Valhan's travelor arrived and with a wave of his arm he boarded it. As it gained speed, he looked back. Odep was a speck on the horizon, still waiting for his travelor. Valhan knew that his ideas about loss and its lessons would have few takers in the city he was hurtling towards.

Aryan

It was raining heavily. Despite the extensive drainage mechanisms, the roads and highways were inundated with water. Lightning seared across the sky and thunder clapped incessantly. It was another day in the long deluge that had overtaken Earth.

'Over the last many decades, there has been a lingering debate on what a cloning parent can order in a clone. Should it only be limited to physical replication or should it also include other attributes and personality traits? Should it be mandated that a clone must look different from its parent? How many clones should a person be allowed to have? As the technology has progressed and refined, so have the questions surrounding this final product.

Keeping in mind a host of issues, such as genetic diversity and other ethical and moral standpoints, we propose that only physical attributes, including health, should be defined, instead of complete replication of looks. Also, no other ability or attribute can be defined.'

Silence prevailed in the darkened room as well as along the screens where participants were live in the conference. Slowly, the lights turned on and Ria looked around while running her hand through her short hair. As head of the bio-infotech programme, her team had worked long and hard on this issue.

'When this issue was discussed some time ago in the Men's Arena, the debate had turned violent. Many of them lost their lives in the turmoil and it remains unresolved till date.' One of the women who were attending the conference virtually on the network informed the other women assembled. 'Do we agree? What the men decide should not impact our decision,' Ria announced confidently, to murmurs of agreement. She knew it was important to have a consensus on this issue for things to move further.

The conference closed without disagreements. Ria stepped out. The downpour was continuing. The city seemed to be creaking under the weight of incessant rains in the month of March.

Boarding a speed train towards the Bio-Infotech Centre, Ria watched the drenched city below. From above, the city looked the same; it did not have any demarcations or lines drawn across it. However, Ria knew exactly from which street and block, the 'Men's Arena' or the areas where men were concentrated, began. The Centre lay beyond the Men's Arena. She got off at the station, while the train sped off towards that area where some men and women, who belonged to another era, still shared a roof.

Aryan disembarked from the train, glided down the escalator and walked the silent street towards the house. In the pale late afternoon sun, the house seemed quiet and serene as opposed to the cacophony at the University. There was a slight chill in the air. Although it was end-June, the weather on their planet was now unrecognizable. His coat, responding to the temperature around him, was getting warmer as Aryan walked slowly. He pulled his cap closer over his thick snowlike hair.

Inside the house, the door of the room where Maya practised her music was ajar. Some lilting strains of a composition were floating around. Aryan walked to the door and peeped in. Maya was sitting by the window, staring at the quiet afternoon. From occupying only the spaces of his mind, Maya had, now, entered his life. They shared a home, creating a space where the stars and the notes of music mixed together to give rise to a mélange of experiences.

Aryan walked to Maya and put his hands on her shoulders. Maya covered his cold hand with her warm ones and asked, 'Cold outside?'

'Very. I have asked Help for some soup. The music is nice. Is it a new piece?'

Aryan sat next to Maya. They looked out of the window at the darkening day.

'Remember, Aryan, there was a time when you never came for any of my performances and did not even know one composition from another. Now look at you! You are learning!'

'It's good, isn't it? You always used to say that I didn't have enthusiasm for new and different things! So, I am changing a bit now. Anyway, do you know there is a solar eclipse on 22 July? It will be nearly as long as the one in

2186. Do you want to come and observe it in the University with me? And, just so we are clear, I want you to see it with your own eyes and not virtually or in any other manner that is constantly being invented.'

Maya laughed, 'We are in 2204 Aryan, and no one experiences anything through their given senses anymore!'

Aryan sank further into the sofa with a long sigh, 'Do you ever wonder why some of us are still alive, Maya? The world has certainly moved on without us. Just because we have the technology to live forever, we don't have to.'

Maya kept silent. This was the kind of rhetorical question that often came from Aryan. He had not found another dream after delivering the new planet, Elone, to humanity. It had garnered some interest and generated a bit of research, but then, it had been consigned to some shelf to be taken out in the future. The developments on Earth occupied humanity much more.

On the other hand, she still found so much to live for. Her music, being with Aryan, and the leaps and bounds by which technology was altering their existence, fascinated her. Maya loved to try out all the things that technology offered—in her compositions and in her life. She felt as if she had lived a thousand different lives already.

Maya held Aryan's hand. It always evoked a feeling of warmth and belonging. She rested her head on his shoulder and they watched the day disappear into the arms of dusk.

'I have noticed a strange thing at the University, Maya. More and more women are dropping out of classes—real as well as virtual. At this rate, only young men would be left in the classes,' Aryan shared his concern with Maya.

Maya was drowsy as she snuggled against his shoulder. Outside, in the early night, lights were brightening the sky in the distance. It seemed normal and routine, but nothing was the same anymore.

'Aryan, your University is between streets 175 and 359. Don't you know, it is slowly becoming an area where only men can live and work.' Maya wondered, sometimes, whether Aryan really did not know or merely chose to ignore all the changes that were happening around them.

Now, one of her old compositions was playing in the room. Aryan had shut his eyes. He did this often these days. Maya watched his profile as he sat there—still and taut. His spectacles, which he clung on to, were perched on his white head. All this tinkering with nature, which was the new world order, troubled him immensely.

A message from Ria arrived on Maya's Trin band. She was shaken out of her languid state. Ria had messaged her after a long time. Her carefree daughter, born of love and passion, with long silky hair, had disappeared. Technology had abducted her along the way and taken her into its fold. Ria was one of the leaders of this new alignment that was emerging slowly, but inexorably.

'The incubation process has begun at the gynake facility. A few months and she should be here. I thought you would like to know.'

So many thoughts and numerous visions passed in Maya's mind in a matter of seconds, like a movie reel. Ria, as a bundle of joy placed in her exhausted lap in another century. Ria, growing up, a smiling toddler, absolutely unique. Ria, a woman with furrows in her brow, changing in a world where change was at a pace that overtook life completely. Ria, the one who celebrated cloning as the ladder to immortality. Ria, who matured in a time when men and women had ceased to look at each other for the primordial need for reproduction. Ria, who never had a clone because she did not want to carry the child herself. And the Ria of today who was eagerly awaiting the arrival of her clone from the incubators that had taken up the job of creation and freed women so they could stake their claim on Earth.

Maya held on tightly to Aryan's hand while he slept with his head resting on the sofa. Maya realized that Ria had never known this simple joy. In fact, she had never experienced so many things that completed the dialogue between a man and a woman.

She suddenly realized that her granddaughter was on her way, completely made from a cell from Ria, being processed, as it were, in an incubator, as Maya sat there. Maya shivered involuntarily. It was chilling to think of the process of creation so dispassionately. Maya shook her head to get away from the negative thoughts. She thought of her granddaughter and smiled. She began looking forward to her arrival. As soon as Aryan woke up, she would tell him.

Life in the winter months was becoming unbearable. Sheets of snow covered the ground. It had been like this for months. The damp, biting cold seemed to seep in despite extensive heating and clothes that stayed warm. A robot with a friendly face, that Ria had christened 'Nun', tended to her five-year-old clone Ami, as she pattered about the small apartment Ria occupied.

Ria sat before a screen, immersed in solidifying the demarcation between areas for men and women where they could live, work and exist. Ami came and stood on her toes next to Ria and peeped into the screen. At times, Ria caught her own imprint in Ami's looks, and at other times, she looked so different. So many like Ami had now been born, if it could be called birth. The men, on the other hand, had also set up their own incubators. Now, both of them spawned their own offspring, without any interface or requirement of the other. It was a deliverance that was unparalleled and Ria believed that it called for a completely different world order.

Sometimes unbidden, when Ria dwelt on the issue of men, she thought of her father. Years ago, he had died in a sporting accident. She believed that he had been spared, in a way. The world he had lived in was simpler, and in a way more innocent. Whenever she thought of him, she always remembered Maya.

It had been long since they had met. She couldn't believe that Aryan and she still lived together. For this day and age, they were truly non-conformists!

It began to snow heavily outside. From her apartment window, it seemed as if a white curtain had been drawn outside. Ria checked the weather forecast. It read like a doomsday warning. The sun would be missing for many days, hiding behind grey, menacing, seemingly never-ending clouds. Ami was running around in circles in the room, with Nun trailing her assiduously.

'Go to the other room,' Ria ordered. She wanted some peace and quiet so she could concentrate properly. Nun promptly went to the door and waited for Ami to join. Ami stopped running around. She first looked at Nun and then at Ria. Then, she shook her head firmly and continued to circle the room, laughing mischievously.

With a sigh, Ria turned her attention back to the workstation. So many islands and areas had been submerged underwater in the last decade. Land and contours were transforming. Ria was scanning the latest reports about the rising water level when a beep announced the arrival of something of interest on the network. Ria clicked on the box. The men were announcing that they had decided to explore the planet 'Elone', that was discovered a few decades ago, as a possible future home for humanity. After all this time, the men still considered and addressed themselves as 'humanity'! And then, it hit her and she froze. Elone—the planet that Aryan had discovered so many years ago. They had almost forgotten about it, but now, the men had brought it back to life.

Ria straightened and thought about it. She knew that the planet Aryan had discovered was habitable. Was Elone the solution to all the problems confronting Earth?

Aryan had been summoned for innumerable discussions and chats about Elone, that bountiful planet he had discovered in the galaxy far away. In the beginning he had been enthused, happy in a way. But, then, as the discussions continued, despair began to rise in him.

That day too, after spending two

hours in front of the screen, he was resting. The men who questioned him were relentless with their questions. 'How do we get there?' seemed to be their primary concern. He had told them repeatedly that he did not build spaceships, nor did he know how to. The coordinates of the planet and his research had become a precious commodity and had been taken over by the men.

Aryan lay down on the bed, tired and exhausted. The image of the cosmos, with a small bluish speck in the far left corner, hung on the opposite wall.

It was ironical; watching the image gave him a strange sense of peace while it was Elone that was the cause of all his despair. It was clear in all the discussions that the men thought of Elone as their planet and believed that the women had no claim on it. This divergence disturbed Aryan deeply. This was not the way men and women were supposed to be. They were partners in the journey of discovering the universe, not competitors. Things would calm down and return to normal. They always did. That was his only hope.

The winds outside were howling, adding to his sense of disquiet. The house system announced softly that Maya had entered with Ami in tow.

Aryan got up hurriedly. He liked it when Ami came over. Ria, on the other hand, had begun to intimidate him. As it is, she rarely visited them but whenever she did, it always seemed like she was carrying a great burden on her shoulders. Ami, fifteen years old now, was a window to the transformations happening all around them. She was bright and inquisitive, and proficient in all the gadgets that surrounded their lives.

A revamped version of Help began buzzing about the house, laying the table for a meal. When Aryan entered the dining area, Ami and Maya were already seated at the table. Maya smiled at him, while Ami was busy on the small screen reflected on her palm, activated by a chip inserted in her little finger. Once dinner was laid, Ami put away her ear device, shut the palm screen, and addressed Aryan, 'You actually discovered Elone? This planet that everyone is talking about these days? Is it true that it can support life as we know it?'

'Yes, Ami. It can support life. But why do you sound so sceptical?'

'I was just wondering because all the efforts to colonize the moon or even Mars fell through. In fact, even the Earth's replicas nearby could not support life. So, maybe this is also a false one. I was just wondering…' Ami shrugged.

Aryan looked across the table at Maya. She was concentrating on her food. He did not want to talk about this issue anymore and waited for Maya to change the topic.

'Ami, please tell Ria to come by sometime. She has not visited us in a long time,' Maya said.

'She is busy trying to find a way to reach Elone. The men are also doing the same, are they not?' Ami said, pointedly looking at Aryan.

Aryan sighed, 'I think so. They keep asking me for a route, so they must be.'

A silence fell across the table.

'Well, you are a man, so you will obviously not tell me the truth!' Ami said nonchalantly and got up from the table. Reclining on the sofa, she activated the palm screen again. Maya and Aryan finished their meal in silence. Maya got up, ran her fingers through Aryan's hair as she passed, went and sat next to Ami, and Aryan retreated into his room.

'What are you looking at, Ami?' Maya tried to engage her attention.

Ami looked around and after assessing that Aryan was out of earshot, she said, 'They are using Buli's brain that is on

202 • *Ascendance*

the machines. Do you remember her? She was the space scientist. They are trying to find ways to build a spaceship that can travel to Elone.'

Maya remembered Buli. Aryan and Buli had collaborated many times in the old days. But, five years back, Buli was one of the few people who had merged with the machines.

Maya had not thought of merger for a long time. At present, her life was complete and content.

Soothing lights bathed the low-lying recliners lining the room. There was complete silence as the few women present were either busy with their palm screens or with the small screen on the tables. Ria stood near a tall window, a glass of wine in her hands, and looked down at the city from the hundredth floor. She often came to this wine bar as she liked looking at the lights. High speed trains, like arteries, connected the city that was constantly growing vertically.

Three days ago, there had been a vicious attack on some women as they had passed by the Men's Arena. It had sent shock waves on both the sides. Security devices, constant surveillance and deathly stealth weaponry, that were readily available at both the ends, had played a big role in deterring violence for many decades.

Ria felt exhausted. The last two days had been spent in discussions with the men virtually on the network. To avoid the possibility of a greater conflagration, the rules of separation had been solidified. What had been an informal division of space and resources had now been demarcated formally.

Dark rumbling clouds, angry and pregnant with torrid rain, were marching across the dark sky. The years now passed in a constant battle with the weather. Their life had been reduced to two kinds of struggles—one with the men and the other with the weather. Ria sat in one of the recliners and gulped down the wine. A robot came promptly and poured some more. She stared into nothingness. It was clear that time was running out for both of them. All the predictions about Earth were changing constantly.

Time—humans now had it in plenty, but the Earth was apparently running out of it.

Aryan got down from the elliptical air-car near the house. He felt dizzy. The air-car hovered above him and then took off. He entered the house, their personal space. While the world around them was constantly changing, he and Maya had tried to keep their world intact. This familiarity of their house always calmed him down. As he crossed the room to his favourite chair, Aryan caught his reflection in a mirror. He moved closer, adjusting his spectacles, for a better look. His hair was dishevelled, as usual, and his eyes looked tired. He looked like an ancient being trapped in an endless life. What was he still doing alive? He wondered.

'Are you hungry? It is such a nice day and that too after such a long time,' Maya called out from her music room.

Aryan forgot his own question, and felt a shiver go down his spine. The men's group dealing with Elone had called him. Even though they didn't look threatening or menacing, their demeanour was certainly forbidding. He was asked to move to the Men's Arena as they were afraid that he would give away the coordinates of Elone. As Aryan had sat there and observed the men, he had wondered if any of them had ever known a woman, even fleetingly. This crop of men, eager, ambitious and quick at lateral thinking planned to colonize Elone, and that too alone. Elone—Aryan had no sense of ownership or pride in that discovery anymore.

Help was setting the table for dinner. Aryan went to the music room. Maya saw him and smiled. She was hunched over her workstation. Should he tell her? But what would he tell her? Maya got up and came to where he was standing near the door. She hugged him and led him to the dining table. Darkness had begun to fall on that rare pleasant sunny day.

'How was your meeting today? Why did they call you there and not conduct it over the network?' Maya asked as Help served them.

At that moment, Aryan decided that he would tell her.

'Maya.' He stopped short as the door opened and Ria walked in. Maya's face lit up. She got up and spread out her arms to hug her daughter. Ria dodged the waiting embrace and walked towards the table. It was the last time Aryan saw Maya ever move to hug her child.

'You have come home after years, Ria. You look so different. Come, join us for dinner,' Maya said quietly.

Ria sat down awkwardly and took a plate from Help.

'How is Ami? She has also not visited us in a long time,' Maya tried to fill the spaces of time with conversation.

Ria chose to address Aryan instead. 'Give me the coordinates of Elone, Aryan,' she demanded. Those were her first words in the house she had entered after many years. By uttering that one sentence Ria brought the strife that was brewing outside right into their home. All the conflict and rage that was floating around came and danced on the table as the three of them sat there. Aryan was stumped.

'Ria, your politics will not be played out at my dining table,' Maya declared firmly.

'Maya, what you dismiss as "politics" is the reality of our world now. Do you know you both are among the last few people who are still allowed to live together? Have you ever stopped to think why? That is only because you are my mother! Aryan is alive only because the men think he might be needed in their futile quest for Elone.' She took a deep breath and continued, 'This is a question of survival. If you want some concessions to continue, then give something back.' Ria's unsmiling and stern face did not resemble the girl Aryan had known for so many years.

In the span of a few seconds, a lifetime of emotions played across Maya's face—incredulity, shock, understanding, acceptance and then love, all over again. Ria kept looking at Aryan, unflinchingly, waiting for his response.

'Ria, finish your dinner. You cannot use your relationship with us to gather information,' Maya decided the issue.

Ria had barely picked anything from the plate. She stood up, 'This is not the end of this conversation, it is only the beginning. I am not hiding behind any relationship, Maya, you are. And the sooner you realize it, the better.'

The door slammed shut behind her. They heard an air-car stop outside and whisk Ria away, who had left behind a haze of uncertainty and confusion hanging in the room.

At night, Aryan lay in bed. His eyes were closed but he was wide awake. The voices of the day reverberated in his head. Late into the night, Maya entered. They had not spoken about what Ria had left hanging between them.

'Stroke my back the way I like it,' Aryan said turning over.

Maya hugged him, caressed his back, and both of them drifted off to sleep.

Next morning, Aryan went to the music

room. Maya was already there, staring out of the glass window. The day was going to be rainy and grey, as predicted by the dark and gloomy dawn.

Without any preamble, Aryan spoke, 'Maya, I will give you the coordinates to Elone and by evening, I will shift to the Men's Arena.'

Aryan had understood that it was time to go behind the walls that had been created. He was a man and Maya was a woman. Their paths had to diverge in this new world order that was overtaking their lives. Maya gently patted the seat next to her on the sofa. Aryan sat down and she entwined their fingers.

'Aryan, this is a battle between the people who are completely different from us, even though they came from us. Let the smarter side win. I am neither for men nor for women. I am for life. And between the two of us, Elone's whereabouts is a closed issue from now on.'

They both sat there for a long time, the second part of Aryan's decision hanging like a thread between them. Dividing and yet tying them together.

Tara began wailing in the next room. Tioni went to attend to her. Hap brought something to eat, and Tara got busy. Iwe continued to sit near the workstation, while Tioni tended to Tara.

The late afternoon sun was shining brightly outside the window. A stream of sunlight was strung across the room like a swathe of golden fabric.

'Maya are you there?' Tioni asked when she returned. She sat in her chair by the window. Iwe stood up, stretched and toyed with the streaming sunshine. The hum of the system seemed to indicate that Maya had left.

'Do you think Seeni knew all this? About how men and women lived together and then diverged on Earth itself? About the slow decay of Earth? Why it happened and how it happened? If yes, why didn't she share it with you, Tioni? Did she share it with someone? Was this knowledge why she was taken?' Iwe asked.

Tioni was still hoping that Maya would come back and finish the story. The interplay between men and women on Earth had been so different. In Elone, they could never even imagine it. This fascinating story had no place in their existence.

'For us, the men have always been on the other side of the Fence. I don't think anyone on either side has any memory of what Maya is describing. Actually, it doesn't matter,' Tioni was trying to get a perspective on the reality of Elone.

'Maybe, you are right, but Tioni, what happened on Earth is important.' Iwe, the sceptical one, was still grappling with the past.

'How will knowing all this change anything, Iwe? Whatever the ties between men and women may have been on Earth, we are not a part of it anymore. How does knowing the past change anything? Can it change the present or the future?'

Tioni, who had been so interested in what the past held, was trying to leave it there.

'I agree. I am not saying that it will change anything. It cannot because the past is over. But ultimately, we must accept that we are the same species,' Iwe stopped when she said that. It was a realization that had struck her only at that moment. Those creatures with their different bodies, their separate existence, were essentially similar to them.

'That was a long time ago, Iwe. It is difficult to relate to those who lived on Earth so many zacs ago,' Tioni said, staring out of the window.

'Imagine Tioni, if we destroy the men, as we have tried to in the past, we would be all alone in the universe. They are the only similar beings that we know of who exist.'

Both were quiet, as the stream of sunshine slowly receded from the room, as if someone was pulling the fabric away.

'We are not thinking of destroying the men, Iwe. It is the men who are up to something. We have to defend ourselves.' Then, as an afterthought, Tioni added, 'Are you going to tell Ultur about all of this?'

'I have not yet decided anything. Maya's story has not answered any questions related to Seeni's taking so far.'

Iwe joined Tioni at the window. They both looked out at the descending evening. Somewhere in the horizon, the Fence stood. It was strange to think that those living on the other side had once been so intricately linked to them.

Decisions

Patix and Valhan sat near a window in a small but exclusive dining centre on the outskirts of the city. The window overlooked a small terrace of green grass awash with colourful flowers. Beyond the terrace, in the darkness, the ocean's rush could be heard. Although muted inside, it made its presence felt.

The food arrived from the serving room on the belt that ran around the dining centre. They picked up their order of kimpayo sandwiches and tibli sauce, along with two glasses of enab. Patix observed Valhan as the latter looked out of the window, at the darkening day. He concluded that the substitutions had done him good.

Despite the distance, Valhan could feel the rush of the ocean as if it was kicking just below his feet. The discussions with Odep at the Gazer building had helped clarify some issues, but in his mind he still felt unsure. Ime was still at the Gazer, working on assessing the possibility of Tai as an alternative home.

'So what was going on at the Gazer? Why were you there?' Patix leaned back in the plush sofa, sipping enab.

'Nothing, just the usual. As you know, it has a high altitude telescope, so we were just gazing at the galaxies,'

Valhan continued to stare outside as he brushed aside the question.

Patix put both his elbows on the table. The lights in the ceiling were reflected on the polished surface, along with Patix's reflection.

'Let us talk clearly with each other, Valhan. Now, more than ever. We have to be on the same side, especially with all that is happening...' Patix trailed off.

Valhan turned his attention to Patix.

'And what is happening exactly, Patix? All this talk of a nex on the other side. Who is putting such things on the lex highways? Have you seen the kind of uproar it has created? Why are we playing with the peace that has served us all these zacs?'

Patix leaned back, again. He had known it was not going to be easy.

'I heard Radul put that on the lex. I plan to meet him soon and ask him why he did it,' he said, dismissingly. 'Now, you tell me, what is going on at the Gazer...and the Matsu.'

Valhan looked at Patix and smiled, 'I agree with you, Patix. We should be clear with each other. That is the only way this meeting will serve any purpose. Firstly, I know you know that the reserves of Nepo are declining. We need other reserves or an alternate material. Secondly, at Gazer, we are exploring if any other planet in the universe could be habitable and if it has Nepo reserves. That is all from my side, now, it is your turn.'

They ate in silence for a while as Valhan waited. Patix thought about what he should share with Valhan.

'There has been a nex on the other side. This is the information that the bubbles have picked up. More importantly, the gynake are putting the blame on us! And yes, I do know that the reserves of Nepo are dwindling. Have you had any success in finding a habitable planet?' Patix knew that the existence of an alternative home could impact his plans greatly. However, he also understood that even if they did manage to find a planet, it would take a long time for any decision to be made.

'Who was nexed, Patix?' asked Valhan, 'Someone important?'

'Not that we can make out. The name seems to be "Seeni". They are saying that we used Vish which is absurd because we decommissioned Vish many zacs ago. And I am sure they know that. The way they are pinning it on us makes me sure that they are planning something, and it involves aggression against us in some way.'

Valhan ate quietly. He could not decide if what Patix was saying was correct. He did not know about Vish being decommissioned or what they had done with the existing stores.

They finished their dinner and exited the dining centre. The three moons were bright and a light breeze was blowing as they walked along the oceanfront. Near the path, the ocean waves crashed on the rocks, spreading foam that gleamed in the silver light.

'I don't know yet if the planet we are exploring will be able to support life. But it does seem to have bright prospects. Will it be as beautiful and bounteous as Elone, we still don't know. At the moment, all I can say is that it is a plan that may or may not work. If it does not, we would have to look for other worlds. Sometimes, I wonder about those people on Earth. It must have taken a lot of effort and research to find

Elone. If they could do it, I'm sure we can too.'

They walked along in silence with the ocean's symphony for company. Patix was convinced that the proposal for the new planet was something for the distant future and would not impact his plan. He was now clear about where he needed to take things.

'What about Radul, Patix? Why are you making him put all these things on the lex? Have you seen the kind of responses his messages have evoked? It seems as if we are going to war with the gynake tomorrow itself.'

'I am not making him put anything on the lex, Valhan. He learnt about the nex on the other side when he visited me at the Etuis some time ago. You know him, he is neither focused nor does he do anything worthwhile. Messing with the lex is his pastime. In fact, I was planning to tell him to be more cautious,' Patix wanted to keep the façade that Radul was acting on his own for a little longer. That was the best way to achieve his aim. Valhan knew Patix was not telling him the complete truth about Radul, but he realized that no purpose would be served by pushing him on this.

'Okay. So now, what are you planning to do about the outpouring of hate against the gynake that is swallowing the lex highways? It is not showing any signs of slowing down. It seems to have acquired a life of its own. This anger either needs to be channelled elsewhere or doused completely, Patix. It is not good for us.'

Patix walked by his side in silence. He had thought long and hard about this. Since the day he had called Radul to the Point and thrown this challenge at him, everything had begun to converge as per his plans.

'I agree with you, Valhan. I think we should call a meeting

of the Syned to discuss all this. Maybe we can meet after a calante?'

Valhan nodded. They had reached the end of the track. They began to walk towards the road from where they would take separate travelors.

'What will be discussed at the meeting, Patix?' Valhan asked.

'I think we should share the information we gathered from the bubbles and the decline in Nepo. What it means for us and what we should do,' Patix replied.

They had nearly reached the road.

'You have a plan?' Valhan asked.

Patix swiftly changed the topic, 'Do you have any news of Odep, Valhan? Do you think he will come if the Syned calls him for this discussion?'

Patix knew Valhan still visited Odep in his house in the hills. Odep might have withdrawn into the hills, but his views still carried a lot of authority in the Syned.

Valhan understood and did not push Patix about his plans. Instead, he thought about Odep—sitting in that forlorn house of his in the hills, giving up substitutions, trying to see how life would change if he knew a nex was coming for him, thinking about the gynake as some fellow travellers in the march of the universe. No one would listen to him anymore. In fact, they did not need to hear his ideas. Since Odep had decided to disappear into the margins, he would have to remain there.

'He is doing all right, Patix. I met him at his home some time ago. As for coming for the discussion at the Syned, he would if we ask him. But do we need to call him? As far as I could make out, he has, in a sense, signed off from things.'

Patix nodded, relieved. So, it had been sealed. The plan was now to be rolled out.

In Ime's absence, the Furawa had looked after his saplings well. They had reached a fair height and were laden with the sea blue bell-shaped flowers that Ime had designed. The deep blue dots on the sides added to their beauty. Ime was on his knees, near the patch, taking in their fragrance. The fresh smell of the seaside in the mornings was wafting from them. Ime was delighted by the flowers, the way they had turned out; he knew where he would plant them along the pathways of the Aeona.

'What is this place, Ime? I have never been here before. What a maze of colours and smells this is!' Radul's shadow covered Ime's patch.

Ime glanced up. Radul looked different from the last time he had seen him. His hair was shorter, and clothes dapper. Now, by merely looking at him, no one could say that he was an inhabitant of a group house anymore. Ime had decided to meet Radul to understand what was going on. He realized that between their last meeting at the Aeona and now, a lot had changed.

'This is the Furawa, Radul. It's an incubator for flowers and plants. When I got your message, I was already on my way here, so I asked you to join me.'

'You were gone away for a long while. Where have you been?' Radul asked as they walked towards benches installed under the huge tree that ruled over the Furawa landscape.

While Ime sat on the bench, Radul continued looking

around, impressed with the kaleidoscope of colours around.

'I had gone to the Gazer building for some work. Anyway, you tell me, why have you been putting strange messages on the lex lately? Is what you said about a nex true?' Ime asked. Radul was delighted. Finally, someone knew that he had put the message on the lex.

'Yes, Ime, I found out from sources in the Syned that a nex has happened on the other side and the gynake are blaming us. What do you think about all the noise that is exploding on the lex these days?' he asked. Ime let the fragrant breeze blow over him for a while. Radul was still standing near the bench, looking across at all the different blooming flowers.

He couldn't fathom what Radul got from all this meddling. Was it his own doing or was he being pushed by someone?

'You had asked me last time if I knew anything about the origin of the hostilities with the gynake. I tried to find out from various sources, but I drew a blank. No one seems to know the history of our shared life on Earth. It is not recorded anywhere. I think it was so far back in time that it has lost its relevance along the way. They are the enemy behind the Fence—that is the only reality today,' Radul said.

Then Ime asked what he had been meaning to ask since the beginning, 'Radul, first you wanted to bring the issue of creation before the Syned. Now, you have started this fear and hate campaign against the gynake. What exactly are you hoping to achieve?'

Finally, Radul sat down with him on the bench. He looked directly at Ime with his electric blue eyes.

'Ownership and absolute ownership of Elone. I want the entire planet for us, Ime. You know whenever fences come up, the prospect of a conflict is already embedded in them.

This era of peace that some of you talk about all the time, it is nothing but a pause while we regroup on both the sides. Think about it…they have started the rumblings with this accusation of us causing a nex on their side. What do you think our response should be? Should we simply hide behind the Fence and wait for their next move? Ime, the time has come to reclaim our planet. We need the other half in more ways than you can even imagine. It's not about space alone. We need the other half for survival.'

Ime watched as Radul spoke with confidence and in an assured manner. When he had come to the Aeona, Ime had completely missed this raw ambition that was now dripping from his entire being. Radul knew about the declining Nepo reserves. That was clear from his words.

'At Gazer, I have been working to find an alternative planet for our survival, Radul. One has already been identified as a distinct possibility. We could think of moving. We could leave this planet, those creatures on the other side and start our lives afresh. We can build a new home, new cities, a whole new existence…with no baggage of Earth or what came with us from there.'

Even as he was speaking, Ime realized he was in a sense pleading with Radul.

'A new planet?' Radul asked incredulously, 'Why do we need it? Everything we need is right here. The more I observe around me, the more I realize that Elone is so beautiful. It is our home, Ime. Why should we even think of moving? But on second thoughts, Ime, locate that new planet of yours. Once we have settled ourselves across all of Elone, then we can think of expanding to the new planet. We will restart creations. We should not limit ourselves in any manner, Ime. I completely agree with you,' Radul turned and stared at the horizon, as if he had already conquered it.

Ime thought of the machine that was currently processing all the data that had been gathered already. In a few days, he would know for sure whether Tai was capable of hosting life. All those planets that winked at him through the pane of the Aeona, were they all possible future colonies of Elone? He had never thought of it like that.

'So, Radul, you believe that it is time to eliminate the gynake from this planet? You want to simply destroy another species? Do you even realize that they are the closest to us in the whole universe? We will be left all alone once they are gone. I have watched and held vigil on the cosmos for numerous zacs; there is only silence, Radul. No one else seems to be out there. Also, have you ever stopped to consider that if the gynake have some knowledge of our shared past, it will vanish with them and we will never even know?'

Radul started laughing as he got up. 'Come Ime, let us go and have some enab in the incubator building. I think the universe and the galaxies you work with are playing with your mind. Don't you realize they are planning the same thing for us? Do you think anyone on that side is even thinking about being left alone in the galaxy? What will you do with knowledge about some ancient shared past? Look at the future, Ime. Who wins this time is going to stay here on Elone, and then, the universe is theirs to conquer. It has to be us.'

Radul started walking towards the incubator building. As they walked together, Ime realized that in the future they would all be following Radul.

The sun was hot as Ime sat at the travelor stop with rolling hills spread out before him. Green trees on the slopes glistened in the bright sunlight. Two travelors had glided past him already, but he continued to sit there, motionless. The path to Odep's house, up in the hills, was clear; he could even see the last travelor winding its way up with a few occupants. But he sat there, wondering why he had come here.

He had been in the Aeona when the results started to stream in from the Gazer building. As he processed them, Ime had been dismayed. It was clear that Tai could not be their alternative home. Analysis of major atmospheric movements revealed a volatile and fragile space. In spells, but for long periods, rapid oxidation took place in its atmosphere that turned the sunshine blue which meant that Tai could not support life. Ime had felt a deep sense of disappointment. His first thought had been to tell Valhan, but the wedge between them had not been bridged. Since he had left the Gazer, they had not communicated. Then, he had thought of Odep.

The sun was beating down harder now and the path in front was beckoning. Finally, Ime got up and started his walk up the hills. Dry leaves crunched beneath his feet and the sun played hide-and-seek amongst the trees. After a long walk, Odep's house became visible around the corner. Ime felt a combination of fear and apprehension. He wondered if more streaks of silver had appeared in Odep's hair since he had left Gazer.

As he approached the house, Odep stepped out. When he saw Ime walking up the path, he smiled. 'Ime, I am glad you came by. I was planning to call you here. It is warm today, come in, come in.'

Once inside, Ime observed the house. It was sparsely done

Decisions • 221

up. From an open window, sunlight was streaming in, livening up the otherwise bare interiors. The structure of the house seemed different from other buildings, in and around the city.

'You designed this, Odep?'

'Obviously. I know it's different; actually, I tried to make it so,' Odep said.

He gestured towards an easy chair and both of them sat down.

'You are doing all right?' Ime was trying not to stare at his hair.

Odep smiled, 'I still have only two silver streaks, Ime. Things don't change so fast even when you stop substitutions. We have refined Nepo to such an extent that organs last us for a large number of zacs. I still have a long way to go.'

They sat in silence for a while. Ime was still wondering why he had come here.

'Odep, Tai cannot be a future home. The analysis has come in. It has a volatile atmosphere, we would have to begin our search again,' Ime blurted out.

'It is a long search, Ime, to explore the universe to find an alternate home. It requires patience and effort. But we have to remember that until we succeed, we have to live on Elone and face the realities.'

'Well, the reality on Elone is not very encouraging, Odep. Since you are disconnected from the lex, you don't know that. We seem to be entering a phase of conflict again. The Syned has members who are waiting to approve such a move. Men seem to have found something to rally around and are now planning to annihilate the gynake. The whole thing is spinning rapidly out of control.'

Odep sighed deeply, 'Ime, we have had a long spell of peace.

A kind of stillness had enveloped our existence. Waking up to a known enemy engages us. War at intervals is like a life force. It brings much needed change in our collective lives. It gives us something to do, something to plan for. Even though it thrives on destruction, war is a unifying force. Maybe this is our way to re-enter the cycle of creation and destruction, which is the basis of the universe.'

'So you approve?' Ime was surprised.

What had he been expecting when he came all the way to Odep's house?

'It doesn't matter if I approve or not, Ime. As Valhan told me when we left Gazer, I have been away for far too long. Now, I am on the margins. Nothing I say or believe matters anymore,' Odep's kind eyes looked at Ime directly. They were neither defeated nor sad. They were accepting.

Ime stood up and walked out of the door, and looked towards the horizon. An orange hue was spreading across the sky as the sun prepared to set.

His lex buzzed. It was a message from Radul.

The Syned is meeting next vihan to discuss the situation. I thought you would like to know.

Ime turned around and walked inside again. Odep was sitting in his chair with his eyes closed. Hearing Ime's footsteps, Odep opened his eyes.

Looking at his concerned face, he said, 'I just hope that in their clamour for action, they do not forget that the gynake are a formidable enemy. They always have been, Ime. They have the same desire to survive and exist that we have. It is a battle of equals,' he shrugged, matter-of-factly.

'Odep, the Syned is meeting next vihan. Why don't you attend the meeting too? They will listen to you even if they don't agree with you.'

'They have not asked me to come, Ime. So, I can't go, but what I will do is send a message to Durk that I would like you to attend on my behalf. At least that way, both of us would know what is happening.'

What would he say or do there? Ime had never actively thought about what went on in the Syned. His place was among the stars and the galaxies. Ime knew that Valhan would not appreciate his attendance as Odep's representative.

'Odep, I have never been involved in all of this. I think you should attend,' Ime tried to argue.

'I am now on the margins of what matters, Ime. You are a part of it. Be there, say what you think is important. A voice of reason is always important. It might not change the decision, but it does impact the process.'

Ime thought of the yellowish Tai, of Elone, of the Fence and their existence as it was. Everything was threatening to change dramatically. He made up his mind.

'Okay, I will go if they agree. But I don't think my presence will make much of a difference. There is a determination to go forward that I find quite forbidding,' Ime said, recalling his conversation with Radul.

'Sometimes, even a few words of caution that articulate a different point of view than the prevalent one can change the course of decision-making,' Odep said, meeting Ime's gaze squarely.

Earth

Maya was sitting on a bench in a thickly wooded patch of the exclusive resort. It was far away from the city, with cottages sprawled over the area. The resort was an expensive place, where men and women could still meet and spend some time together. As far as she could see, leaves formed a carpet on the floor. Maya rested her head against the back of the wooden bench. There was a deathly silence all around her, broken only by the sound of rustling leaves. She tried to remember what the twitter of birds sounded like. But she couldn't recollect. Most of the birds and animals had gradually disappeared, lost to humanity and the Earth in the process that they now called life.

Maya opened her eyes and looked at the sky. The

clouds floating above seemed almost the same, the air that swept across carried smells and fragrances, the sun in the peak of summer still managed some heat. On the surface everything appeared the same, but it had all changed. Maya's Trin band was silent because she had switched it off the day before, when she had left the city for this resort. She had taken the speed train to reach here. Before she had disembarked at the station, at the foot of the hills, and had started to walk up, she had activated the band for a while. There was a message from Ria.

I know where you have gone and why your outdated band is shut. Why are you doing such things, Maya? Why are you being a traitor to our cause? Don't forget, men are not merely our competitors anymore; they are the declared enemy. You know it too. He will not come. He will never desert his ilk to consort with the enemy. Stop fooling yourself.

Men and women as enemies? It was such a painful thought. However, in their new world, this was the emerging perspective from both sides. The knowledge that Ria knew where she was had sent shivers down Maya's spine. It had almost made her change her plans. What if Ria had Aryan arrested?

But then, Maya had weighed her options. She needed to meet Aryan. The risk was worth taking. And she had climbed slowly up the hill towards the resort.

She was much older now, as was Aryan. It was 2230. What were they doing in this strange world where young men and women lived separately, in their own ghettos? A world where resources, money and power were a battleground, but not between countries, ideologies or groups, rather between men and women. After millennia of needing each other for procreation, they had fallen apart once their reproductive dependencies had vanished.

Maya got up from the bench and started humming as she walked through the clearing. At a little distance, a small stream was gurgling down the hill. Its water was pristine and clear. The resort would have paid huge sums of money to let it remain a part of their property. Water bodies of any kind were bitterly fought for by the two sides. In fact, everything was fought for. Their shrinking world, beleaguered by surging waters and dimming sunshine, was creaking under the burden of warring sides.

A full day had passed since their appointed time to meet. Maya wondered whether Ria had been right. Would Aryan not come? She shook her head and dispelled the thoughts. A shared lifetime could not be erased so easily and surrendered to this new equation that had emerged between men and women.

Maya sat near the stream and let the music of the tumbling water drench her in its melody. In this new world, where wombs had been replaced by machines and a mere cell from a man or a woman could clone a baby, very few like them remained—men and women who had brought life into this world through passion and love.

As the stream gurgled past, Maya wondered how they had not seen it coming. This conflict and divide between men and women. Earlier they had been tied together by biology, but as technology progressed, that tie had loosened and ultimately it had broken completely. It divided the world. The stream somehow reminded her of her younger days, when desire surged in her veins much like the gush of water. What a delicious feeling it used to be!

Maya had learnt long ago that humans were social animals that needed each other to live. It had been turned upside down. Too many factors in the equation had changed. Now, all alone, with the help of technology, a man or a woman could produce another being. And not just any being, someone who was an extension of their own genome sequence. They could replicate themselves, become immortal. Humanity's long-standing quest for eternal life had been achieved, in a manner of speaking. In a most basic way, humans had become self-sufficient. Thus gradually, but surely, the solitary individual had become the norm.

In their sprawling house in the female ghetto, which was now called the 'Gynake Hub', Maya often felt sad. Ria was a high-ranking official in the female world, sought-after for her technical skills and her decision-making abilities. Her daughter, the one with a tinkling laugh, had now been transformed into a determined strategist in the conflict. Ami, her granddaughter, who grew up in a world where men were the enemy, was being hailed as the new woman, the harbinger of the future.

Ami lived alone in an apartment in the Gynake Hub and was waiting for her turn to get a clone. Desires, sexuality, the need for another's touch had slowly, but surely, begun to wither away from the genes of this new generation.

'What a loss,' she remembered Aryan saying this to her in what seemed like another lifetime.

The sun was setting on the horizon. Maya walked to the edge of the hill to watch its majestic journey. The sky was a flaming orange with the burning sun like a spotlight in the middle. The hues changed like a kaleidoscope as the sun dipped further and further. It was breathtaking. She decided that she would wait for Aryan for at least a week. He would come. She knew that, despite what Ria said.

She had not returned. It had been almost three days since Maya's band had fallen silent. Ria felt a cold anger envelop her. Ria got up from her chair and looked out of the window at the expanse spread out below. The Gynake Hub was surrounded by a wall on three sides and the sea on the fourth. Outside those walls was a corridor that was used intermittently by both the sides, and beyond that, began the Men's Arena. The men still controlled the major share of the habitable part of the planet, and that was unlikely to change.

Earth—how quickly it had shrunk and shrivelled in the last few years. Now, only a small part of the original land was inhabited, the rest had been submerged by continuously rising waters from the melted glaciers and snowcaps. Everyone knew that this patch would also disappear soon; the sun was wilting and life as they knew it was surely coming to an end. Earth was unravelling at breakneck speed.

Ria looked at the sky in the direction of their hope, at Elone. Initially, its discovery had not caught the imagination of anyone, but now, years later, it was the only hope for human survival. Now, that distant planet had become their goal. Men armed with the coordinates of Elone were building their spaceships. The women were trying to identify its location while working on their own spaceships. The side that won the race would leave the other behind to become extinct along with the dying planet.

Ria turned towards the three screens on the opposite wall. The one in the top-left corner gave her the details of the development of the spaceships. The second gave a continuous feed on anything of importance that was happening in the Men's Arena. The third updated her about the happenings in the Hub.

Aryan had still not reached the resort

where her mother imagined she was hidden, waiting for him. Maya's stubborn behaviour angered Ria. Maya clearly understood the reality of their world. She knew that it was a crime for her to meet a man, even if he was someone whom she had loved all her life. Ria shook her head at that thought. Maya could not leave him even now. Now, when the world around them was reverberating with conflict and it was a matter of life and death. What if others in the Hub learnt that her old, frail mother was frolicking in the hills with a man?

She knew that Aryan was completely true to his side. Over the last few years, Ria had tried to persuade Maya to get Aryan to reveal the coordinates of Elone. That was why she had let them meet occasionally. But she had not succeeded.

People of the vintage era like Aryan and Maya were of no use to either side. However, Maya, one of the oldest women alive, could be considered a source of information about the old way of life, when men and women lived together.

Ria was pondering over this thought when there was a knock on her door. She unlocked it from her desk and her assistant, Naqi, walked in.

'The Council is meeting tomorrow to

discuss the utilization of the water bodies. I have sent you the draft.' Then, she suddenly asked, 'Something troubling you, Ria?'

Ria shook her head, 'What? No. Why do you ask?'

'Well, you always put on Maya's music when you are thinking.'

Ria was surprised. She had not even noticed when she had started playing the music.

'Nothing much. I was wondering about Maya. Sometimes, it seems that she is out of touch with the reality around us.'

'Maya is grounded, Ria. She might be old and belong to another time, but she knows what is happening. And the best part is that she accepts new realities. I was thinking that you should seriously talk to her about merging. You can see for yourself how Buli's merger has benefitted our space programme. Maya is a musician par excellence. We need to have her around to animate the new world we plan to go to.'

'Hmm... I have broached the topic with her. Anyway, let's see what is on the agenda for tomorrow.'

Naqi left the room.

Maya's music was still wafting through the room. It made Ria think about what

Naqi had said. She had already given the suggestion to Maya, but she had remained non-committal. Merger, used sparingly, was no longer a technological step in the quest for immortality. Replacement therapies and the availability of cloning had changed the game. Merger now was a process to preserve exceptional brains.

The thoughts of Maya and Elone led her back to the present problem. Should she get Aryan arrested if he reached the resort? After all, the resort was within the jurisdiction of the Hub. Then they could grind him to the ground for the coordinates of Elone.

The skies were overcast, as usual. It looked as if the rains would come in torrents for the next few days. Standing in the balcony, Aryan scanned the pitch dark sky for a glimpse of the stars. For the third day in a row, he had not seen them break through the dense cloud cover. He needed to squint his eyes to scan the sky these days, especially when he did not use his silver-rimmed spectacles. His eyesight had deteriorated and he had a constant nagging pain in his shoulder. Disappointed with what he saw, he went inside and sat on the bed in the cluttered room. This one-room apartment in a decrepit building in the Men's Arena contained the sum of his long life. On the left wall, hung his favourite image—the cosmos with a small bluish speck in the left corner. That was how Elone had looked from the viewfinder of the telescope in the astronomy tower—the vision Maya and he had seen together so long ago.

The moment he thought of Maya, Aryan felt a pang. He knew she would be waiting for him. Four days had passed since the appointed day. He had not yet set out. Aryan was tired, he was exhausted with this world he found himself trapped in. He had given Elone to the world, to humanity, so that they could create a future. But instead, it had become a prize for which the two sides were battling, bitterly. A new life waiting on that faraway planet had become the anthem. He was forgotten, the original purpose was lost and what remained disgusted him.

For some years now, Maya and he, caught in the crossfire, lived in the separate spaces that men and women inhabited. From his life, Maya had again moved to the spaces of his mind.

On a screen mounted on the wall, news was streaming in. It was something about the Gynake Hub. Ria's face flashed across the screen. How much had that child changed? The determined crusader had been a cheerful and happy girl. Much like her mother, she was once a free spirit. But now, Ria was caged in the web they had created for themselves.

In a way, it had never mattered to Aryan who won this race. He had decided long ago that he was not a part of it. Whether men and women were going to annihilate each other here or somewhere in space—it was irrelevant to him. Aryan, the struggler with change, had found that this indifference helped him cope. Now, he sought solace in the dim stars he saw from his balcony. They were the only things that remained constant in the chaos around him.

The other aspect that mattered to him was the woman waiting for him in a hillside resort. In all the years that they had been together, Maya had always given him a sense of hope. It was a terrible loss that Ria and those who would come after her would never know this feeling. Not know how even at this age, when no part of his body surged when he thought of her, he still felt a warmth around his soul when he thought of Maya.

From his forlorn balcony, Aryan often observed the men rushing below in the streets. They were alone, confused and in a constant state of war—with themselves, with change and with women. When he was younger, he remembered everyone always used to talk about the dangers of having hordes of single, unattached males in any society. It was considered the start of all sorts of problems. Now, their community was simply that—a cohort of single, unattached males. And they all believed it to be a glorious high in civilization's growth as men no longer needed women for anything. It was considered the pinnacle of success. Nothing made sense to Aryan anymore. There were no ideological battles, no wars for territory, and no cries for freedom. Women were finally the enemy, formally and openly.

Maya—he thought of her in that dark thundering night while raindrops were falling like stones on the roof. Her smiling face, her lilting music, her lust for life, her energy and her sense of hope. He remembered how she looked when she ran her fingers through his hair. He loved her. It had taken him a lifetime to accept it. What a wondrous feeling it was. He wondered what would take its place in the new world that was struggling to be born.

Maya was sitting near the stream. More than a week had passed and Aryan had not come. But she continued to wait. Somewhere in the distance, she could feel Ria's anger brewing. There were times when she forgot that Ria was her own; she generally thought of her as one of the leaders. It had been many years since they had hugged or had any personal conversation.

The afternoon sun was quite strong but it was a welcome change after two days of continuous rain. The smell of drenched vegetation hung in the air like a curtain. Maya rested her head on her arms and let a melody play in her mind. Music was her eternal companion. It renewed its embrace the moment she reached out.

There was a light tap on her shoulder. She looked up and against the sun, saw Aryan standing there. She held out her hand and he helped her get up, gently.

'So you finally came?' Maya said, a little unsteady on her feet.

'Yes. I started walking two days ago. Sorry, I am late.'

Aryan looked completely exhausted.

'You walked all the way?' she asked incredulously, 'Why didn't you take the air-car till the border of the Hub and then walk?'

'Well, simply because I did not have the fare. In all the chaos that is around us, pensions are not being paid. Unlike your music, I live off my pension now. We are old now, Maya. The younger ones don't need us. How many times have I told you this?' he replied, slightly agitated.

They walked to the little bench in the clearing and sat there. Hand in hand, in silence. Aryan was still breathless from the climb.

After a while, Maya said, 'You must be hungry. Let us go inside and eat something.' Maya was getting up, but Aryan pulled her back on to the bench.

'No, I ate something. Let us sit here for a while. It feels nice...almost like old times. How have you been? Let me see you clearly. It was nearly two years ago when we last met, right?' Aryan turned, placed his silver-rimmed spectacles on his snow-white head, and looked at her. His eyes smiled at her. Now that they were together, it felt like they had never been apart.

'Yes…two years. I wasn't sure if you had got my message. But I am glad that we managed to communicate. I am sure Ria was monitoring the conversation though,' Maya said and put her head on his shoulder. And in that moment, the strange world around them evaporated, and they were an old couple, sunning themselves, enveloped by a blanket of companionable silence. Each sat there with their separate thoughts, but still together.

'Maya, do you remember they taught us that life emerged on Earth after Big Bang? From single cell organisms to other complicated life forms? How men and women, and the children they begot, made the world? There were wars, strife, conflict, peace and prosperity in phases. But through all the changes and turmoil, we were always together, as humans. Of course, we ravaged other species, even brought them to extinction. But whatever was done, it was done for humanity. Then, this Earth that was so bounteous and beautiful began to crumble with overuse. We still fought together to perpetuate ourselves as human beings. Climate transformation, increasing pollution, submerging land, vanishing sunshine—they were all common battles. But millennia of unity have given way in the matter of half a century. Why? Because we managed to change one factor in the equation of nature. Men and women stopped needing each other for procreation. They do not even need their own bodies to nurture future generations. A mere cell and a well-equipped incubator is all that is needed. We achieved the ultimate outsourcing solution. As a result, both sides believe with ferocity that the other is a different species. Remember, Maya, I said this to you many years ago when we saw Elone for the first time together. To be honest with you, that time, I was more preoccupied with the long lifetime we had invented for ourselves. But I never thought I would see my apprehensions come true while I was alive.'

Maya opened her eyes. The sky was getting overcast again. She tilted her head, resting on Aryan's shoulder to see his profile.

'What about this hurts you so much, Aryan?'

'The loss, Maya, we lost the basis of human civilization. It is a disaster. Don't you see it?' Maya held his hand and played with his long fingers, while Aryan squinted into the distance. Maya nestled into the crook of Aryan's shoulder. There was so much peace in that space.

'This is the man in you speaking, Aryan. There has been an underlying conflict between us since the time men were hunter-gatherers and women kept the fires burning. For centuries, men had the upper hand because of physical differences. It was biology that ensured that it remained a man's world. Biology was the basis on which all the social constructs that made women second-class citizens were built. Rape was used as a weapon for centuries with no one acknowledging it as one of the means of warfare. Sexual violence against women was a punishment, a way to assert power, a means to belittle and dishonour, and to reinforce a sense of misplaced masculinity. I still remember the time when a woman's body was not her own. Whether she could choose to have a child or not, what she wore, where she went, who had the right to touch her—everything was mandated and sanctioned in some way or the other by men. It was never her choice. For centuries, men colonized women as their right and with a sense of entitlement.

'Aryan, the centuries you talk of, when we coexisted, only denied the inherent conflict that has always existed between men and women. It was just contained and caged in. It was only in abeyance. Then, slowly, things began to change. As buttons replaced horsepower, as machines began to do what was done by humans, as the equilibrium began to shift, women emerged from the shadows. It was a continuing struggle, Aryan. Misogyny and patriarchy, entrenched within us for millennia, were not easy to fight. How can you forget the phase when the known gender constructs began to change and homosexuality became mainstream? Gender boundaries began to blur, identities were confused—there was a lot of flux. Sexuality, heterosexual and in other alternative forms, continued to thrive. However, in all that time, men and women continued to exist in the same space because reproduction still needed both of them to succeed, whether you were gay, lesbian or straight. We were an exponentially evolving species, being pushed by technology. Not many people saw the immense change technology would bring in the future. We hid behind our ideologies and organized faiths and thought the future would never arrive. But it did. One fine day, it all changed.

'Our dependence on each other ended. Men could have their offspring and women theirs. What a downward spiral it has been for desire. What we labelled as our "primordial urge" for centuries disappeared, just like that, from our landscape. What we have lost, as a species, is sexuality, Aryan. That basic instinct that tied us together despite all odds has disappeared. We have diverged completely, giving rise to a new creature—this lone human, male or female, who can live, procreate and die, in a solitary manner, is the new motif. Add to that a long and fairly healthy life; well, we are moving to another pattern of human life. Our life revolves around machines, they have become our tools of engagement. Technology is the ultimate leveller, Aryan. All known constructs will further disappear; in a way, they already have.'

Maya paused to take a breath.

'This divide between men and women and what you think of as a loss, is in fact a victory for women that took a long time coming. The Earth belonged to the men for too long, Aryan. Humanity changed biology, which changed the pattern of ownership. There is bound to be clash and conflict. This is going to be a long-drawn battle, especially if both men and women make it to Elone.'

The first drops of rain had begun to fall.

Aryan's eyes were closed. He adjusted his spectacles and said quietly, 'I have never thought of things in this manner. Maybe what you say is true, but it is no victory, Maya. Of that I am certain.'

Maya stood up and ran her fingers through his thick crop of snow-white hair. It was a wonder that it had remained so thick even at his age. And she still loved running her fingers through his hair.

'You love doing that, don't you, Maya? I always liked the feel of it even though I have never told you so.'

'Come Aryan, let's go in. We will get drenched otherwise,' Maya said, holding out her hand.

Aryan looked up. Sitting there in the gathering rain, he simply gazed at Maya silently. All the years they had seen together seemed to float by in front of him. As the rain began to fall more persistently, Maya finally said, 'I love you too.' His eyes smiling, Aryan got up. They began to walk hand in hand towards the cottage, as the raindrops got bigger.

'Do you think men and women will ever come together again, Maya? Maybe in some distant time or space?'

They had neared the cottage door. It opened at their arrival and they stepped into the warm and dry interiors.

'Go and wear a robe, Aryan. You are soaking wet. I will also change. And let us not worry about the future so much. As you always say, we belong to the past.'

It was pitch dark outside by the time they finished their dinner and lay down, side by side, in the dim light on the sprawling bed.

'Why did you call me so urgently, Maya? Are you unwell?' Aryan asked.

Maya moved her head and rested it on his shoulder, the way he liked it.

'Ria asked me if I would like to go in for a merger. She says since I am a renowned musician I can fall in the category of a "special mind". That is the official version,' she smiled in the dark before continuing, 'more importantly, she tells me that they are close to a breakthrough regarding your precious Elone. She doesn't want to leave me here to die alone and I cannot take the physical journey to the planet. What do you think?'

Aryan lay there in silence. He knew what was going to come next and he knew his answer too. His shoulder was throbbing more than usual that day. He stroked Maya's forehead as she lay next to him. How could she still not perceive the loss for humanity? What in her being made her so eager to explore unknown frontiers?

'What do you want to do, Maya?'

'It was always easier to answer that when I was younger. Maybe even twenty years ago, I would have said I want to go to that new planet and see how we live our life there. Merging my consciousness with the machine never frightened me, as it does many others. But now, I don't know. Will you also go in for merger, Aryan? We could be together, you know.'

Aryan turned over and said, 'Stroke my back, Maya…the way I like it.'

The rain was creating a cacophony outside and Maya waited for Aryan's response in the silence of the room. Her hand was running slowly along his back.

'Maya, stay back and let us die together on this planet. You just said some time ago that we belong to the past. The past indeed creates the pathway to the future, but it has no place in it. When they leave, we can be together again. Here, on this Earth, and wait out our time. This is where we belong, Maya. However shrunk and shrivelled it may be, or cold it may become, this is the only home we have known. Also, there is great peace in knowing that an end will come. Even you know that now, Maya. This idea of an endless existence on a machine is not for me. I would rather die holding you.'

The rain outside was like the drumbeat of a marching band. What Aryan had said did not surprise Maya. It did not even hurt her, like it would have done many years ago. Somewhere, deep inside, she understood the weariness with living and coping with unending change. Why was it that the idea of life being limitless did not enamour her anymore? Was it because the life that was on offer was radically different from her own conception? This fight that had erupted between men and women had never been a part of her imagination. Maybe this change was too much for her. Or was it that she was too old now and, like Aryan, wanted this journey to finally end? Stay back on Earth and wait the time out with Aryan. It seemed like such a wonderful future to look forward to. Aryan seemed to have drifted off to sleep. Maya stopped caressing his back. She turned and lay on her back. Aryan caught hold of her hand and murmured, 'Don't go.'

He pulled her arm over him and she turned to him again. Maya's cheek touched his back and she rested. With the drumbeats of the rain and Aryan's heavy breathing playing like a symphony, Maya drifted into a quiet sleep.

A sharp knock on the door awoke her abruptly. The day had broken and somewhere the sun had managed to break through the clouds. Its glory was sprinkled on the hills, visible from the long glass panes of the room. Aryan was still asleep. Despite the sunshine, Maya felt a cold hand curling around her heart.

The door swung open and two female soldiers, smartly attired and fully armed, walked in.

'Sorry Maya, we have come to take him.'

Night had fallen and the Vault was absolutely silent. The hum of the system was all that they could hear. Iwe and Tioni sat there, eyes shut, waiting for the story to unfold. However, there was only silence.

Tioni opened her eyes and felt as if she could see the two female soldiers escorting Aryan out of the door. She shook her head and blinked a few times to come back to Elone.

'Maya, are you there? What happened to Aryan? Don't go just yet,' Tioni pleaded at the blank screen of Iwe's workstation. There was, however, no response.

'She seems to have gone, Tioni,' Iwe said, opening her eyes.

The solitude of the Vault was somehow overwhelming. Iwe stood up and began pacing around the room.

'I wonder, Tioni, if men know all that Maya has told us,' Iwe said, as she walked around.

'I do too. Do you think life on this planet would have turned out differently if both the sides had remembered the past?' Maya's voice boomed in the room. Iwe hurried back to her chair.

'Tell us Maya, what do you know about Seeni's taking? Don't go away this time without completing your story,' Iwe wanted this uncertainty to end.

'I had not left. I was simply caught up in the past. Iwe, like I have said before, I know nothing about Seeni's death. In fact, she never even learnt the whole story. I miss having her around, though.'

'What happened next, Maya?' Iwe asked, although she was very disappointed that Maya could shed no light on Seeni's taking.

'The story from here is simple and short. They couldn't arrest Aryan because he had already been taken. He died that night in my arms. He had always wanted to die on Earth, although all his life he lived amongst the stars. I was not as lucky. I lived to watch the race till the end. Then, when it was time to make the journey to Elone, I thought a lot. If I could not spend my last days with Aryan, at least, I would reach his planet. So, I decided to merge. Ria brought me here as part of our heritage during the Great Escape. And, here I am still… roaming time and space and all the other dimensions as the endless consciousness of a woman.'

'And…?' Iwe was waiting for more.

'The rest, since our arrival on Elone, you know. The first open conflict between the men and women claimed Ria and Ami.'

'Are there more like you in our system, Maya? Did any of the men who merged also come to Elone?' Iwe was getting impatient. There were so many questions swirling around in her head and Maya was not being expansive in her responses. Was it actually a programme put in by the men? The old doubt began creeping in again.

'A few of the merged women had been brought and installed in the common system. However, it got destroyed in the first War. Ria kept me in her gapped home system and so I survived. And regarding the men? No Iwe, when it was time to board the spaceships, the men left useless machines with old brains on them behind. Men were adept at changing rules to suit their needs.'

'Do you still think about Aryan, Maya?' asked Tioni.

Iwe couldn't believe that Tioni had asked such an irrelevant question. There were so many things to ask Maya before she disappeared into the system again. It had already taken her many vihans to reach this instalment of the story.

'It was a different time, Tioni. Back then, when you loved someone, as much as and for as long as I had loved Aryan, they became a part of you. They never left the spaces of your mind. So yes, even today, he is a part of my awareness.'

'Maya…' Iwe wanted to bring the discussion back to more important areas.

'I haven't finished yet, Iwe. This awareness of another is difficult for you to understand. You are wired for an individual existence. Your own self is the extent of your awareness. What drives you is the desire to remain and exist. That is the passion of your world, your reality, your value. What a civilization values and pursues is determined by its realities. For a long time, we swore by a different set of core human values, and believed that they were universal and eternal. However, once the basis of civilization changed, they disappeared. A new set of values took root, for both the sides. Change the realities and the values change. It took me a long time to understand this.'

'Maya, how come men and women travelled here together? Why?' Iwe asked, after waiting for a moment.

'Girls, just see how you both have different questions about the same story. It gives me hope. Having different perspectives and ideas is the basis of growth.'

There was silence. Both of them waited patiently for Maya to speak again. Meanwhile, through the tag, Tioni checked up on Tara. She was sleeping peacefully, watched over by Hap. She breathed a sigh of relief; she could be at the Vault for some more time.

'Maya?' Tioni whispered softly.

'I am here, Tioni. It has been a long time since that overwhelming journey from Earth to Elone. I was simply gathering the details. Why did we come together? Simple Iwe, because there was no other way the Great Escape could have succeeded. Time was running out, the sun was getting weaker, the terrain as well as the weather more inhospitable. Our survival was at stake. The women had the spaceships that could travel the distance and the men had the coordinates and the route to Elone. Eventually, they realized that if they waited to win this race against each other, they would all die on Earth. So they came together, one last time, and shared their respective knowledge. After all, they could not dismiss millennia of sharing, loving, hating, conflict, cohabitation and coexistence in half a century. One act of cooperation and the human race survived and made it to Elone, albeit as two separate species,' Maya said.

'That epic journey happened thousands of years or zacs ago. Now, on their respective sides of the Fence, men and women live as different species which, in a way, they have become. No one, on either side, remembers or even cares to know about our shared past,' Maya concluded.

'Although it is an interesting story, it has no relevance in our world, Maya. The only thing that has stayed with me from your narrative is that the men are a similar species to us; that we share a common gene sequence!' Iwe declared.

'I agree that the past has no bearing on your way of life on Elone. However, the past is never over in a sense. It might not change in any way how you live or your future, but it does have the ability to impact the way you deal with your present. The thought that the men are the only ones in the whole universe who are similar to you could herald a different way of dealing with those living across the Fence,' Maya's statement reverberated in the silent Vault.

Entirety

When the travelor stopped at the entrance of the imposing Syned building, Patix was engrossed in the latest item on the lex.

Did you know that Nepo reserves are dwindling fast? Yes, Nepo, the basis of our existence. And, where can we find untouched reserves of Nepo? ON THE OTHER SIDE OF THE FENCE! Some would say that we can search the galaxies for a new planet. But I ask you—do we want to wait that long under a cloud of uncertainty? What do you think we should choose?

Radul

Patix disembarked from the travelor and entered the Syned building briskly. On the second floor, at the end of a long corridor, a small discreet room served as the chamber of the Unumo. He punched in a secret code to gain access. The critical Syned meeting was the next day and Patix was angry with Radul for bringing the issue of Nepo out in the open. The decline was supposed to be leveraged at the right moment. Radul was overstepping the mandate given to him. How did Radul even know about the search for another planet?

He thought about removing the entry from the lex altogether but then decided against it as many men would have already seen it.

He started up his workstation and began to review the traffic on the lex. A term thrown up in the outpouring —'Down with the Fence'—had already taken on the proportions of an anthem.

The screen was displaying all the attendees for the forthcoming Syned meeting. Patix scanned it carefully. There were no absentees but there was a new addition.

Ime will be attending as a representative of Odep.

Patix was surprised. When did Ime meet Odep? And why was he representing him? Patix shrugged it off. Odep was anyway on the margins of decision-making and Ime did not matter in the least. There were more important things to consider.

He was positive that the Syned would not need much convincing. The cacophony on the lex had to be addressed. What Patix needed was some time to execute his plan. The Unumo had been working relentlessly these past few calantes gauging the preparedness of the gynake. They were readying for something too and would not be taken by surprise. Patix sat in silence with the machines humming around him. At long last, they were moving towards his vision. The plan that he had been developing for the last dozens of zacs would finally be put into action. The half globe at the Point flashed before him. It was going to become whole soon.

Sitting in the Matsu building at his workstation, Valhan looked out of the window. Although it was early morning, darkness prevailed as the sun was blocked by a thick layer of clouds.

The Syned was meeting in the afternoon. The gloomy, dark morning brought with itself a strange sense of foreboding. Valhan opened the list of attendees at the meeting and noticed the addition of Ime. All the zacs, he had sought out Odep for help and guidance, but at this crucial juncture, Odep had chosen Ime to represent himself. Valhan stared at the list for a while wondering when had he crossed over to the other side and had started ignoring everything that Odep said.

As the machines churned data, Valhan opened the screen and looked for the area around the Fence. Draped with vegetation, the opaque space was calm and serene. Along its path, bushes were blooming with colourful flowers and trees were waiting for the rain. The image on the screen was tranquil and peaceful. Were they doing the right thing by destroying this peace, the calm of zacs? Was there no other way out of this?

As Valhan continued watching the quiet area around the Fence, graphics about the available Nepo reserves and their projected utilization popped up. Nepo would certainly run out unless they found a substitute and that too, fast. Valhan closed the image of the Fence. Sometimes bad choices had to be made for the greater good.

It began to pour outside. Valhan stepped out. In the wet, dark morning, he waited for a travelor to take him to the Syned.

Radul was glad to see the clouds in the morning sky. It meant that the day would not be hot like the past few had been. He dressed with care. He wanted to look like one of them so that they would listen to him. Radul had been working assiduously since he had met Ime. His final move had been to put the issue of Nepo on the lex. The Syned was bound to take a decision with all the noise on the highways echoing loud and clear. It was time to set Patix aside. Radul had made up his mind; he would take over and lead the expansion of Elone.

As Radul ate the usual meal of parina and craw in the common dining space of the group house, the other occupants, instead of lounging about, stood around the table. There was a hushed silence when they saw him in a well-fitting grey shirt with dark blue pants, ready for the meeting. Radul knew these were his last few days as an occupant of the group house. After finishing the meal, he stepped out into the rain, ran after a travelor and jumped in. He brushed off a few raindrops from his head and sat down. It was going to be a long ride to the Syned building.

The Syned building looked like a sulking hulk in the grey rainy afternoon. The lights from within the building were streaming on the falling rain. Inside, a sense of urgency pervaded the building's plush interiors; everyone seemed to be hurrying towards the main chamber.

Radul was also running; he had barely made it. When he walked in, all the members of the Syned were already seated. Ime was sitting next to a vacant spot. Radul smiled at him and sat down. Ime was representing someone called Odep. Radul had checked him out. One of the most important men on Elone, he had dropped out many zacs ago. He knew it was just a matter of time before Ime would be on his side. In the new world, when they ruled all of Elone, he would task Ime with his favourite work—looking for newer worlds. Together, they were going to conquer the universe.

Ime looked around the chamber. He had never entered the Syned before. The luxury and grandeur of the interiors struck him with awe. The silence of his lex was deafening. He did shut it down when he was working, but it still buzzed constantly. However, in the Syned, it was as if the lex did not exist at all. Ime felt out of place, he didn't know anyone. And the one person he did know, Valhan, had acknowledged his presence with a grudging shrug of his shoulders.

A hush fell around the room once everyone had arrived. Everyone sensed this was an important meeting. Durk opened the meeting and then handed over the mantle to Patix since the call for the unscheduled meeting had come from him.

'This is an unforeseen time for Elone. Such times call for drastic decisions and firm action. Let me put the facts before you in the way that they have occurred. As some of you are aware, I also head the Unumo. Sometime back, we, at the Unumo, picked up chatter from the other side about a nex there. It was not of an important gynake, but what they believe to be the cause of the nex is definitely important. They believe it is we who caused that nex through Vish. This is both absurd and impossible since we have decommissioned Vish many zacs ago. As head of the Unumo, I would like to state to the Syned that we had nothing whatsoever to do with the nex we have been accused of,' Patix paused to let his words sink in. 'This perception on their side alarmed us because it meant that they believe that we have committed a hostile act, or more importantly, that they are using this accusation, amongst themselves, to plan something against us. Either way,

I would state clearly that the peace of the Fence is over. It has taken more than hundreds of zacs, but it has finally happened,' Patix stopped. His beady grey eyes darted around the room. All the men were looking at him with rapt attention. A few mouths had fallen open.

'The other matter of utmost importance to be placed before the Syned is that the reserves of Nepo are running out. Data regarding this has been put on the screens before you,' he paused as everyone scanned their screens.

'Now, what does this mean for us? If we do not find alternative reserves, we are heading for extinction,' Patix looked around the room. Since the information about Nepo had already appeared on the lex, it did not have the impact Patix had hoped and planned for.

'What these facts mean for us and what choices we have before us would be explained by Valhan,' Patix said and sat down. Valhan was surprised. He looked towards Patix with a questioning glance. Valhan was not prepared for this role. He did not know any details of Patix's plan. His understanding was that he was supposed to support any proposals made by Patix. But now, by asking him to speak on the choices, the onus of carrying forward the meeting was on Valhan.

Radul was observing the proceedings with great care. Looking at Valhan's expression, he guessed that Valhan was not prepared to address the Syned. Essentially, Patix was working alone. He decided that as soon as Patix unveiled his plan, he would move in. Ime sat straight in his chair wondering what Valhan was going to reveal.

'The more important issue at hand is the declining reserves of Nepo,' began Valhan. 'How do we resolve this issue? There are two alternatives: first would be finding other reserves of

Nepo on our planet or developing a substitute. This first alternative could be considered a short-term plan while we continue to work on the second long-term plan which would be to search for another home in the universe that could support us. Now, the first two alternatives exist right across the Fence. The gynake have large reserves of Nepo because they found a substitute many zacs ago,' Valhan stopped.

The angst and anger of the men that had been appearing on the lex highways seemed to flash on the face of every member in the room. But Valhan was not going to be the first to put this anger into words. An eerie silence descended over the room as everyone waited for the other to say what was going through the minds of most of them. Patix looked towards Radul, his eyes urging him to speak. But Radul remained quiet. Patix decided to fill the silence. He could not let the moment pass.

'The choice is either to wait and see what the gynake do or take action ourselves. This time the end of the conflict must be decisive and we should aim to have Elone to ourselves. When I say this, I am echoing the collective desire that is being expressed repeatedly on the lex highways. We need to decide now.'

He let out a long breath; it was finally out in the open.

All the men around the table looked at each other. Agreeing with a viewpoint on the lex was different than hearing it within the Syned. They all knew that the decision regarding this issue would change their lives immensely. The sense of responsibility had rendered everyone speechless.

Ime felt as if he should say something. Odep would want him to, but he did not know what to say. He looked around and saw the sense of hesitation etched on many faces. He realized that this was the only time when a voice of caution would be heard. Later, it would be too late.

So, he began, 'While deciding on our next course of action we should keep two things in mind. First, it is not going to be easy. Let us not forget that the gynake are a formidable force. It is not as if we decide to overrun the planet and they would just let it happen. Second, think of the planet if we succeed in wiping them out. We would have destroyed the only other species in the whole universe that is similar to us; a species with whom we have a shared past. There has to be another way to solve the problem of the declining Nepo reserves. Can we not consider talking to them? Transform our antagonistic relation into one of collaboration on certain issues. Why are we thinking only of war? Let us not forget that many of us will also be nexed in this process. In fact, both the sides will lose with the way we are planning to approach this issue. It is also not certain that we will be the victorious ones. The future we are imagining could be very different. Before we break an existing equilibrium, we should explore all the choices, other than the most obvious ones.' Ime was earnest in his appeal. His face was flushed, and his red hair was dishevelled from running his fingers through them as he spoke.

He looked around. A look of collective relief seemed to have swept around the table. But it did not mean what he thought it did. Now that another viewpoint had been placed on the table, it was easy to brush it aside. They were waiting for what seemed to be inevitable.

'We haven't had any collaboration with them or any discourse with them for hundreds of zacs. The problem is ours, why would they even think of helping us?' Gebo, one of the older members, said.

'I agree. We have to take a chance,' Durk nudged the discussions forward.

Ime sat back with a deep sense of sadness. It was clear where the Olders of the Syned were headed. His role in this meeting was over.

Patix looked across at Radul with questioning eyes, but Radul merely shook his head. He was waiting for Patix to unveil the plan before he spoke. He would address the Syned on his own terms and not at Patix's bidding.

'So Patix, do we have a plan? How do we ensure that the planet will become only ours?' Valhan had taken the issue to the next level. Despite many attempts, Patix had never revealed his plan to him. Valhan observed that everyone seemed keen to know about the plan. Only Ime sat disappointed and sad.

All heads turned towards Patix. His head was down as he peered at the screen on the table. Patix felt a wave of exhilaration go down his spine. The decision had been agreed to without being voted upon or much discussion. He suddenly realized that Radul's idea of putting matters on the lex for public discourse had helped a lot. He took a deep breath and spelled out in as few words as possible what he had been working on for countless zacs.

'We have thought of a manoeuvre that would ensure that we have no losses. This plan would work despite the fact that the gynake are also working on something. We will use a weapon called Astra. Developed over the last few zacs in utmost secrecy, this scenario will be the first and last time we would have to use it. Airborne carriers will rise to the edge of the atmosphere of Elone and release the Astra which will lead to a billow fall. It will be like a cloud covering all of Elone and would cause rainfall for two whole days. The rain will contain a particle that we call Snap. It would attach itself to anything with the genome of species like the gynake and in a flash, destroy it. When the cloud dissipates and the sun comes out, the Snap particles will vaporize from the surface of land and water. Being lighter than our air, they will escape into space beyond our atmosphere in a day. Basically, they would be gone without a trace. It will not affect our vegetation or crops or water bodies in any manner,' Patix braced himself for a barrage of questions, but was greeted by a deep silence. No one moved a muscle. Everyone sat stunned by the vista being spread out before them. They had never heard of this weapon Astra before. It sounded like a fantasy. It was even frightening to an extent.

Ime remembered the blooming Furawa with all its flowers and plants, the trees on the hills where Odep's house was located. Was what Patix saying true? Would they survive the death fantasy called 'billow fall'? He looked around the room. Did no one comprehend that not only did they share time and space, but they also shared their genome with the gynake? How could this group of talented men not see what was happening? This was a plan to destroy the planet, not claim it. But he could sense no resistance to what was being proposed.

'What about us, Patix? How will we survive the Snap?' Gebo voiced the question that was raging in all their minds.

'I am sure all of you must have realized that the Snap will also attach itself to us because we come from the same genetic stock. Keeping this fact in mind, we will build protective chambers underground stocked with provisions to last us one zac at least. A few days before the proposed launch, all the residents will enter them. Then, after three days, when all the Snap particles would have vaporized, we will emerge and claim our planet. It will be our final ascendance. Believe me, the gynake do not stand a chance. They would be anticipating the Fence to be breached or some other violent attack. An attack of stealth from the space above our atmosphere disguised as innocent rain is not something they would expect. When the crafts would rise, it would appear as a gust of wind. No probe can discern these crafts. It is foolproof, doable, and we have researched and simulated it to perfection.'

A murmur went around the room. It was a huge step and most of them felt inadequate to take such a momentous decision. The Astra and its billow fall were not even in the realm of their imagination.

Valhan was astounded by the revelation. He wondered why Patix had not spent the considerable resources at his disposal on researching for an alternative to Nepo instead. It would have solved all their problems. There would have been no need to plan this endgame conflict. They all would have been saved.

He suddenly remembered Odep. He wished he would have been present. Odep, unlike Ime, would have been heard. In this apprehensive space that the spectre of the Astra had created, Odep would have found takers for his views.

'So, if there is an agreement about using the Astra, I ask for six calantes from the Syned to make all the preparations. We will then come back to the Syned before taking any action,' Patix said, waiting for any voice of dissent. He had decided that if no one raised any questions, he would close the meeting.

'I would like to say something,' Radul spoke. Everyone looked at him.

'Yes, we should hear the views of the new members on this,' someone said. There was a sigh of relief around the room.

Patix glowered at Radul from across the room. He couldn't

understand why he was interfering when matters had almost been decided, just as he had wanted them to be?

However, Radul did not even glance at him. This was his moment. He had listened to every word Patix had uttered, and in a flash, he had identified when he could take over.

'We are forgetting that the gynake are also planning something. I do not think we have six calantes to spare. So, I offer to take the responsibility of preparing the underground chambers in two calantes; of stocking them, preparing the men to go inside and saving all the things we need to. I propose that in the third calante, on the night when the three moons hide, we attack, since it is also the start of the rainy season. Our deception will be perfectly hidden. Furthermore, when we emerge, we should have a plan of action to take over and get the other part of the planet going as soon as possible. In that regard, I offer to form a small group that will move there and get the place up and running. I understand it will need a lot of work. I would present regular progress reports to the Syned,' Radul had seized his moment.

The meeting chamber felt like a time machine. In an instant, Radul had brought the future on the table before them. No one had gone that far, not even Patix. It seemed as if the Fence had already come down and the other half of Elone seemed to beckon. The Astra and its dreadful effects wore off and the men began to look for the rainbow after the dissipation of the billow clouds.

'We can think about all these things next time,' Patix said irritably, in an effort to pull the men back into the present.

'No, Radul is right. I think we can agree to everything that he is proposing. We agree to take action in the third calante from today and the arrangements proposed for the aftermath.

We will meet again only if there is a change in the plan. Do we all agree?' Durk asked.

'Let us meet again in the next vihan and decide on this. These are huge decisions. Let us all think about this a bit,' Valhan said, almost pleading. He felt that matters had escalated too quickly.

Patix remained silent. He could not openly agree with Valhan, but deep down, he did. In the course of the next vihan, he would ensure Radul clearly understood his place in this emerging scenario.

'We don't have the luxury of postponing decisions. Who knows what the gynake are planning? The Syned owes it to the men, who feel threatened and are waiting for some action to be decided upon,' Radul said, playing on the fear of the members who were aware that for some time now, the Syned had been viewed as ineffective.

'What we decide now is not likely to change in a vihan. So, let us agree upon the action proposed by Patix and the time frame suggested by Radul. Is there any opposition?' Durk wanted the meeting to close with some positive action. The men clamouring outside needed to hear that some concrete steps had been decided upon. The future ensures it comes into existence when it looms large on the present. No one spoke.

'So, we agree. The men will be informed that the Syned has decided to take steps to counter any aggression from the gynake. A group consisting of Patix, Valhan, Gebo, Radul and me will monitor the progress,' Durk closed the momentous meeting.

Radul knew that the future belonged to him now. Patix and Valhan had been relegated to the present. He looked across the room—Patix was fuming, Valhan was confused and Ime, dismayed. These men were going to pave the way to the other side of the Fence. But what would be built there and beyond, he would design. The subdued group dispersed. It had stopped raining and the sun was shining on a wet landscape.

'Radul, would you accompany me to the second floor? I need to have a word with you about this whole thing,' Patix's voice had lost that tone of authority.

As they moved towards the discreet office of the Unumo, Patix asked, 'You have taken a lot of responsibility on yourself and you did not even think of discussing this with me. But nothing to worry about, we will work it out together.'

'Patix, I already have a team in mind to take this forward. And I thought since we were working towards the same thing, there was no need to discuss. Is this not what you had wanted since the day we met at the Point? You wanted the men of the Syned to agree on some decisive action and now you have that. Why don't you focus on the plan of action and I will work towards the time after the action. Don't worry, I will keep you briefed,' Radul said.

'All right, Radul. We will see this through.'

They had reached the door to the office and the conversation was already over. Radul had made his intentions perfectly clear to Patix. He simply turned and walked down the corridor. Patix's grey eyes followed his retreating back. There would be time to deal with him.

Radul moved towards the exit. Once outside, he walked briskly towards the travelor stop. He had a lot of work to do. At the stop, he turned around and looked at the Syned building. From a sulking hulk, in the bright sunshine, the grand building had transformed into a glorious symbol of what men aspired to be.

Forgetting their differences, Valhan and Ime left together. At the travelor stop, they looked back at the grand Syned building. It was meant to house the best minds on Elone, to take beneficial decisions for men. But now, both of them had the same question on their mind—was the decision taken that day going to be good for them?

'Let us go to the Aeona, Valhan, and have some enab. It has been a tiring day. It has made me sad. Also, I never did get a chance to tell you that Tai has failed our tests. It cannot be a future home for us. Not that we will need one now.'

Valhan nodded silently and together they took the travelor headed to the Aeona. Now that the action had been decided upon, Valhan did not know if he had been on the right side. Was the upcoming conclusive attack what he wanted? Valhan looked out of the window at the buildings flashing past.

'I still don't understand, Valhan, why we did not consider negotiations or opening a conversation for even a moment? Why is there this urge to destroy and expand? To what end?' asked Ime.

'Maybe it is an instinct that we carry forward from our ancestors. Who knows, Ime? We only know the end that we are aiming for, that is, we want to survive, to remain...to the exclusion of all else.'

For two calantes, Radul travelled extensively to understand and map the contours, the physical landscape and the number of men residing all over Elone. Now, he could recite figures and statistics without even referring to the lex.

From getting the protective chambers built to perfection, to finding the right machines to do the job and meeting the deadline, he realized that he had taken on an enormous task. About two vihans were left till the night when the moons would hide and Radul was ready. The chambers had been constructed. Every site had two interconnected underground rooms; one would house the men, the other provisions. Most of the provisions had already been stored. The entire schedule of the men going into the chambers had been worked out. The retreat would start nearly four days before the appointed day. That would ensure that the descent took place without chaos and confusion.

The construction had been carried out in a routine manner. When men saw the machines at work around them, they did not seem concerned. It was decided that men would be asked to retreat into the chambers right before the planned day. They would be told that these were routine security measures as there were some suspicions regarding an attack from the gynake. The plan of the retreat and the billow fall was kept entirely outside the lex highways. It was made absolutely clear that their plan was not to be picked up by the other side under any circumstances. The preparations were finally complete and Radul was sure he had not missed anything.

Often the audacity of the plan would keep Radul up at night. One mistake or miscalculation and they could be annihilated along with the gynake. Patix and he had met frequently to discuss the preparations for their attack. Nothing about the future was ever spoken about. That was a different battle for another day and both men knew it.

But Radul had not forgotten the task that lay ahead. All

his energies were spent on working out, in detail, the steps that needed to be taken when they emerged on the fourth day. As per the plan, on the third day, after the rain would stop, the Fence would be blown up by a nano-electric surge. When they would ascend to ground level again, the way to the future would be wide open.

Radul had decided that he would move to the other side with his team and set up a base there. From the unknown part of Elone, he would shape a new existence for men.

I would like you to be a part of the future group. I want you to identify someone who can help you in all the tasks that await us, from understanding the systems to exploring new terrains.

When the message from Radul popped up on Ime's lex, he felt a strange tug at his insides. Ime was sitting in the Aeona trying to lose himself in the cosmos that was visible through the telescope. The meticulous manner in which the destruction of the gynake was being planned was unreal and unbelievable. The inevitability of it and the sense of ruthlessness accompanying it were incredible.

Ime had withdrawn completely from the activities that had begun since the fateful Syned meeting. He had even tried to ignore the digging and construction taking place some distance from his home. He had stopped looking for alternative homes in the universe though.

Ime read the message again. He looked out desultorily at the distant vision of stars and planets in the morning light. Increasingly, Ime had begun to understand Odep's quest. The fear of loss leads to the realization of the importance of what exists. Ime had never thought or bothered about the gynake, but their imminent destruction made him think about them all the time. He wondered about their world, how they lived and what they imagined about their future.

He had informed Odep about the decisions of the Syned. He had only received the acknowledgement of receipt and nothing ever since. Ime had also not tried to reach him, or even Valhan. Instead, he had closeted himself in the Aeona. He was mourning the passing of life as he knew it although he did not know it to be so.

The more the message replayed in his head, the more convinced Ime became that he wanted no part in what was waiting to unfold. Before he conveyed his response to Radul, Ime decided to send the message to Valhan. It was disheartening to know that even now, Valhan did not know which side he was on. He oscillated in between, dismayed at times and at other times, looking forward, albeit with some trepidation, to the new world that was threatening to be born. Not on some faraway planet, but on their own.

Valhan was on his way to Odep's home when he read the message. Along the way, from the travelor, he had seen many signs indicating the route to the nearest protective chamber. He couldn't believe only one vihan was left. All the preparations were already complete. There was no going back, no changing of minds. It was a certainty now. Valhan had accepted this reality a while ago and had decided to visit Odep. He would convince Odep to retreat with him into a chamber. He knew that Odep would decide to stay outside and he was not going to let that happen.

The old order was going to change. The rumblings had

already begun. The takeover of the whole of Elone was just the first step. Next, they would build a world that was distinct from the already established paradigms. He realized that once the known and common enemy was vanquished, the lurking ones that might emerge could be more devastating. At that time, they would need men like Odep who would help create a world which would be acceptable to all.

Valhan thought of Radul's message to Ime. It was not to be ignored. Even Radul knew that Ime did not support their plan, but still he had reached out to him. Valhan sent the message to Patix. He would know what to do. After all, Patix had drafted Radul into the Syned. It was a different matter that somewhere along the way, Radul had managed to wrench the leadership from Patix. He knew that their skirmish would be out in the open, once the future arrived.

The Astra was ready to be launched. The airborne carriers were loaded, ready for take-off. Two days were left for the actual action to take place. Patix had spent the last two calantes perfecting the launch of the Astra. Discussions on the launch were only verbal and face-to-face, so that the other side would not get even a whisper of it on the information highways.

All along, as things moved ahead according to plan, Patix considered how he would oust Radul from the decision-making process once they had occupied the other side. There was no way that upstart from a group house, whom he had given a chance, could relegate him into the background.

When Patix saw Radul's message, he saw an opportunity. This was their chance to enter the new structure and get a lead on the substitution material used by the gynake. It should not to be missed. Since there was no time to meet Ime, he sent him a message.

Accept it. We need people like you. Think what could happen if all the information that is revealed falls into the wrong hands. I hope you know what I mean. You have got the chance to play an important role. Agree to the proposal.

The day, when the three moons were going to hide, dawned bright and clear. The sun was shining and a cool breeze was blowing. But their side of Elone was empty and desolate. The cities were deserted; no one was in the streets or in the buildings to see the glorious day. No travelors criss-crossed the landscape. All was silent and still. The sun moved on its eternal ride, crossed the sky and dipped into the horizon. Night came, and an eerie, deathly silence continued to envelop half of Elone in its tight grip.

Below the surface, in the protective chambers, the men huddled, waiting. Some were scared; others felt it was a false alarm since nothing seemed to be happening. The day had seemed long and endless. At nightfall, a hush fell over most of the chambers.

As the night deepened, some men thought they heard airborne crafts rise high above the atmosphere. They felt the release of the Astra and imagined billowing clouds. Then, through the sound sensors that had been installed on the ground, they finally heard the pattering rain. For the next three days, they waited for the rain to stop and their final ascent to begin.

Farewell

Clouds had taken over the skies and were threatening to pour. Ultur was standing near the Fence at the spot where Seeni had been taken. The rain started with a few drops, but soon, turned into a downpour. Ultur walked briskly towards a building across the street and stepped under its awning. It was early morning, and life had still not stirred on the streets. In the grey of the pouring sky, the long empty street looked forlorn and lonely.

Ultur wondered about the men across the Fence. What a long and tumultuous journey it had been with and against them. Ultur, too, had processed Maya's story. They had shared so much with them and fought with them for so much more. It was a trajectory of loss for both the sides. Across the rain-drenched street, the area the Fence occupied looked like a shroud. Even though she tried as hard as she could, she still felt no connect with the men on the other side. She had seen the characters of the past play out their drama; she could even understand what had happened, but, at the end, it had happened to someone else. For her, the narrative of life on Earth was in effect only a story. The feelings and emotions that had defined life on Earth did not resonate in their world. The conflict with the men, the fight with them for territory and resources were familiar and comprehensible. Those men and women on Earth, who had travelled to this planet—they were akin to fictional characters. Once the story finished, they ceased to have meaning.

The men behind the Fence—they had been fighting them across galaxies and planets, and space and time. But, it had to end sometime. The peace that the Fence had enforced was merely a pause in that long-standing conflict. This was the reality of their lives and Ultur understood it clearly. Seeni—her beautiful and talented creation—had been the first casualty of the latest clash.

The rain had stopped. Ultur stepped out from under the protective cover and began to walk back to her apartment. Raindrops still fell from the edges of the buildings, causing her to walk quickly. Ultur rode up to the walkway to cross the city through one of its skywalks. From high up in the sky, nearly at the same level as the rooftops of the tall buildings, she looked down. The streets below had begun to bustle. Shuttles criss-crossed the streets, pedestrians walked briskly, as a new day dawned.

She realized that all this was going to change. A clash was coming and they needed to prepare for it. It was time to set aside her grief over Seeni and start thinking about what was going to happen to them. Ultur straightened her back and resolutely resumed her walk. The days of questions and wondering were over. Reality had dawned, crystal clear.

Iwe and Tioni had come to the same rooftop café where Tioni

and Seeni had met a long time ago. It was their first meeting after the completion of Maya's story. Iwe watched Tioni as she was constantly on her tag, monitoring what was happening to Tara. Iwe wondered why Tioni never voiced her irritation over the burden of bringing up Tara. It seemed quite a tiresome job.

'Tioni, don't you get tired of caring for Tara?'

Tioni sighed, 'Oh, I do, Iwe. But, that is part of the protocol one agrees to before the right to a creation is granted. Sometimes I feel so exhausted but there are also times when her presence relaxes me. I like the sound of her cackles and her laughter,' she smiled.

Both of them sat together in silence for a while.

'Iwe, do you think about what Maya told us? It plays quite unendingly in my mind, although I try to banish it. I realize that the past has no place in our lives.'

Iwe looked down through the railing next to their table. Lights were clearly visible in the streets below. In the distance, when she looked up, the three moons were beginning their evening ride of the sky.

She had replayed the story many times over. She understood a lot of it, but mostly it still seemed like a fantasy.

'Tioni, I shared Maya's story with Ultur since she had put me on to the quest for Maya. I felt that she needed to know even though finding Maya did not solve the problem of Seeni's taking.'

Seeni flashed before Tioni's eyes… elegant and beautiful with her inquisitive mind. The thread of Seeni's message had revealed a story with such an intricate tapestry and a tremendous impact.

'You still believe that the men had something to do with Seeni? Maybe we do not want to accept that it could have been a mishap, Iwe.'

'Tioni, after all that we know, we cannot disregard any doubt or suspicion with regard to men. You seem to be influenced by the story of Maya and Aryan. You have to remember that in our world, no such interaction has ever existed. That is fiction, Tioni, something that may or may not be true. Who knows how much of the memory of a consciousness on a machine is real and how much is manufactured.'

Tioni sipped the sparkling wine placed before her by a tobok. She didn't agree with Iwe completely. The dynamics between the two species, how creations had happened, the depth of emotion that came through between Maya and Aryan—it all had been real at some time. The story of their shared past and subsequent divergence explained their current existence.

'I agree, Iwe. I am influenced. It must have been an interesting interplay to have. We have nothing close to it in our lives anymore. Maya was right. No one matters to us other than "oneself". Maybe, as she says, we do live and exist like islands and aspire to remain for eternity. Our existence is so different from what our ancestors had on Earth,' Tioni sighed.

'That is exactly my point, Tioni. That was a different time, a different space, with its own challenges. We are in a different time and space. We have our own ways of living, defined by what our world offers us. Our relationship with those creatures on the other side is one of open competition and conflict. We have no mutual dependencies. So, there is no simmering power play like the one that went on for countless zacs on Earth. Those men and women Maya talks about are extinct. We are the new species on a new planet with our own dynamics.'

'But Iwe, it was the efforts of the women and men on Earth

towards life extension that led to our replacement technology. It was their discovery of cloning that gave us the ability to create. At least we should appreciate that,' Tioni said.

The links to Earth were manifold and varied; Elone had grown from the roots that had begun on that extinct planet. However, Tioni agreed with what Iwe was saying. The story of the past was to be known and understood, but it had no role in the present, or in the future, for that matter. Dwelling on the past would cloud their thinking and interfere with their present.

Iwe finished her drink. What had happened between men and women in another galaxy in some nebulous distant past had no relevance. What they had done was for their survival. What they on Elone, needed to do now was for theirs.

'Let us put Maya's story behind us, Tioni. It answered many questions, which was a benefit. Now we need to see what is happening around us. Ultur tells me the Council is going to meet soon to decide our response and course of action. It will be an important meeting. It seems we are heading for some uncertain times.'

The shuttle was winding through the thickly wooded high mountain ranges. Promly was sitting by the window, watching the sunlight playing hide-and-seek in the trees. Music was playing through the tag. Promly often listened to the piece sent by Seeni. The music was indeed superlative. It amazed her that the Enodus had still not found Maya—that elusive musician. The system was not able to trace that intruder, despite extensive efforts. Soon, it would not matter. Promly knew that.

Elone was beautiful. Ever since Promly had moved to the countryside she had become an avid appreciator of the natural grace of the planet. The high mountain ranges that the shuttle was passing through were majestic. Some of the tall trees had a magical fluff of white flowers. It seemed like specks of snow clung to the green trees even in the warm weather. Whenever she saw the glory of Elone, Promly wondered if she was taking the correct course. It had been a lonely road. She had traversed it alone, thinking that at an appropriate time she would involve Ultur. The shuttle raced across the range and began its descent into the valley. If Seeni had not been taken…maybe Ultur would have been with her on this journey.

She processed Clepo's message again.

It is important to review the progress at the site. I am waiting for you. Do come.

Promly had dropped everything and had proceeded to the site. The shuttle was descending rapidly. The valley between the mountains had a large river flowing through it. All along the banks of the swirling river, flowers of various hues were blooming. In the distance, on the opposite side of the valley, habitations dotted the slopes of the mountains. It was picturesque. The music added to the serenity of her journey.

When the shuttle reached her destination, Promly disembarked. She saw the unassuming building that looked more like a lodge. The building had three levels. Behind it, grew a thick forest, providing a lush setting to the drab structure. A shiver of anticipation went down Promly's spine. She had come here at the start of the last zac when the plan was in mid-course. Now, it was on the verge of culmination. Promly stood rooted to the spot where the shuttle had dropped her;

the unmarked building across the road waited for her.

The journey to this destination had begun when Promly had taken over the Enodus. While she was familiarizing herself with the new work assigned to her, she had processed tomes of information and data housed in the unit. Poring over all the facts she had never known about earlier, Promly had realized that the Fence was not a solution; it was a mere barrier that bought them time before the occurrence of the inevitable. The prevailing peace was akin to a long lull, a pause. An endgame confrontation was still waiting to happen. During this long break, both the sides had regrouped and evolved technologically by leaps and bounds. Over the last few zacs, Promly had weighed the options. Gradually, as events had unfolded, she had finalized a plan and pursued it relentlessly.

The cool breeze of the mountain ranges ruffled Promly's ash hair, caressed her cheeks and whispered in her ears. She reached the door and looked into a small device on the left-hand corner. The door swung open and Promly walked briskly into a room at the end of the corridor. Before she could reach the room, the door opened and Clepo stepped out.

'Good to see you, Promly. How was the journey?' Clepo's straight hair swung around the sides of her head as she anxiously followed Promly into the room.

Promly sank into a luxurious sofa in the large room. There was a solitary workstation in a corner and a large table surrounded by chairs stood in the centre.

'This certainly doesn't look like the control centre of the operation, Clepo. Things have changed around here.'

'The mainframe and controls have been shifted to the second floor. This room has been kept for any unannounced visitor or passer-by,' Clepo was standing awkwardly in the centre of the room.

'Sit down, Clepo. So tell me, why did you call me?'

'Promly, your journey to reach here must have been a long one. Why don't you eat something and then I will take you around.'

Clepo was out of the door as soon as Promly nodded her assent.

Promly stood up and went to the window that opened on to the back of the building. Outside, the trees were glistening green over a sprawling, thick patch of wood that stretched towards the mountains. Clepo came in with a tray and placed it on the desk. Promly began to eat the asipo and rice.

'When is the Council meeting, Promly? Are we taking it before the Council this time? If we go by what we have picked up from the men's side, we don't have much time,' Clepo said.

'I will decide that after today's visit. How many from the unit are deployed here?'

'There are only two more women. Between the three of us, we are managing well.'

Clepo watched as Promly ate briskly. They had been working very hard these last two zacs. She could not think of a better plan than what Promly had suggested to face their future. Promly finished eating. She ran her hand over her head to smoothen her dishevelled hair. Clepo noticed that they had grown and needed to be trimmed.

'Let's go. First, I want to know what has come in from the other side over the last vihan. After that, I will assess our preparations.'

They stepped out of the room and took the elevator to the second floor. Clepo swiped her thumb, pressed the security codes and then the door of the elevator slid open.

It was a different world. The mainframe and controls were placed on the right side of the room and were bathed in a violet light. On the left, there was a row of workstations. Five toboks were busy at the machines. Clepo walked to one of the workstations and it flickered to life. Both of them sat before the screen and processed the data coming in. By the time all the data had been sifted through, evening had fallen.

Promly leaned back in her chair, 'They had an important meeting last vihan. Something big is going to happen after two calantes. That is for certain. As you said, the window available seems to be closing down.'

Clepo nodded her head in agreement and continued to work to get some additional precise details. Promly looked around the room. Their future was locked in the innards of these machines. It seemed that the time to unlock it had arrived. By setting the deadline, the men were in a way pushing her to take action.

'It is not clear what will happen after two calantes. The chatter we picked up goes quiet after the meeting. Some talk of rain and clouds is all we are getting. What could this mean, Promly?'

Promly stood up and walked towards the machines. 'This means that we have to take it to the Council now. Are we prepared to launch? And how much time will it take? Walk me through the progress.'

They went back to the workstations and pored over the plan. Outside, night fell, turning the mountains into menacing edifices. The sky was littered with stars and the habitations, seen in the distance, twinkled with lights. It was just another quiet and peaceful night in the mountains of Elone which seemed to envelop the building with serenity, belying the storm brewing within.

Where was Promly? Ultur had been tagging her consistently for the last three days, since her visit to the Fence. Promly's tag had been switched off. She was neither in the city nor at the farm. There was no way to reach out to her. Promly was becoming rather adept at doing this. Ultur got up restlessly and walked into the outer room. The colours that were splashed around the room seemed to taunt her for giving up on Seeni. But Ultur had not forgotten Seeni. She had only put her aside for the moment.

Ultur went and sat on the chair near the window and looked out. It was early evening. From the height of her apartment window, she could clearly see the deserted street below. Once the evening deepened, activity would increase. The sky was clear except for a few tufts of clouds wandering across.

Ultur remembered that Maya's story had mentioned other species like birds and animals. Ultur wondered what they looked like. They had no image or memory of any other species on Elone. There were only two of them—the men and the women. When they had arrived no living thing had been found on this bounteous planet. What inhabited it were the wanderers from Earth. Why had the people on Earth destroyed all the other species? Would Elone have been different if there had been other living things? Would they have added colours, movement and sounds to their life? The story of Earth seemed to be one of slow and inexorable loss.

Ultur shook herself. Dwelling on Maya's story was not the need of the hour. It was their future that was being threatened. Ultur knew it was time to bury all misgivings about Promly and work together like they had done for countless zacs. Both of them had faced many challenges and had found solutions along the way. And now, it was time to do so again.

If a clash happened, Ultur wondered how it might play out. Would it happen on the ground, in the air, across both, or would there be stealth involved? What would remain after the clash? Or rather who would remain? How many? Were they heading for a time like the last days on Earth? Would Elone become a dead planet incapable of supporting life? The questions swirling around in her mind were endless.

Ultur felt exhausted. Their lives on Elone were demarcated by the clashes with the men. Tranquil phases intervened, some long, some short, but the defining moments had always been the clashes. This pattern had to change; this time it had to be a fight to the finish. The planet could belong to only one of them.

Her life floated past as Ultur sat by the window, waiting for Promly to return to the system. What was sharply etched in her memory was the time after Seeni had come. The long journey that lay behind her was like a coil that wound endlessly. And now, a long endless road stood ahead…unless the forthcoming clash changed it. Ultur tried to suppress the sense of relief the thought gave her. Why did this thought about an end crop up surreptitiously in her mind at regular intervals?

On the screen, Promly appeared on the encrypted channel. Ultur hurriedly activated it and said, 'Where have you been, Promly? We need to plan many things before the Council meeting next calante.'

'I was busy with some important work. First, Ultur, the Council meeting has to take place next vihan, and not next calante. Second, let us meet at the Irana Hub tomorrow. I am glad you have got out of your grieving phase. A lot has to be done, Ultur. Our future awaits us.'

The yellowish walls of the Council building were glistening in the morning sun as Ultur made her way towards it. She reached the dark doors which swung open as she swiped her tag. A quiet sense of calm permeated the corridors. The door of the main room, where the Council usually met, was open. When Ultur entered, not many members had come. The high, transparent roof flooded the meeting room with sunlight.

Ultur sat at her designated position. The table in front of her was flashing the agenda for today's discussion. It was concise—urgent meeting. Discussions only. Crati, the current head of the Council, walked in. Seeing Ultur, she came and sat down next to her.

'What is the urgency, Ultur? Why are we meeting one calante ahead of schedule?'

'Promly wants to bring something urgent to our attention,' Ultur replied. The look of pinched sadness that had shrouded Ultur's countenance since Seeni's taking had dissipated. She was looking more at ease.

'Is it something about what happened to Seeni?'

'No, Crati. Not yet. There are, I guess, more important things that Promly wants to discuss.'

As Ultur was speaking, most of the other members walked

in. They all sat down, waiting for Promly. Crati took her chair, in readiness to start the moment Promly arrived. A hush hung around the room. Some were looking at the skylight, others at the designs that adorned the walls. There was a mix of anticipation, anxiety and curiosity in the air as they all waited for the meeting to start.

Promly entered the room on the dot. She was smartly attired for the meeting in a black tunic and black trousers. Her ash hair neatly framed her face. She came and sat at her appointed place. Only one chair was still empty.

'Who is missing, Crati?' Promly asked.

'Tuela. She has asked to be excused as she is away at a Remplazo.'

Everyone looked at Promly for consent. It was clear that she was the nominal head of the meeting.

'All right. This is a closed meeting so all tags will be off. Crati, should we begin?' Promly asked.

Once Crati nodded, Promly was ready to speak but was cut off by Ultur.

'Before you begin, Promly, I would like to know if there is any information about what happened to Seeni.' Surprised, Promly looked at Ultur, but Ultur was determinedly looking at the screen in front of her. When they had met at the Irana Hub prior to the meeting, Ultur had listened calmly. She had asked many questions, but none about Seeni which had relieved Promly. She could not understand the logic behind Ultur's sudden question now. Ultur kept looking at the screen even though the display had been shut. The meeting was indeed closed in every sense. Ultur knew Promly did not expect this question at this juncture. But she had to know. The others kept silent and waited.

'I am sorry, Ultur. We have no clear answer yet as to why Seeni was taken. What we do know is that it was Vish and that it came from the other side. Whatever I am bringing before the Council has actually been precipitated by what happened to Seeni.'

Promly looked around. Everyone seemed convinced by this response. Ultur was now looking directly at her; but she slowly moved her gaze away. It was clear to both in that instant that Seeni was still hovering between them.

'Promly, you may now begin with why you have called us so urgently,' Crati wanted the meeting to move forward. Promly looked around the room. They were all looking at her impatiently. She took a deep breath and began.

'This meeting is not about us alone. It is also about those on the other side of the Fence, the men. I think for long we have ignored their existence, lived as if we were alone on this planet. The peace of the last hundreds of zacs has lulled us into thinking that this is how it is going to be. But that is incorrect. It is a completely false notion.'

She looked around at the confused faces and continued, 'If I were to give you two alternative futures, which one would you choose? In one future, we live with a Fence between us and the men. We clash with them at intermittent intervals and then have peace for some time. In the other proposed future, there is only us. There are no men, no Fence, no clashes…ever.'

Promly paused once more and let her words sink in. Suddenly, the silence was broken and the responses began to fly around the room like a torrent. It was difficult to track who was saying what.

'What is wrong with the way things are? We haven't clashed for so long. Why do you think we will now?'

'Promly, you were always a combative person. Do not bring your own desires into our lives.'

'Well, I would go for the second alternative. It would be a great relief not to have to bother about the men.'

'I don't want a clash, now or ever. Let things be.'

'Are you trying to say we should plan to simply annihilate the men? Wipe them off the face of the planet?'

'No men, no Fence, the planet all to ourselves? Sounds really good to me!'

Promly let everyone have their say. It was important. She knew the debate could be led to the designated conclusion only if everyone felt that they had spoken and been heard. When the storm had blown over and a hush had descended on the room, Promly spoke again.

'Will it help you choose if I were to tell you that as we sit debating in this room about what our desirable future should be, the men have already made a decision? They are, at this moment, working towards a plan that will ensure that the planet is theirs.'

The silence in the room deepened. Then, Crati asked, 'If what you are saying is true, Promly, why have they suddenly decided this? I agree that we have lived a conflict-ridden existence with the men since our arrival here. We have clashed and fought bitterly, but the battle has always receded.'

'Yes, it has, Crati. This decision has come because their reserves of Nepo are dwindling. And, unlike us, they still depend on Nepo for replacements. Since we stopped using it many zacs ago, in favour of Amar, our side has large reserves of Nepo; and that is what they want. You can ask Ultur. I have shown the data we have scrambled from the other side to her,' Promly stopped. As she had expected, everyone looked towards Ultur. As the oldest member, she carried authority and credence.

Ultur spoke slowly, 'It is a battle for survival now. The men need this part of Elone to continue to exist. We all know that both sides would do anything for that. If we had not found Amar and had faced a similar situation, we would have gone the same way. So, let me put it clearly before the council. We are staring at a clash that will be aimed at owning the planet at any cost.'

Ultur was clear and concise.

'Why don't we share with them the discovery of Amar? Then, there would be no clash and we could all continue to live as we have been living.'

'What do we do? In a clash, a lot of us would also be taken.'

'Are you trying to frighten us into agreeing to something?'

'How do we plan to annihilate the men? We have not done any weapon development in so many zacs.'

The questions and accusations were once again hurtling around the room; the temperature was rising despite the cool interiors.

Promly had to stand up to get them to stop.

'There is a plan that I want you to consider. But first, let us look back at our existence on Elone for so many zacs. We have had two clashes with the men. In each, both the sides lost heavily. After a clash, it was like starting all over again. Since the Fence came up, we have lived peacefully and our development has been fast-paced. We discovered Amar, made breakthroughs in technology and did not need to waste resources on weapons. In effect, when there were no men on the horizon, we prospered. So, according to me, for us women, as a species, doing away with the men is the best option. Now, coming to your suggestion of sharing Amar with them. Have the men ever shared any resource, any new invention with us? No. Then, why should we share Amar with them? They will take the knowledge and use it against us in the future. Don't forget, like us, they have used this time to develop and regroup too. We have no clear idea as to what their weapons are or what they want in their future. What we do know is that, at the moment, their existence is in peril and the solution to that is on our side of Elone.'

Promly stopped and a murmur went around as the group whispered among themselves. As Promly observed the reactions of the group, she began to feel confident that her plan would be accepted. Fear of the unknown combined with the feeling that they were going to be targeted because of some mineral hiding below the ground would swing the decision in her favour.

A cloud passed over the skylight and the room darkened for a while, but soon, the sun shone again and bathed the room in its glorious light. This play of light and shadows seemed to reflect the mindset of the agitated members.

'So, what do you suggest we should do? Suppose, for a moment, that we want to consider the second future? What then?' Tabi, who normally never spoke up, asked.

'I have a plan if we want our future to be devoid of men. It may sound implausible and fantastic, but let me assure you, it is achievable.'

Promly wanted to reassure them before revealing the plan she had been working on for so many zacs.

'Have you developed some weapon in secret that would annihilate them? They are a formidable force, don't forget,' Crati spoke at last. She was heading the Council and was firm that no absurd or fanciful idea was going to be accepted.

Promly took a deep breath, and running her fingers through her hair, she started, 'We have been on Elone for thousands of zacs now. It is a beautiful planet. We have exploited its resources, lived off its bounty and existed here amidst plenty. But we must remember that we are, in essence, travellers. We came here from Earth, a species seeking refuge and survival. Think for a moment, maybe it is time to leave once more. And this time, we will go alone to a new planet that would entirely be ours.'

Promly paused. There was a sigh of relief around the room because the new plan did not entail a battle. Slowly, the members seemed to be enthralled with this new idea. After a long gap, something new and unheard of was being contemplated.

As the mood in the room began to transform, Promly continued. She wanted to spell out everything before the questions began.

'We have the spaceships ready. The route has been mapped. We have been working for the last ten zacs on this project. The list of all the residents of Elone has been drawn up. All the equipment, knowledge and materials that we need to take with us have been identified and marked. Specimens of trees, plants, flowers and of course, Amar, have been collected. As per our calculations, we would need three spaceships which are already ready and waiting.'

Suddenly, the room was transformed into a bubble that was floating in the future. The idea Promly had thrown at the group had them transfixed; many of the members were envisioning a journey that seemed to begin in the room itself. No one spoke and there was complete silence, everyone was lost in their own thoughts.

'Can you show us the spaceships?' Gela, one of the younger members of the Council, broke the silence. Promly clicked on the table, the skylight shut down and the lights dimmed. In the middle of the room, a multidimensional image of the building in the mountain ranges that Promly had recently visited began to float. The focus shifted to the woods behind the building. The forest parted and three huge spaceships came into view. The multilayered oblong structures in the soothing shade of blue, mirroring the colour of the sky, looked like some imaginary creatures. The three gigantic, gleaming carriers perched on the ground held a promise that seemed real and achievable. Slowly, the forest came down like a curtain again.

'The woods are an illusion we have created so that nothing can pick up the view of the spaceships. We need about three calantes to prepare for embarkation and then we can leave,' Promly said as the vision dissolved and the lights came on. The skylight remained covered.

'But where are we going to go, Promly?' This was again Crati. The importance of this meeting was slowly dawning on her.

'Ten zacs ago, the space mission cell of the Enodus came across a planet that seemed habitable. It is in another galaxy very far from ours. We have investigated and researched it. We even sent a small probe to pick up data, soil samples and atmospheric variables. Two zacs ago, we were able to confirm that it can indeed support life. We have it mapped down to its last crevice and river. We know where we will land and where we can put up our first camp. From there, we will spread out. We are headed there…to start a new life, a new world. Let me present to you, our new destination.'

The lights dimmed again and the image of a planet began to twirl in the centre of the room. It had a bluish tinge and from the topography, it was clear that there was land, water and lots of vegetation.

As their future revolved in front of them slowly, Promly said, 'This planet has a big sun, only one moon and the time it takes to revolve around its sun is shorter than our zac. This journey will be longer than the one from Earth to Elone, as the planet is further away, in another galaxy. But at the end of that journey, a new world awaits us.

'I know this is not an easy choice, but right now, for us, it is the best one available. We have always been resourceful and creative. The time has come for us to finally shed the baggage we carried from Earth, that is, the men. Let us move on and go to our own world, our own place in the universe. Why is it better than trying to vanquish them in a clash? Because in a clash, we lose many of our own. Also, there is a chance that some of them would survive. We would be picking up the pieces, rebuilding our lives and then, after some zacs, another clash would be knocking at our doorsteps. This journey that I am proposing would be our final ascendance to our own home, our own place in the sun.'

The skylight opened and in the bright sunlight, the image of the mesmerizing planet wilted away. They all looked at each other. It was a momentous decision. In the familiar sunshine, each one began to think of their life on Elone. Of all the small and big things they liked about it. Could they just leave it all and move away to an unknown planet and start all over again?

As the silent musings continued, Promly waited. She looked towards Ultur. Ultur knew the best time to influence a decision was when views had not evolved firmly.

'Do we agree to Promly's plan? I have thought about it. Let me assure you that we are not leaving because we cannot fight the men or vanquish them. We are choosing to move on. We have nothing that ties us to those creatures on the other side of the Fence but conflict. Let us leave them behind and build our own world. The men are planning to attack us soon. It is clear. Let us break this cycle, once and for all.'

Ultur threw her weight behind Promly's proposal. They both waited for the group to respond. Reluctantly, but slowly, they began to get nods and agreements.

'What do we tell the women outside? Where are we going? Does this new home have a name?' Gela asked.

They all looked towards Ultur. This christening had to be done by the most respected resident. Ultur thought for a while and then, she smiled. In a long while, no one had seen her smile.

'We are going to Earth. That is what we will call our new home. That is where it all began, so it is logical that is where we should end up. The original Earth spawned us and disintegrated. We will now build a new Earth.'

The processors at the Vault were working non-stop. It was not easy to compress all the information into the formats specified. All of them were busy packing, compressing, fitting data and information into smaller units. Iwe had been working continuously. It had been more than a calante since the Council had decided that they would move to another planet, to Earth. To Iwe, it seemed like an absurd plan, but the immediate directions had been precise and clear.

It was a clear day. Iwe stopped what she was doing and went to the window. All that was familiar was being left behind and that too in such a hurry. Two calantes more and they would be on their epic journey. The trees across the road, the Vayunum on the corner…everything was going to remain here; only they were going away.

At the beginning of the last calante, they had all been asked to be physically present at specific locations near their homes and had been informed of the directive. Iwe had listened silently but she could not believe it. The details had been fleshed out and they were warned not to put anything about the planned journey on the tag. And suddenly, this incredulous plan had become real. At intervals, they were called to the same locations and instructions were given verbally.

Iwe sighed as she thought about it. They were going away and leaving the planet for the men. Rather than fighting them, it had been decided to abandon them. The more she thought about it, the more Iwe resented the idea. It felt like they were running away and leaving everything known and familiar for an unseen place. They would have to start from scratch and create everything—the buildings, the roads, the systems—everything. It was an unimaginable displacement…all in a matter of three calantes.

Another thing she couldn't fathom was the name—Earth! Why had they named the new planet Earth? None of them had been given a choice. All the women were leaving; it was decided and final. A new world awaited them.

Complying with the meticulous instructions kept them busy. Soon, like all the others, Iwe was involved with what had to be done to make the exit successful. It left no space or time to think of all that was being left behind. Earth—preparing to go there had become the all-consuming activity.

As the calante had passed, and she had almost wound up things at the Vault, Iwe had accepted the move. She wanted to finish with the Vault by the end of the next vihan. After which, she would look at her personal things. In the last meeting, they had been told that only one item of personal baggage was to be carried.

Tioni, Tara and she had decided to travel to the mountains next calante when the rainy season would begin with the hiding of the three moons. It was sort of like a farewell to Elone. By then, Iwe would be done with all the preparations.

The night before the launch, the system that connected their world, the processers, the tags and the workstations, would be destroyed. The men, as and when they would come to this side, would be greeted by an empty shell.

It was a strange feeling. As the prospect of the journey became inevitable, Elone began receding. Everything was evaluated for its need or importance on the new Earth. In a way, in their minds, they had already reached Earth.

As Iwe thought of Earth, she suddenly remembered Maya. If the system was destroyed, what would happen to Maya? They needed to tell her about the impending departure. Should they ask Maya to come along? Iwe tagged Tioni.

Do we ask Maya to join us?

While Iwe was working furiously, Tioni too had been busy. Replacement technology and equipment had to be transported. The idea of leaving for a planet that would belong exclusively to them excited Tioni. For her, the best part of this plan was that there would be no clashes with the men, so there would be no losses, no pain and no rebuilding of Elone periodically. On Earth, they would research newer ways of extending life without the constant fear of men getting their hands on it. They would go in for creations, build a new life and a new world.

Tara was busy with Hap in the other room; Tioni could hear the sounds of her chuckles. She went and stood near the door. Tara was jumping on the bed while Hap was standing attentively nearby. Tara would grow in a world that would be free of the shadows of conflict and unnecessary competition. The future creations would inhabit a world that was entirely their own. Tioni suddenly thought about Ria and all those women who had fought, planned and brought themselves to Elone. In a way, this space ride to the new Earth was a culmination of the journey that had begun on the original Earth.

Tioni moved back to her workstation when Iwe's message about Maya came in.

Maya—what would they do about her? Let her be destroyed in the system or ask her if she would like to accompany them? They could try and reach out to her to ask.

There was not much she wanted to take. All the colours and dimensions added to her home by Seeni were going to be left behind, except for a tapestry of myriad colours that had been Seeni's favourite. Ultur stood in the middle of a room that did not seem like the theatre of an iconic departure, and wondered if she really wanted to go. The question had been chasing her. She had continued to prepare, pack and obey all the instructions, but somehow, she had never felt that she would actually leave Elone. She felt a strange reluctance and fatigue at the thought of the long journey and the longer period of uncertainty ahead. Did she want to be a part of building a new world and all the accompanying tensions? Setting up a new life in an unknown terrain was a huge challenge. There would be hits and misses, losses and gains, before slowly, over time, they would settle down.

In the last calante, Ultur had walked to the spot near the Fence innumerable times. She had travelled to all the places Seeni and she had enjoyed going to such as the sea, the hills and the gardens. She had visited the Irana Hub and the Nividum where Seeni had worked. Sometimes, Ultur wondered if it was the pang of leaving the place that had memories of Seeni or the planet itself that pulled her back.

In the night, when she lay awake and heard the silence of Elone, she wondered whether the air on the new Earth would be as crisp, if the skies would be as blue and the flowers as charming.

Ultur was taking down the tapestry that she wanted to pack when the door of her apartment swung open. Seeni used to walk in like that. Only she knew the code to the door… along with Promly. Ultur swung around and, sure enough, Promly stood at the door.

'I see you are getting ready,' Promly said as she sank into a reclining chair near the window.

'What about you? Have you packed all the things you want to take with you?' Ultur came and sat next to her. She wondered why Promly had come. There was so much for her to do regarding the launch. The meticulous planning that had preceded the Council meeting was impressive. It had ensured that once the decision was taken, things swung into action immediately.

'I have come to your place after a long time, Ultur. It has not changed much in all these zacs,' Promly sank further into the chair and shut her eyes. She looked tired and drawn. Ultur waited for her to continue.

'I don't have much to take. We have to take a lot from Elone. I have taken all the processed Amar from the manufacturing units, taken the components for new crops, and set the standing crops, if any, for destruction prior to departure. I don't want the men to find anything of use when they cross the Fence. I wanted to destroy the reserves of Nepo too, but for that, I would need the Council's clearance. And I know that you would veto it like you did my other proposal. Why did you do that, Ultur?' she asked.

So, that was why she had come. Ultur stood up, laid out asipo and loaves of inola along with a glass of wine, and placed it before Promly. She opened her eyes and began to eat.

Ultur sat and watched Promly. They had worked together on projects, collaborated in the Council and taken an avid interest in Seeni as she had grown. Things had changed when Promly moved to the Enodus.

Once again, for this strange journey to uncharted frontiers, they had worked together. Ultur had supported the plan. Although it was fraught with uncertainty, it represented an ideal solution to the endless strife that surrounded their lives. It was a chance worth taking.

'If you want to know why I vetoed the last segment of your plan, Promly, you need to tell me the truth about what happened to Seeni,' Ultur's voice was firm and quiet.

Promly continued to eat. She had known all along that

she would have to answer this question, sooner or later. She looked around the room. The blank space on the wall where Seeni's favourite tapestry had hung seemed to starkly mark Seeni's absence. It was sad that Seeni was not with them on this journey. She would have revelled in establishing the new world order. So much talent had gone to waste. But had it? In fact, it was her absence which had set in motion the chain of events that had led them to the forthcoming journey.

'Sometime towards the end of the last zac, the unit that was working on this plan got a message that asked whether we have discovered a planet that could be another home for us. It was a great shock for the Enodus, as all the research and planning was under a shroud of complete secrecy, encrypted and protected. They tried to trace the sender of the message, but could not do so. The originator eluded them and certainly knew the informatics system well,' Promly fell silent.

Ultur was waiting. It was obvious from the way she sat, erect and still, that she was not going to let it go till the end.

'They kept getting messages, off and on, seeking information. At first they assumed someone had entered the system. The men were the first suspects, but were soon ruled out. After a lot of effort, finally, the messages were traced to the Irana Hub and more precisely to a particular workstation. At that point, Ultur, the plan was still being worked out. The route map, the number of spaceships, the loads, the supplies, it was at a vulnerable stage. A debate could not be started about it; it would have put an end to the plan. After a lot of deliberation and thought, the originator was silenced.'

Ultur shut her eyes. Seeni as a young girl flitting in and out of the house; Seeni as a grown woman busy with her work, her long beautiful hair and her inquisitive mind—all these images danced before her. She felt a slow fury growing within her.

'Promly, did you authorize the silencing knowing that it was Seeni?'

'Yes, I did,' Promly's voice was firm and quiet.

'Why, Promly? You could have taken her into confidence. You could have spoken to me. She would never have betrayed your trust. You know that. She had a curious mind. She always had. You punished her for something she never did, you punished her for her curiosity. She never mentioned this to me. She did not even know you headed the Enodus. She believed you had taken up farming,' Ultur was weeping and she did not even realize it.

'Ultur, I could not take any chances. This was not something personal. The whole plan was at stake. Our future, our existence was dependent on that plan. If at that stage, even a whisper of this plan had come out or even been wondered about, there would have been many like you in the Council ready to trash it. So many questions would have been raised. It would never have fructified. If it had been anyone else, even you, I would have decided the same thing,' Promly looked at Ultur, who continued to weep copiously.

'Ultur, with the men in an aggressive mode, waiting to attack us, the plan sailed through the Council.'

They sat and looked at each other across the room. Ultur remembered the time she had felt Promly had become as unreal as her image on the system. She felt the same again. When had Promly undergone such a transformation? Ultur battled with the feelings of rage, sadness and disgust that were rising like waves within her. Slowly, through the tempest that was brewing inside her, an understanding began to dawn.

'Promly, you did that to Seeni so that you could build it all up to this point, right? You blamed the men and convinced us that they caused it. And then, you ensured that this accusation was conveyed to them. Slowly, everything fell into place. The dwindling reserves of Nepo were a bonus for you. You brought the plan to the Council at just the right time. Promly, you did not perceive Seeni as a threat; you used her inquisitiveness to set the stage for your plan to succeed. Why was it so important? Why did it have to succeed at any cost?' Ultur was nearly shouting.

'Ask yourself that, Ultur. Forget for a moment what happened to Seeni. The fact is that for the men, Nepo is running out. Even Enodus did not know of this till a while ago. If not now, then sometime later, they would have turned on us. This forthcoming clash that they are plotting is inevitable, Ultur. You also know it. Going to Earth is the best way to get rid of all of this once and for all. Maybe some events accelerated this decision, but it had to be made, sooner or later. Seeni or no Seeni. You also know that this is a chance we must take.'

Promly watched as Ultur's tears rolled down her cheeks. She had to understand the futility of her chain of thought. By the time Clepo had identified the message sender as Seeni, most of the plan had been put into place. The results of the probe had been analysed. The destination and the mode of travel had been identified. When Promly found out about Seeni, she had been uncertain at first. She had grappled with many conflicting thoughts. But then, she saw the opportunity. Thereafter, she didn't have to think twice. Some losses were needed for the greater good.

Promly stood up. She felt relieved that Seeni's episode had been sorted on Elone itself. She and Ultur would make a fresh start on the journey to Earth. She walked towards the door.

'I will tell you why I vetoed your last proposal, Promly. Maybe this opportunity will never arise again. So, sit down,' it was Ultur's last attempt to reach out to the earlier version of Promly; before she had decided to change the destiny of women.

Surprised, Promly went and sat in the chair near the window again. Outside, the sun was slowly setting and an orange hue permeated the sky.

'Promly, you had proposed that before departing we should launch a final assault on the men. Inflict as much damage as possible, destroy as many as we can. And then, we could be on our way. If any men survived they could pick up the pieces and rebuild their life. I vetoed it, the first time that I ever used this privilege given to me by the Council. I have a very strong reason for doing so. Promly, we have a complex and intertwined past with the men. After Seeni's taking, I have been doing a lot of research. I discovered the intricacy and fluctuating tenor of our shared lives on Earth. It has been a journey of dependence, cooperation, conflict and separation. We did come together to Elone to survive the destruction of Earth. We have lived for thousands of zacs on this planet, fighting and still finding ways to survive. They are a similar species—we share the same genome sequence. We have a much larger commonality of biology, although it was the differences that ruled our interaction. We aspire for the same things and work towards similar futures. In the present context, we both want a future without the other. As we separate finally, in every possible way, let us leave them with a chance to survive and continue to exist. Who knows, in some distant future, the mere knowledge that some others like us exist and remain in this universe would be the key to survival. That is why I vetoed your proposal.'

Promly did not understand completely, but there seemed to be some thread of reason in what Ultur said. She got up and went to the door. She stopped and said, 'Ultur, you will come to Earth. I also came to tell you that we are going to leave in the next ten days, not next calante. The directive has gone out.'

'I haven't heard about this. Why this sudden change?'

'There will be a cosmic storm along the route we are embarking on during the next calante. If we wait for it to pass, our departure will be delayed by nearly another calante. So we decided to move earlier. We leave the night the three moons are hiding.'

'Will everything and everybody be ready?' Ultur wondered.

'They have to be. That includes you, Ultur. Let us leave behind all the baggage here on Elone. Don't even think about staying back. The new world we build will need someone like you.'

The apartment was nearly empty. As per the directives, all the things that were to be left behind had been consigned to the incinerators. Only three days were left till departure. Tara was running around the almost empty space with glee. Hap had also been sent to the incinerator. They would create all the machines they needed anew once they reached Earth. The system was still humming. It was scheduled to be destroyed the next day at midnight. Outside, it was dark; from where

Tioni and Iwe sat near the workstation, the three moons were not visible as they were hidden by dark clouds. This was the third night in a row they were waiting for Maya. If she did not appear that night it would not be possible to take her along.

At regular intervals, Tioni called out into the darkness, 'Maya, please come. We would like to talk to you.'

It seemed strange, but Maya had often responded to such calls. Tara came ambling up and tried to clamber up on to Tioni's lap. Tioni picked her up and began to rock her against her shoulder. Iwe watched the two of them in the light of the workstation.

'How will you take her on the journey, Tioni? It will be difficult as the spaceship would be quite confining for her.'

'She will learn to manage, Iwe. She has to. We will all have to learn to manage in strange surroundings...not only on the journey, but on Earth too.'

'Sometimes I feel angry, Tioni. Why are we displacing ourselves and leaving everything to the men?' Iwe expressed her resentment at long last.

'I do not perceive it as such. I look at it as deliverance... as an opportunity to own our world. Imagine a planet of our own to build and create as per our aspirations with no limits imposed by a Fence. No men lurking in the shadows as some indeterminate enemy. It is what we need as a species. Just imagine the freedom it offers. It's a wondrous feeling.'

Tara had fallen asleep. Tioni went and put her on the solitary bed that remained in the apartment. Outside, the clouds seemed menacing as they spread across the horizon.

'What is a wondrous feeling, Tioni? I thought only love felt like that,' Maya's metallic voice broke through the system.

'Where have you been, Maya? We have been waiting for

you,' Iwe was slightly irritated.

'Maya, it is so good to hear from you. I have been missing our long chats,' Tioni was glad to finally hear Maya's voice boom from the system.

'I was busy creating some music. I always forget everything else when I am doing that. You want to hear?' And, without waiting for a response, Maya's music began to play. It was a different melody; it sounded like the beating of drums in a distant land while it rained somewhere nearby. Both Iwe and Tioni were transfixed. It seemed as if a shower of rain had entered the room and caressed their faces.

The music faded slowly and Maya asked, 'Did you like it? I copied it to your tags.'

Tioni looked out of the window, it was humid but it had not yet started raining. The room remained silent.

'What happened, girls? If you don't like it, that's fine. Music is a very subjective thing. And this piece does belong to my time. I tried to capture the mood of the last time I was with Aryan. Before he departed, and in a strange way, I did too.'

'Maya, we are leaving this vihan. In three days, to be precise. Come with us,' Iwe put it in the only way she could.

'Going where? Of course, I will come with you. Wherever you are on Elone, I can join you on the system,' Maya's voice was slightly surprised.

'Maya, the women are leaving Elone. All of us. We are going to a new planet in another galaxy. The men will stay behind on this planet. We are going to find our own place in the universe,' Tioni's voice carried a strange sense of excitement.

The humming of the system came across the silent room, loud and clear. There was no response from Maya.

'Maya, are you there? Tomorrow this system will be

destroyed. I can take you on the circuits we are carrying. Come with us,' Iwe pleaded.

'Where are you going?' Maya asked.

'We have named this new planet Earth. It is in a galaxy very far from here.'

Maya's tinkling laughter rang out loud and clear. It was a soothing sound to hear.

'So women are going to claim Earth at last. How happy Ria and her ilk would have been to know this. The time when Earth belongs only to women has finally arrived. I never imagined it would end like this. Go girls, go to this new world that will completely be yours. Make your own rules and values, enjoy the fruits of your labour, live a life free of violence and oppression. Live out of the shadow of men.'

'You are not coming with us?' Both Iwe and Tioni asked the question simultaneously.

'Tioni, explain to her that she will be destroyed with the system.'

'I understand that much, Iwe. And no, I will not come with you. I have transferred the knowledge I had to you. That is what a consciousness is supposed to do. From where I came, the future we could see for ourselves was fairly limited. I stretched that vision far enough to come to Elone because one night, long ago, I had seen a bluish object in the sky with Aryan. It was his discovery, but I was the one who eventually made it here. This is how far my vision of the future is. I do not want to go to a planet that has no link to or memories of the people I loved. What has always driven me is love—for music, for life, for Aryan. I have roamed for what has seemed like an eternity. But I come from a time when, although we aspired for eternal life, we believed it was merely a dream. Aryan was right when he said there is much peace in knowing that there is an end. I feel that peace today.'

'Maya, your music will also vanish with you. How will we hear such beautiful melodies if you decide to stay here? You said you are a woman's consciousness, you need to be with us,' Tioni was trying to convince her. Maya had become a part of their lives.

'Someone else will create better music on your new Earth, Tioni. And the two of you will carry the torch of consciousness to your new world. Farewell, my friends. I am happy to die here…at last.'

The system began to hum again. They both waited. The rain began to fall slowly in large drops that created a clatter as they gathered speed.

'She has gone, Tioni. Imagine, she will be destroyed tomorrow.'

Iwe stood up and went to the window. She was suddenly feeling tired.

'We gave her a chance, Iwe. We probably do not understand what Elone means to her. For her, this was a destination. For us, it is part of a much longer journey.'

The sun was shining brightly on the day when the journey to Earth was to commence. All the residents had gathered on the mountain ranges. Equipment, machines, implements and other items that they were taking along with them had been loaded on to the two supply ships over the last couple of days. The system had been destroyed. Furniture, workstations and other items had been incinerated entirely. As soon as the spaceships would take off, the last energy reactor would combust and darkness would fall on their half of Elone. What would remain would be empty buildings, stationary shuttles, silent roads and quiet woods.

Preparations for the ascent of the residents into the spacecrafts had begun in the morning. Each carried a single small item of baggage representing their existence on Elone. It had not been easy to squeeze a long lifetime into one item. Their tags had been destroyed and for many, this silence was deafening. Quietly, slightly bemused and somewhat afraid, the residents were lined up, awaiting the opening of the spacecraft's enormous doors. The sun had completed its ride in the sky and darkness had enveloped them as the three moons were hiding that day. As night fell, their ascent into the spacecrafts began.

However, midway through, clouds began to gather in the sky, billowing and mushrooming across the horizon. Fierce winds began to blow across the mountainside and the weather turned menacing. An urgency to finish the embarkation swept the gathering and they hurried to get into the spacecraft before the rain began to fall.

Promly had boarded early, while Ultur was at the rear to ensure complete embarkation. Tioni, holding tightly to Tara, was at the tail end of the waiting group. The skies were threatening to burst as the lines diminished.

'Ultur, has Iwe boarded? I have not seen her,' Tioni asked.

The clouds had come very low, and only a handful of women remained on the ground.

'Hurry those ahead of you, Tioni, she must have boarded,' Ultur urged from behind. No one wanted to get wet before the start of a long and arduous journey.

'Can we ask Promly if Iwe has gone in?' Tioni said, as she picked up Tara and climbed the first step.

'No, there is no tag. It's going to pour, Tioni, run up the steps. There is no one here. The area is deserted, I checked. Now, go quickly,' Ultur was pushing Tioni into the interior of the huge spaceship.

As the first drops of rain began to fall, the doors of the spaceships shut and the engines revved up silently. Outside, the clouds burst amidst howling wind, and it began to pour. Tioni reached her designated perch and looked around. In the sea of bemused, confused faces all around, she could not spot Iwe. Promly was with her team somewhere on the higher floors of the spacecraft.

Everyone was strapping up for the journey to escape Elone's atmosphere. After that, they would wear the gear for the long journey across time and space. Tioni was worried. Tara and she had settled down for the initial phase, but Iwe's space next to them was still vacant. As the illusory forest parted, the spacecrafts rose swiftly. On the screens before them, the last glimpse of Elone became visible. The sparkling sea of light got murkier because of the rain and then, suddenly, an inky blackness spread across the screen as the lights went off. Ultur felt a pang of sadness and felt a tear roll down her cheek. Tioni was busy trying to spot Iwe and did not see the blackout. Finally, she saw Iwe emerge from the elevator that came from the higher floors. She sat down quickly and strapped herself.

'Where did you disappear? I was worried you got left behind!' Tioni was relieved.

'I embarked early. I wanted to see Earth in the mainframe of the spaceship. We are leaving everything familiar behind and

I wanted to see where we are headed. I am going to document our time on Elone, this journey and our struggle on reaching Earth meticulously. It is important for the creations that will happen in our new home to know about their past.'

Iwe was staring transfixed at the screen. The spacecrafts had nearly cleared the atmosphere of Elone. A huge cloud covered most of the planet, not even allowing a final farewell.

'That means you are planning to keep the men alive, at least in memory,' Ultur remarked, as their home for countless zacs disappeared from view.

Iwe continued to stare at the screen which was showing an increasingly smaller cloud. She wondered who would first flick open the switch at the Vault. Nothing would turn on except a screen. She had left a message for them to see. Iwe had to do it. The men needed to know at least that about the past.

'I think we should stop looking back and look ahead. A new world awaits us. Let us embrace it with happiness. As Maya would have said, "What a wondrous thing to happen, just like love."' Tioni flicked on a switch. The skies above were reflected on the screen, twinkling with innumerable stars.

Elone

Two days had passed and the rain had stopped. The men had spent a restless four days, cocooned in the chambers, cut off from sunshine, fresh air and their lives. A cursory announcement had been made that a skirmish had taken place and the gynake had suffered huge losses. Finally, the chambers were opened and they were let out. The sun was shining and there was no vestige of the rainfall that had pattered on for two days. The city was glistening after a good shower. The travelors began to move and hectic activity began. Men rushed to their homes and workplaces to see if anything had been damaged or affected. Within no time, the cities were hustling and bustling, as if the silence had been a dream.

In the afternoon, Radul and his team, which included Ime, moved towards the Fence. As per the plan it had been destroyed the night before and now lay in shambles. All the vegetation that had grown around it had been burnt down. Through the gaping holes in the opaque space, they saw the other side for the first time. As they crossed through the gaps, they stopped and wondered at the beautiful city before them. There were tall buildings that disappeared into the mists of the skies, walkways that connected them, and many tree-lined avenues and gardens. The grace and imagination in the buildings was different from the sheer grandeur of their side.

Tentatively, they moved towards the streets not knowing what they would behold. The city was eerily silent, as they had expected. The stillness and calm seemed to proclaim that the plan had been successful. As Ime walked the vacant streets, he felt as if his chest was tightening. He did not know what he would do if he actually came upon a nexed gynake. Down the street a wood-coloured vehicle, resembling their travelor was standing still. Radul signalled for three of them to go and look inside, while he and six others moved towards a medium-sized yellow building surrounded by a park.

Ime walked up to the shuttle and stopped. One of the other three went inside. 'Empty. No one is inside.'

Ime realized that he had been holding his breath. He moved inside the shuttle which was sleek and elegant but completely empty. He tried to activate it, but found that there was no source of energy for it to draw on.

Radul and his team entered the yellow building. Its door was swaying in the eerie silence. He could see the security sensor on the left side of the door, but it was obviously not functioning. Inside, it was absolutely quiet. The building was empty. It was shorn of any furniture or machines. They tried to switch on the lights, but nothing worked. The skylight in the main room was the only source of light. Radul realized something was deeply amiss.

Where had they gone? Where could they hide? Had they known about the attack? He tried to lex Ime, but in this space, their lex system did not work. When they came out of the building, the other three were rushing towards them.

'There is no one here, Radul. They have shut down the systems and removed everything from inside all these structures. They have just vanished,' Ime felt a strange sense of relief as he said it.

Radul nodded, 'I know. Let us see if we come across anyone anywhere over the next two days. Let us occupy this yellow building and start out. Comb the place. Even if one is found, we will know where they are hiding.'

He was sure that they would find them because there was no place for them to hide anymore. They fanned out individually into the many streets and lanes of the city. Everywhere, they were met with empty shells. Nothing was working, nothing remained. More importantly, no one remained. Their airborne travelors combed the length and breadth of Elone. The seabed and water bodies were also investigated. There was no sign of any life. The gynake had simply disappeared.

On the second night, it was still absolutely dark as there was no power. They had been trying to link their energy channels, but the systems were different. Through the gaps in the Fence, lights from their side were visible. They had all returned to the yellow building. Radul was hearing each one's identical report on what was out there. It began to dawn on him that although they had not been annihilated, the gynake had abandoned Elone and gone away somewhere.

Once that became evident, Radul decided it was time to start making this part of Elone functional again. They would deal with the whereabouts of the gynake later. Elone was in their possession completely. Their plan had succeeded, even though the outcome was different from what they had hoped for. He looked for Ime, but he had not yet joined the group.

Ime had also been searching for the last two days, combing every building he came across, trying switches and buttons. All the buildings were open, empty and silent. It was clear that the gynake had gone forever. No one who planned to return destroyed their own belongings so meticulously and completely. A part of him was overjoyed that they had escaped the horrible end the men had planned for them; the other part felt alone and afraid. They had Elone to themselves now—just what Radul, Patix, Valhan and most of the men had wanted. But he also knew that soon enough the men would start fighting over it among themselves. The seeds for that conflict had already been sown.

By nightfall, Ime stood before an imposing building. In the darkness it looked foreboding and sinister. His hand-held light had lost power. He entered the Vault, and groped around in darkness. Sliding along the wall, he tried to see if there were any buttons or switches he could turn on. His hand fell on a switch and he flicked it. Nothing happened. He moved in the opposite direction across a long empty space till his hands touched a wall. Again, he began to grope his way along the wall till his fingers touched a button. He pressed it. Suddenly, a screen on the far end of the wall sprang to life. Ime nearly fell. In the flickering light of the screen, he looked around to see if there was anyone in the space. The dimly lit hall was empty. Then, he turned back to the screen and saw that some words were scrolling on it.

He ran across the huge hall and stood in front of the screen, peering at the words.

If you are seeing this, it means you have arrived on our side. We are leaving this planet for you. It's all yours. After all, on Earth, it was a man named Aryan who discovered this planet.

Ime stood rooted to the spot. He read the message again and again. Soon, the power, on which this last screen was working, ran out. Ime continued to stand in the inky darkness.

He waited for any other screen to activate; for some other sign or message from that elusive species.

After a while, when only the dark surrounded him, Ime moved towards the exit. The door swung open and Ime stepped outside. In the sky, the three moons were shining and many stars were twinkling. He sank down on to the steps of the building, exhausted. The message replayed in his head incessantly. They had known about Earth. They knew things that even the men were unaware of, such as the name of the man who had discovered Elone.

Ime looked up into the sky. Only that limitless space could have swallowed them up. They had found a new home and had gone there, leaving them behind forever. It was a strange sensation. A sense of complete abandonment was enveloping him. The last link in the chain to Earth had been severed.

Ime continued to stare at the twinkling stars. Somewhere in the galaxies, they lived and existed. He stood up as a feeling of reassurance began sweeping over him. The gynake existed in the universe. One day, he would find them. He was absolutely certain about that.

Acknowledgements

Writing *Ascendance* has been a long journey—in time and of the mind.

Thanks to Kapish Mehra and his team at Rupa Publications for all the advice and encouragement.

Along the way, Dnyaneshwar M Mulay, Lov Verma, Arvind Shrivastav, Suki Iyer, Sangeeta Verma, Karan Nim, Giulia Zaratti, and Arushi Malhotra provided invaluable inputs. Thanks.

The journey would not have been possible without the support of Ziya Us Salam, Ajeet Dwivedi, Sanjay Kumar, Venkatesh Upadhyay, Dolly Sharan, Abhinav Verma, Abha Asthana, Anshu Prakash, Latha Ayyar, Deepak Bagla, Pritika Chatterjee, Ravi Batra, Upjit Singh Sachdeva, Kavir Moza, Pravin Kumar, Anuradha Mishra, Ramesh Yadav, Vijay Kumar Gautam, Harinder Gill, Pramila Sharan, P.K. Prushty, Payal Malik, Ajay Shukla, Ajay and Arpana Bhutani, Shrikant Jain, Sukesh Mishra, Anita Rana, Pravin Basoiya and the Income Tax Department. I am grateful.

Thanks to Ravi Pawar, Shashi Nim and Kunal Moza for design ideas.

Pujya, my daughter, this voyage was enriched with your engagement and companionship throughout!

Glossary

Amar	A plant that provides raw material for replacement organs
Astra	The name of a weapon
Calante	A month on the planet Elone
Clarent	A cloning parent
Creation	A child produced through cloning
Elone	The name of a planet
Enab	An intoxicating drink
Gynake	The term men use to denote women
Inola, Asipo, Parina, Kimpayo, Korive, Tibli, Craw	Names of different foods
Lex and Tag	Communication devices
Nepo	A mineral that provides raw material for replacement organs
Nex and Taken	Terms used to denote death
Tobok and Tobot	Mechanical aids
Vihan	One week on the planet Elone
Vish	A poisonous substance
Zac	One year on the planet Elone (one zac is equivalent to approximately eight years on Earth)